HE SEEMED TO THINK
HER A MERE CHILD. . . .

"Damme, but you're a relief, Fanny!" Charles glanced at her with an oddly twisted smile. "Five or six years hence, when you have all London at your feet, let the beaux see your natural self. . . ."

"I shall never have London at my feet—not with my red hair. It will not matter how well I dance or play the piano, which Almy says is all the gentlemen want."

"Hah, does she so?" he snorted. "It just goes to show, don't it? Don't you believe her, Fanny —and your hair isn't *red*. It's—it's sort of golden summer sunset." He eyed her appraisingly. "I shouldn't wonder if you took London by storm—and I hope I'm around to witness your triumph."

An Eligible Connection

Elsie Lee

A DELL BOOK

To Faith Baldwin
for the enduring
Auld Lang Syne

Published by
Dell Publishing Co., Inc.
1 Dag Hammarskjold Plaza
New York, New York 10017
Published originally in abridged form
by Cedric Chivers, Ltd., England

Dell ® TM 681510, Dell Publishing Co., Inc.

ISBN: 0-440-12821

Printed in the United States of America
One Previous Dell printing
New Dell printing—April 1980

CHAPTER I

Fanny Cherill stood at the window of what was euphemistically termed "The Young Ladies' Sitting Room." With the curtain discreetly opened one inch, she observed the Honorable Mrs. Edgar Cherill, attired in a pansy purple half-gown embellished with silk fringe, descending the street steps toward the waiting town carriage. Behind mama was Miss Almina Cherill, her ebony curls concealed beneath a wickedly becoming bonnet of lemon yellow that matched her dress of worked muslin. Fanny was unable to see her older sister's beautiful face, but she knew it by heart. So did the rest of London. From the moment of her first curtsey, Almina had been hailed as the Dark Incomparable, and although this was her second season, the fashion was still for brunettes; Miss Cherill remained the Incomparable in the *haut ton*.

With a sigh, Fanny watched the carriage drive away, leaving her to yet another dull expanse of hours. If only she had known . . . well, she had, but not *enough* of the rigid restrictions for younger sisters. When the Honorable Edgar Cherill abruptly decreed dismissal of the governess—"Fanny is too grown for lessons; bring her to London with a maid"—in her elation at being in, if not of, the *ton,* Fanny had joyously ignored her mother's grave face and warnings of curtailed freedom—only to find they were all too true. The few young people within the family acquaintance were barely out of the nursery. Fanny was reduced to such glimpses of town as could be gained by walks in the park with Janet, or an occasional stroll to Hookham's Lending Library.

After two months, Fanny admitted to herself she was bloody well *sick* of it—not that she would acknowledge cognizance of such an expression, learned from her elder brother, Harry. He and his bosom crony were currently with the Light Bobs, known respectively as Major 'Arry-Goddam and Capting Sir Robin-Redbreast . . . and if only either of them was in England! Instead, they were relaxing in Bordeaux after the rigors of pushing Frenchies up and down the Pyrenees, but richly deserving some fun, now that Napoleon was being packed off to an island.

Fanny straightened the curtain and turned to face herself in the cheval glass used for straightening hems and flounces. Her reflection did not inspire confidence: a slip of a girl with blue eyes too large for her tiny triangular face, and only the merest suggestion of a bosom. Mama said it would develop, but Almina's had been finished when she was Fanny's age. Porcelain white skin, delicate bones, and to top all, a mop of *red* hair—papa said his mother had had the same, and she had come all the way down from Scotland, appeared once at Almack's, and married the Earl of Aranshire— but that was years ago when Mr. Almack was still alive. Today was entirely different. The taste of the *haut ton* might veer from blonde to brunette for a year or two. It *never* swung to red.

For the twentieth time, Fanny yearned to go home and stay there. It was not in her power. When she asked, it was to learn that Cherley had been closed. Worse still, her timid request produced one of her father's uproars, until Mrs. Cherill hastily called Fanny out of the breakfast room.

"Yes, the house is empty. There is no point in a staff when we are away for months. I'm sorry, Fanny, but you see how it is: always so much on the calendar, and Almina must come first. Now, do not be teasing papa again," warningly. "Nothing upsets him more, he becomes stubborn at once, and he is not in good frame at the moment."

"Neither is anyone else," Fanny blurted. "You looked fagged to death, mama, and Almina is so tired that she snaps at the least word. It sounded exciting to read of routs and assemblies in the *Gazette*, but now—I don't think I want a season. You don't seem really to be enjoying yourselves, it's just something you have to do—but why?"

"How else is a girl to be suitably established? During her season, a young female is presented to society gathered from every part of the country, and has a chance to form an eligible connection among gentlemen of the *haut ton*."

"I think it sounds like one of those terrible slave auctions in the Colonies," Fanny muttered, "where they put them up on a block and sell them off to the highest bidder."

Mrs. Cherill's lips twitched. "A good many people agree with you," she remarked dryly, "but there is another aspect. Think, Fanny: who is there in the neighborhood of Cherley to suit Almina?"

"I always thought she favored Robin Elvey."

"Boy-and-girl," Mrs. Cherill shrugged, "and only a younger son. Besides, he's off to the wars with Harry, and there's no one else but petty squires and farmers. In London, Almina can be seen by gentlemen from everywhere. Does this not give her a far better chance to find a husband to her taste?"

"Yes, except that she doesn't seem to like any of them."

Her mother sighed unhappily. "I know, and papa says she must be settled this season. The expense, you know—it is very large. I'm sure I practice every economy, but Almina cannot be wearing the same gowns for three months—and the price of green peas is exorbitant, but one must have them or be thought a nip-cheese."

"Well, I always knew papa wasn't very beforehand with the world."

"Where, pray, did you hear such a thing?" Mrs. Cherill gasped.

"Harry told me," Fanny said simply. "When he inherited from his godfather and was buying his colors for Spain, papa was in an uproar, but later he said he was demmed glad to have *one* child off his purse."

"Well—well, I daresay he may have done," Mrs. Cherill strove for authority. "Your father often says far more than he means, and it is no easy matter that his heir should be risking his life in a war. In any case, you should know nothing of such things at your age."

"Yes, mama," but with nothing to occupy her, Fanny could not avoid *noticing*.

In the close confines of a fashionable London house, her father's flushed face and irascibility were more evident. Almina's weariness made her sharp-tongued. Mrs. Cherill was interposed uneasily between daughter and husband. Fanny did her best to be unobtrusive, but more and more she wondered about marriage: had mama ever loved papa, or was he simply an eligible connection?

No country-bred girl could be ignorant of the facts of life, but for humans, was the eligible connection *all*? Suppose, once made, you didn't like what went with it? Slowly, Fanny began to suspect this was Almina's problem. Among all the Tulips, Nonpareils, and Corinthians paying her court, there wasn't one she wished to bed with—which led to the further suspicion that Almina's mind was fixed on some man who was *not* paying her court.

Fanny's tender heart ached for her sister, she forgave Almina every quick retort and prayed earnestly that Almina could find someone bearable. The days passed with snail-like slowness. Fanny crossed each one off her calendar, waiting for the first of July when they would leave London for Bath. She nearly abandoned her diary, there was never anything to write in it. "If only *something* would happen," she sighed, observing the departure of her mother and sister for Almack's that evening.

Fanny got her wish. About eleven that night, Mr. Cherill's residence on Hill Street caught fire, due (it later developed) to the tweeny smuggling a candle end to her bedroom, where the curtains were set ablaze. Luckily, it was discovered swiftly both within and without. Fanny awoke to hoarse shouts and a great bustle that brought her out of bed to search hurriedly for flint and candle. Hastily she donned her dressing gown and ran to the door, but when she opened it she recoiled, gasping at the cloud of acrid smoke pouring through the hall. With no idea whether the fire was above or below her, Fanny slammed the door and raced to throw wide the window. "Help, help!" she cried.

There was a number of dim figures milling about below her, but they were making so much excited noise her voice was lost. The fire was apparently in the rear, for the crowd jostled its way through the side garden to connect with other helpers from the stable mews. Fanny tried the hall once more; it was still murky with smoke that swirled into her room toward the opened windows. With a sob, she shut the door and tore back to scream piteously, *"Please,* help!"

She was half faint with relief when a hearty male voice replied, "One moment, ma'am." There ensued a tremendous thrashing, and the voice commanded, "Give me a leg up, you fool. There's a child up there."

By the activity to the rear, Fanny judged the fire to be in one of the servants' rooms, although this was not reassuring. All the staff slept either on the floor above or in the back on her own level. She found slippers and had just got them on when Janet dashed into the room, choking and holding a damp cloth to her nose. "Oh, Miss Fanny, it's all right," she gasped. "It was Maria's room—a fair mess she's made! And screaming like a silly fool, fainting and carrying on, when it's all her fault. She deserved to be burnt in her bed, but

Pitcock's got her out and the fire's not spreading. Eeeeeeeee!" Janet's eyes widened, staring behind Fanny.

Fanny whirled in time to see a well-turned masculine leg in primrose satin knee breeches thrown over the windowsill, followed immediately by a slightly disheveled young man with a mop of black curls and merry brown eyes. "Whooo!" he panted, shaking himself erect and grinning at her. "Well—what's to do here?"

"N-nothing," Fanny stammered, pulling her robe closely about her. "That is, if you came to save me, I thank you, but it proves unnecessary. The fire is controlled."

He was occupied in straightening the sleeves of his amber velvet evening coat, but at her words he stared at her indignantly. "Then why did you scream for help?" he demanded. "Let me tell you, it is no easy matter to crawl up your ivy for a child's prank. I've ruined my suit, torn a ruffle, scraped my slippers—and all for nothing?"

"I didn't know the fire wasn't dangerous," she said defensively, "and I feel you underestimate your ability for scaling walls. To one of your physique, it should be the merest nothing."

"A quick-tongued miss," he remarked, still miffed. "I suppose there really was a fire?"

"Certainly there was. Open the hall door . . ."

He strode across, opened and closed rapidly. "There was a fire," he agreed. "Phew, devilish smell, ain't it?"

"Yes."

"Dash it, I shall still look a muff, climbing up walls to rescue a child in no need of it," he frowned, drawing a comb from his pocket and absently bending to the dressing mirror, where he restored a semblance of order to his hair. "The thing is, how can I contrive to get out of here? Don't want this to get about town, you know—never live it down!"

"You could go back as you came," but he shook his head firmly.

"Once was enough! Isn't there a back stair?"

"Everyone's awake, Miss Fanny," Janet whispered.

"The side stairs," said Fanny. "I'm afraid you'll have to wait until the servants have settled down, sir."

"Damme, what a devilish nuisance," he complained, throwing himself into the slipper chair. "It's the last time I'll play Galahad, I can tell you." Then he hauled up again, "I say, allow me to introduce myself: Lord Charles Waterbury, at your service, ma'am."

Fanny sketched a curtsey. "I am Fanny Cherill."

"Cherill? You are Miss Almina's sister?"

"Yes. Pray be seated, milord. I am deeply sorry to delay your engagements, but once the staff is quiet, Janet will smuggle you down to the garden door."

"Oh, that's all right." He laughed suddenly, "The longer I stay, the less I'll lose." He looked about him curiously, and Fanny flushed as his eye passed over the tumbled bedclothes.

"I regret I have no sitting room where you could be more comfortable, milord."

He chuckled, and sat down again. "I must admit I have never before been in so—virginal a bedchamber," he remarked, "and I suppose it is not customary to find a glass of port in a night nursery."

"No, it is not," Fanny agreed, "but I should not wish to be lacking in hospitality. Janet, bring a glass of port for Lord Waterbury."

"*Port,* Miss Fanny?" Janet quavered, her candle tilting dangerously.

"Port," Fanny commanded superbly. "First draw the curtains and mend the fire. It would be a poor return for Lord Waterbury's gallantry if he should catch a cold in the nursery."

"Oh," said Janet. "Nursery. Of course, Miss Fanny."

In a twinkling the room was a cozy sight, with candles shining bravely from mantel and table. The curtains were closed, the fire well stirred. "Now the port," said Fanny.

Janet hung her head. "Where shall I find it?" she

whispered. "Mr. Pitcock keeps the keys."

Lord Waterbury looked at the crestfallen pair and chuckled. "I should try Mr. Cherill's study, and if there is more than one decanter, the one you want contains a ruby red liquid."

"Wot if he catches me?" Janet hesitated.

"He won't. I left him an hour ago, settled for the night at Watier's."

Accordingly, Janet cautiously opened the door and scuttled off. Fanny stood undecidedly in the center of the room, and could not repress a shiver.

"Why, you must be chilled," His Lordship said bluffly. "Here, child, hop into bed again. Let me put out some candles, or you'll be too heavy-lidded to attend to your lessons tomorrow."

For a second she wavered. "I feel sure it is not at all the thing for a lady to entertain from her bed, milord."

"You would be surprised at how many of 'em do it," he snorted sardonically. Observing her faint blush, he added, "There, I don't mean to tease you, child. Just remember that circumstances alter cases, and a true lady may do many unusual things without impropriety."

"Well, I will then—but don't put out the candles," Fanny begged as he took up the snuffer. "Never mind lessons."

He grinned at her boyishly. "Dreary things, ain't they? I suppose you have a horrid female like my sisters. Why is it that all governesses are dragons?"

"They are a plaguey nuisance, aren't they? Have you several sisters, milord?"

"Lud, yes! Five of 'em, each sillier than the next."

"How sad," Fanny sighed. "I collect you have a low opinion of females?"

"Oh, as for that," he hmmmphed, "it's a fine thing when a fellow's own sisters make a fool of him, screaming and having the vapors at the most exciting moment. Now I put it to you: anyone would want to see a balloon ascension, wouldn't they? Even if it burst and dropped the chap into the pond."

"*Especially* if it burst and dropped the chap into the pond," Fanny agreed with an enjoyable shudder.

"Exactly! But the basket was no more than off the ground when m'sister Georgie began to go into hysterics and demand to be taken away . . . and in the excitement of getting her into the demmed carriage and finding the demmed vinaigrette, I missed the best part of it."

"*Did* the balloon burst?" she asked breathlessly.

"Well, no," he admitted, "but it was borne the devil of a ways up and only came down three days ago."

Fanny sighed. "How I should like to see a man go up in a balloon!"

"There's to be another try next week. I'll take you," he offered handsomely. "That is, if you promise you'll not have the vapors."

"Oh, indeed, *indeed* I shall not!"

"Then that's settled: next Thursday noon," he said, and as an afterthought, "What about the old tabby? Will she set up a screech?"

"I—think I won't tell her," Fanny murmured, "but where shall we meet, and when?"

His Lordship's forehead wrinkled in thought as Janet came whisking into the room, every bow on her nightcap erect with agitation. "Oh, Miss Fanny," she breathed; "Mr. Pitcock nearly caught me! I had to stay behind the study door for the longest while—and then he snuffed the candles, so I don't know if I got the right bottle."

Gingerly, she produced a fine crystal decanter from beneath her robe. It was nearly full—of a deep golden liquid.

"You've got the sherry, my girl," Lord Waterbury said good-humoredly. "Never mind. A glass of sherry will warm as well as port."

Janet looked stricken. "I forgot the glass," she whispered.

"I do not think she should try again, she may be

missed from the servants' wing," Fanny said anxiously. "Should you object to drinking from a tooth mug, milord?"

"Lud, no—reminds me of Eton," he chuckled. While Janet rinsed the mug, His Lordship sniffed appreciatively at the glass stopper. "Your father has a sound taste in wines. This is the stuff for concocting plans!"

"Ah? Thank you, Janet. Go and unlock the garden door."

"Wot if Mr. Pitcock catches me? He's all about, trying to be rid of the smoke smell afore the family gets home," Janet quavered.

"You've only to say you came to be certain I wasn't frightened," Fanny told her firmly. "Good night, Janet."

"Yes, miss." Janet bobbed a reluctant curtsey, but under Fanny's stern eye, she finally slid into the hall and closed the door.

Lord Waterbury sampled the sherry with approval. "Very smooth! Now, how do we arrange?"

"I shall go for a walk with Janet, we shall have errands, but first we will go to the park, where you will meet us at the first side path to the left of Hyde Park Corner," Fanny said serenely. "Then you will take me to the balloon ascension, Janet will do the errands. You return me to the park, I meet Janet and come home—and no one will be the wiser."

Lord Waterbury choked slightly. "That's what staggers me about females," he remarked. "Females are born devious. You find a child in a nursery, and inside of ten minutes she's hatching schemes and plots better than that Italian chappie—whats'isname."

"Machiavelli," Fanny murmured, "but really, milord, if you mean to take me, what other plan would be better?"

"Oh, none," he rolled a mouthful of sherry under his tongue and swallowed happily. Suddenly he sat up, "What about your dragon—and suppose it rains?"

Fanny crossed her fingers surreptitiously beneath the covers. "Miss Bolting will be only too happy to avoid a walk. She has the rheumatism, you know, and is always glad to send me with Janet. And if it rains, you will send your man with a note for Janet to say when to meet you another day."

Lord Waterbury looked at her with undisguised admiration. "Never thought of that. By Jove, you're a clever puss!"

Fanny hugged the quilt to her chin and giggled softly, "But I want very much to go, and yearning is a powerful spur to contriving."

"Why, so it is," he tossed off the remaining sherry with a sardonic laugh. The little French mantel clock softly chimed twelve. "Lord, I'd best be off before your governess comes to see you're safe."

"She's away, she had leave to visit her mother," Fanny improvised glibly, hopping out of bed and rapidly snuffing all but one candle. When she cautiously opened the door, all was quiet. "The coast is clear. Go down these stairs," she whispered, "then to the right for the street, or to the left into the mews. Good night, milord."

"Hah, you're a plucky youngster," he said softly. "Wish my little sisters had your sense! Don't forget: next Thursday."

"I won't. Be quick, milord—they may not all be abed." She lingered tremulously at the top of the steps, while he felt his way down with various creaks and bumps, but eventually the door was opened and closed with a click. She sped back to her bedroom window, kneeling down to peer through a crack of the curtains and giggling silently at the blundering sounds below. "Oh, me, his suit will never be the same!"

As she was absorbed in watching his stumbling retreat, the approaching horses' hooves and carriage rumbling took her unaware. "Mercy on me, it's mama and Almina! Did he hear? Those satin breeches shine like the moon . . . no, he's found the shrubbery!" She pulled the curtains closed and turned—to face the sherry decanter. "Good God, I forgot that!" Impossible to get it into its place in the study—Fanny swiftly raced it down to her father's bedroom and set it unobtrusively on a side table. Chances were Mr. Cherill would never notice it when he got home, and when Pitcock found it tomorrow, he would assume the master had brought it up from the study.

The noise of admitting Almina and Mrs. Cherill covered Fanny's flight upward, and she'd regained her room before they noticed any motion. Closing the door softly, she leaned against it with a beating heart. "Lud, what an adventure!" She kicked off her slippers, tossed the robe on the bed, and slid beneath the covers with a final puff to blow out her candle. In the darkness, she wriggled her toes together luxuriously.

"I wonder who he is," Fanny thought—and was almost instantly asleep.

CHAPTER II

Beyond asking if Fanny had been frightened and praising Janet for staying with her, Mrs. Cherill said nothing. She had enough on her hands with the Honorable Edgar, who made a monumental uproar over the ruined bedroom, the smoke stench throughout the house, and the general ineptitude of everyone but himself . . . following which he took himself off to the club, leaving exhaustion behind him. Almina was not much easier to handle.

"All my gowns *smell,* mama, and how will we ever be rid of the odor in time for the musicale on Monday?" she wailed. "It is too vexatious, when Wyvern has promised to attend. He even asked most particularly if he might bring Lord and Lady Ambrose 'to make my sister known to you!' Only think what that may mean, mama."

Fanny herself was wise enough to know what it meant, and her mother's eager inquiry "When said he this, Almina?" confirmed it.

"Last night, during the final waltz. I had not time to tell you, for we were in the carriage and you know the shambles we found at home. I had decided to wear the presentation gown, and by the greatest good luck, Wyvern is particularly fond of English country airs," Almina sniffled unhappily. "I meant to practice a few, and perhaps—after Madame Gemmé and Signor Altori—there might be a *suggestion* . . . but now all is ruined. We must cancel the whole. Oh, mama!"

"Now, now, my love, do not despair. We will contrive something."

"The Duke of Wyvern," Fanny breathed, wide-eyed. "You never mentioned him before."

"I didn't know him before. That is, we were introduced last season, but on the very next day he departed for their properties in the West Indies and has only just returned." Almina smirked in open triumph. "He appeared at the assembly last night, and came directly to me when he'd concluded the reception line."

"Oh, *Almy:* he's never forgotten you, he's thought of you constantly while he was doing his dull old business, and on his first evening—there you were, more beautiful than ever," Fanny sighed with pleasure. "Is he handsome, does he dance well? What do you talk about? How much he must know of the islands that would be of interest."

Almina's face was expressionless. "Oh, as for that, I've heard it all before. Lud, don't you remember Ullastone sent Robin out for a twelvemonth, and when he came home he never stopped talking until one was sick of the names."

"So much the better," Fanny returned. "Whatever Wyvern has to tell will be familiar, allow you to share his memories in some sort. How fortunately it all falls out! Don't you recall that Boltie always used to say 'Nothing you ever learn but it will come in handy sometime'? How right she was," Fanny crowed. *"I know how to get rid of the odors, what d'you think of that!"*

"How?"

"Pastilles in every room, and burning sugar on the fire shovel, and we will hang all Almy's dresses in the old schoolroom with the windows opened wide. You'll see. Do let me, mama—I'm sure I can freshen in time for the musicale, if I may have the carriage for an hour to visit the pharmacy, and Janet released to help me."

"Well, anything is worth trying, I suppose," Mrs. Cherill said feebly. "I declare I'm at wit's end—one thing after another, just as all looks more hopeful. Very well, you and Janet will come with us this morning. When Almina and I are left at Lady Gilmartin's the carriage will continue on, but I don't know, I hope it will answer."

"So do I," Almina observed, "although how on earth Fanny should know more than Pitcock defeats my intelligence."

"Cats!" Fanny stated oracularly, and chuckled at their faces. "When they are frightened, they—spray. It's the most dreadful odor, far worse than smoke. The time you were visiting Aunt Emma and papa had Pitcock here, I had three house cats in the schoolroom at Cherley."

"I remember you preferred cats to dogs, but *three?*"

"Once I had five," Fanny admitted, "but they were only to be in my rooms . . . except that they followed me around. That day they came down to the salon while I was practicing on the good piano, and as luck had it, Harry came bursting in with his great stupid dogs . . . and you know very well *they* weren't supposed to be there, either, mama. But however, they scared the cats, who ran up the curtains and perched on the poles, and by the time we'd got rid of the dogs and picked the cats from the tops of the windows," Fanny laughed helplessly. "Oh, the salon was topsy-turvy.

"Boltie and Mrs. Mitton scrubbed everything, and for days we burned pastilles until it was fresh again—and the proof is that you never suspected! I'll wager I can get this house ready, and no one will ever realize we had a fire."

She threw herself wholeheartedly into doing it. Aided by a fresh spring breeze, Almina's clothes swayed before open casements that also aired the rooms. A bewildered Pitcock waved fire shovels of burning sugar in salons and halls. Janet and Fanny set smoldering pastilles in every corner, and replenished constantly. The sweetening extended to the servants' rooms, "for if they are not free of odor, it will return to the main section every time the passage doors are opened," Fanny said. "Besides, there is no reason for the staff to endure such a reek. If we do not like it, neither do they."

"No, Miss Fanny." Pitcock looked at her thoughtfully. "What do you wish done?"

"I'd better look for myself," she decided, "after lunch, Pitcock, when it won't interfere with cook's preparations for dinner. Come and get me."

Pitcock looked even more thoughtful, "Yes, Miss Fanny. Shall we say two o'clock?"

"Say anything you like," she returned impatiently. "I'll be ready whenever the staff is ready and we'll get it out of the way quickly enough to give them still some rest. Heaven knows they must need it, Pitcock, and I've nothing more important."

"Yes, Miss Fanny." The butler permitted himself an august smile, but had she known, his regal report in the servants' hall struck the staff dumb. "Miss Fanny wishes to inspect the fire damage this afternoon," he stated. "The inspection is to be at our convenience after luncheon, in order to allow as much of the usual rest period as possible. Miss Fanny says we must need it, and she is available when we are."

There was a slight pause before cook said, "Say what you like, it's the little one that's the lady—not like some I could name. Well . . ." she set her hamlike arms on the table and hauled herself erect, "I'll finish up and be ready in a half hour, Mr. Pitcock. Edith, you and Janet give me a hand. Perkins, help tweeny with the pots, and if you'll be so kind as to place the table for tonight, Mr. Pitcock, we'll be through in no time."

Fanny's eyes widened as she went through the servants' halls, sniffing. "Ugh, how can you sleep? Have the tweeny's room stripped, scrubbed, and whitewashed," she ordered efficiently. "Have the stableboy scrub every bit of wood everywhere with hot water and soap. Take out all the curtains and bedcovers to be washed. Air your clothes as I've done Miss Almina's.

Choose a fresh breezy day, and *open* all windows from breakfast to dinner. You can close them when you go to bed, although you ought to have air at night," she added. "It is *not* unhealthy and you will sleep better, but however, do as you please when the rooms are well aired."

"Yes, Miss Fanny," the staff murmured respectfully.

"I expect with all you have to do, it may be hard to spare the time," Fanny smiled apologetically, "but try to get all fresh before Monday's musicale. Pitcock, I'll give you some pastilles, and you can send Perkins to get more. What happened to the tweeny, she wasn't hurt?"

"She went back where she come from," cook stated. "A'norphan she was, and no use to anyone, Miss Fanny. Trying to *read*—in bed!"

"Poor child, I suppose it was the only time she had to herself, and now it's a black mark against her, when all she wanted was to improve herself." Fanny looked at their bewildered faces and said reasonably, "Well, you can all read and write, can't you? Why shouldn't she? How is she ever to advance otherwise? She can't be a tweeny *forever*, Mrs. Hodge; she'd grow too big for it in a few years. Then what's she to do?"

"Lawks, I dunno," cook returned slowly. "They've sent us another one worse than Maria. Deaf she is, and wanting in the top story to boot. You tell her something, she either doesn't hear or she doesn't understand, just stares at you frightened-like."

"She probably is," Fanny grinned wickedly. "If I were a twelve-year-old orphan, you'd scare *me* to death, Mrs. Hodge." There was an involuntary titter from the others, and the cook bridled slightly before her lips twitched in a reluctant smile. Fanny laughed, "If this one wants to read, make her do it in a corner of the servants' hall, where she'll be seen if she falls asleep." She cast an appraising eye around the group. "I can tell no one of you is unkind," she said softly. "If you had a little sister, or niece or cousin, starting in service, wouldn't you want her to be helped? I expect it's a nuisance when you're all so very busy, but perhaps, if you could just *show* her quietly and calmly—if she could have the feeling that everyone was friendly, she might go on better.

"It must be so lonely to be an orphan, not to have anyone in the world to belong to," she finished. "Pitcock, if you'll come with me, I'll give you the pastilles, and," she smiled at the staff, "thank you for giving up part of your rest period. I'm so sorry to ask it, but mama has left the freshening to me, you know, and I am on my mettle to prove myself."

There was a prolonged silence when Fanny had gone. Finally, Mrs. Hodge said heavily, "There's one fit to be a duchess, and I hope I'll be here when her turn comes. A pleasure it'll be to prepare the dinners and ball suppers for Miss Fanny. She's the sort to make a personal visit to the kitchen to thank you—like Lady Agatha, when I was cook for the Duke of Penniman. Did I ever tell you . . ."

"Yes, you did," Edith inserted, "and I don't want to hear it again. I'm going to start airing my clothes."

During the cleaning process, there was unaccustomed harmony between the Cherills. Fanny was busy, Mrs. Cherill was relieved of her husband's complaints, and Almina was so titillated by her new conquest as to be very nearly sweet-natured. There seemed no doubt of the Duke's serious interest. At each encounter he singled out Miss Cherill. While he was courteous in distributing his favors to daughters of a hostess or talking to various elderly friends of his mother, it was observed that as soon as his devoirs were finished, he was beside Miss Cherill.

Fanny hoped with all her heart that Almina could attach him, she seemed to want him so badly. On Monday she curled on her sister's bed out of the way and watched Almina's robing in the court presentation gown. It was pure white, the richly figured brocade overdress caught by diamond clasps over thinnest silk that molded seductively to Almina's body. Long white gloves sheathed her arms, white slippers with winking paste buckles peeped beneath her skirt, and a diamond crescent rode proudly beside the topknot of black hair dressed *à la Grecque*.

"How very beautiful you are, Almy," Fanny murmured sincerely. "Thank you for letting me stay. At least I shall know how to go on, not that I'll ever be an Incomparable."

Almina smiled through the mirror at the tiny figure hugging its knees admiringly on the counterpane. "You'll do well enough when the time comes," she said. "Red hair is never fashionable, but yours isn't *carroty*, and one thing about mama: she knows exactly how to dress one. I shouldn't wonder if you weren't the most tremendous success, Fanny. You dance beautifully, you play the piano very well, and papa says you've a good seat on a horse."

"It doesn't sound like much to attract an eligible connection, does it?" Fanny looked dubious.

Almina laughed dryly. "It's all that's wanted, I assure you. Gentlemen do not like anything *brainy* in females, it's too apt to outshine them. Look at papa!" She swept to her feet, sliding a tiny fan and a reticule on one wrist.

"Papa?"

"If he could bring himself to admit that mama knows more than he of management, the whole family would benefit. Never mind—you're too young to understand. Once I'm settled, you are the last of us, and as mama always says, we will contrive something."

Fanny sat silent, startled by the sudden thin-lipped determination with which her sister picked up a filigree holder and fitted it about a bouquet of white roses. Almina held them to her nose briefly and sighed. "Hothouse . . . they never have any scent. Well . . ." she revolved for her audience, "can you see aught amiss?"

"Not a thing," said Fanny, hopping off the bed and

running to kiss her sister lightly. *"Dear* Almy, I do hope you'll get him if you want him."

"I must want him, mustn't I? So rich and handsome, in the first stare of the *ton,* with a castle, a major estate, a mansion in London, and heaven knows how many shooting boxes and fishing lodges and properties in the Indies," Almina laughed harshly. "East or West, it doesn't matter."

"It sounds formidable, shall you know how to go on? I suppose you'll have housekeepers and stewards, but Boltie always said you have to know how to do it yourself in order to supervise properly. Of course, it'd be exciting to travel—but you are afflicted by the sea."

"I am," Almina grimaced, "but it don't signify—and I don't know why we're talking in this way. I haven't got him yet." She took a final glance in the mirror and turned to the door. "Good night, Fanny."

Watching Almina's graceful descent to the salon, Fanny was deeply troubled, she knew not why. Nestled in her customary spot at the curve of the stairs from which to observe the entrance of guests, Fanny was interested only in one: His Grace, the Duke of Wyvern. By now she could recognize a number of people to be announced by Pitcock's most sonorous tones. "Lord this, Lady that, the Earl of so-and-so" passed into the salon, and for once papa was on hand. He would stay until the music began, when he would either retreat to the cardroom with some cronies or vanish away to a club. Apparently this was customary in the *haut ton:* it was Gothic, positively shocking, for husbands and wives to betray the least sign of affection or be constantly seen in each other's company.

Fanny could not understand this. Were there no "eligible connections" that included love, or at least some sort of understanding and pleasure in being together?

There—that group of three coming up the stairs. Fanny leaned forward with a certainty it was Wyvern. His sister was dumpy, a squat little woman with protuberant pale blue eyes and a haughty expression. Her gown of silver lace was elegant, but embellished with so many bits of jewelry that she was a walking Christmas tree. "If I looked like that, I wouldn't call attention to myself!" Which of the men was the Duke? They were like as two peas, with nothing to recommend either of them to Fanny: light brown hair, pale blue eyes, florid complexions, stout and stolid. She was conscious of shock. Almina had called him rich and *handsome*.

Pitcock announced, "Lord and Lady Ambrose, the Duke of Wyvern," and the group sailed forward into the salon while Fanny sat back and pondered. Could Almina really like such a pompous, self-consequent man, or was it simply the most "eligible connection"?

"He may be more conversable than he looks," Fanny told herself hopefully, "and Almy's requirements may be different from mine. After all, she has been Out, and we are not at all similar in tastes. Perhaps when I have my season and become familiar with society, I shall think differently, too—but I wouldn't want Lady Ambrose for *my* sister-in-law."

She continued to cuddle sleepily at the top of the stairs, listening to the professional singers unleashing complicated arias replete with trills and high notes. Halfway through the first one, Mr. Cherill backed unobtrusively through the salon door and came up the stairs. "Eh, who's there? Oh, it's you, kitten. What are you doing here?"

"I like music, papa."

"Infernal racket!" he snorted, "I have to pay for this?" He disappeared into his dressing room, returned shortly in coat and high-crowned hat, patting Fanny's shoulder as he stumped downstairs. "I'm off to the club," he announced unnecessarily, "not that anyone will ask. My only value here is furnishing the money for these fol-lols—and after what I've spent, your sister had better make a brilliant marriage."

"Yes, papa, but I expect she will. She's so beautiful."

"Hah! It's only skin-deep," he muttered, plodding heavily from one step to another and eventually vanishing through the street door.

Fanny's eyelids drooped lower and lower, until there was a general bustle and shifting in the salon. By twos and threes, the guests crossed to the supper room for the delicate *vol-au-vents* of sweetbreads and those expensive green peas, broiled mushrooms, sweet jellies, and dressed *salats*, the platters of tiny rout cakes and meringue, baskets of fruits. Suddenly Almina came hastily up the stairs. "Fanny! Thank heavens—be a dear," she begged, "I've torn a ruffle, help me pin it."

"Into mama's room," Fanny sprang to her feet, "or shall I run up for needle and thread?"

"Not time. I left Wyvern talking to people, but he'll be looking for me to go in to supper."

"How does it go?" Fanny was rapidly pinning the torn edges together.

"Excellently! Lord and Lady Ambrose are all condescension, the music is entirely to their taste, and Wyvern himself has said he hopes I will favor them after tea," Almina crowed.

"Oh, Almy, how wonderful!"

"You should be abed, Fanny."

"Not until you've finished singing. Don't tell mama, *please?*"

"Well, I won't then," Almina laughed amusedly, and went down again. Shortly, Fanny observed her sister passing across the hall and was enabled to determine that the Duke of Wyvern was the one in a blue swallow-tailed coat; Lord Ambrose wore green. After that there was nothing to do but wait until tea was ended, and Fanny was fighting sleep once more when footsteps roused her: Janet with a small tray.

"Miss Almina sent word to bring you some supper," she whispered. "Oooo, it's a lovely party, Miss Fanny!"

"Yes, and Almy's been asked to sing! Mmmm," indistinctly, "tell Mrs. Hodge everything is delicious, Janet. The pastry is light as a feather, the sauce is perfectly seasoned."

"Yes, miss."

Fanny sipped the fruit punch, nibbled the cakes contentedly—kind of Almy to remember her. The whole evening was turning into a triumph, to be climaxed by Almy's singing. Fanny knew herself the better pianist, but unlike the average society miss, Almina had a superb voice. She really sang, and if the Duke truly enjoyed music, he could not fail to be impressed.

So were the professionals. Both Madame Gemmé and Signor Altori entreated permission to join Miss Cherill in duets—unheard-of presumption, but Almina was so flown with success that she overbore her mama's resistance. To Fanny, it was the high point of felicity. Almina had never been in finer voice; the songs displayed her mastery of French and Italian, as well as her versatility; the musicians played the accompaniments as though inspired, and the final applause was hearty. At last the guests streamed away, but Fanny noticed the Duke of Wyvern was among the last to leave!

For the next few days, nothing was talked of but Wyvern: every word he had said, every glance, every mark of attention was thoroughly reviewed and its possible significance debated. The report of Mrs. Cherill's musicale in the *Gazette* was a paean of praise, which drew a frown from that lady. "So many details—someone of the guests must be an informant," she said darkly. "I have always wondered how they contrived such items. Pitcock is supposed to give the invitation list, as well as the planned entertainment and supper menu—and one assumes a servant might add a few titbits on gowns or decorations, it is how they pocket a few shillings extra—but only a guest in the salon could know that Almina laid aside her flowers, or the particular songs, for they were not announced, you know. Do not tell me that *Pitcock* would recognize foreign operatic arias, yet here is a complete list and correctly spelled!"

"Be grateful for it, and what does it matter?" Almina asked impatiently.

"One does not like to think that someone of one's acquaintance would stoop so low," Mrs. Cherill returned, shocked. "One expects it of servants, and I'm sure they pocket a handsome sum for tittle-tattle, but a member of the *ton?* I declare it makes me very uneasy, for who knows what may be overheard of an unguarded remark to a close friend?"

"A ballroom is scarce the place for intimate chat, mama. I wish you will attend to me: may I have a new bonnet for Friday's drive with Wyvern—and I think I should order a gown for Lady Ambrose's ball."

"Yes, my love," Mrs. Cherill replied absently. "I wonder who it can be—Lady Mungo, perhaps. I confess I've never known how she contrives . . ."

Fanny listened in silence, absorbing every word and studying the *Gazette* avidly as soon as it was tossed aside—but Lord Waterbury was never on any guest list. She felt puzzled, half fearful that he seemed not accepted in society. Yet—his clothing, manners, voice: all were well-bred. He'd smelled slightly of wine, but nothing like papa's fetid morning breath, nor had he drunk more than a modest portion of sherry—in the tooth mug that reminded him of Eton. That reference was obscurely reassuring.

Under cover of the absorption in Wyvern, she seesawed mentally: to go on Thursday, or not to go? At the outset, it was total ruin for Fanny if discovered. Lord Waterbury thought her about twelve—but a girl of seventeen required a chaperone. Of course, if he were not in the *ton,* perhaps nobody would notice who was with him. Conversely, he might be a rakehell whom no young lady should recognize, with or without duenna. *Pooh,* said Fanny's common sense. There'd been not one word or gesture when Lord Waterbury was in what he supposed was the night nursery. She'd felt as comfortable as if he were Harry—and if he were a depraved character, what on earth could he do to her in broad daylight?

It was settled: she would *go,* "and ten to one he'll have forgotten the whole thing."

* * *

On Thursday, Mrs. Cherill and Almina departed for Bond Street and new finery to tempt the Duke. There was no suggestion that Fanny should accompany them; once finished with shopping, they were engaged for a Venetian breakfast. Fanny saw them off with a sigh. Until that moment it was touch and go. Had they thought to take her with them as a break in the boredom of her days—for the carriage could have well returned her to Hill Street before calling for them later—she would have abandoned the balloon ascension, but they had not thought of Fanny. The coast was clear, with nothing to prevent a walk in the park.

Fanny took a deep breath, and quietly put on the oldest dress she possessed: a round gown of pink muslin, with only a single flounce and much faded from washing. She chose the plainest of her bonnets, and stealing into Almina's room for a view in the cheval glass, she was satisfied that she looked like a nursery child. So much so, in fact, that Pitcock frowned slightly when he saw her coming downstairs with Janet behind her.

"We are going to walk and do a few errands, Pitcock," Fanny held her voice steady. "It may be several hours before we return. In such nice weather I like to saunter."

"Yes, Miss Fanny." The butler stared after the small figure, marching down to the street and turning sedately toward Park Lane, with a troubled sense that all was not right. Surely Miss Fanny had something more modish than that old country dress? He would have been even more disturbed if he'd been able to observe her progress once round the corner.

Fanny quickened her pace toward the park, with Janet trotting along in bewilderment. Fanny was nearly as breathless as the maid, but from the suspense of "will he, won't he?" They had just gained the appointed path into the shrubbery when she spied Lord Waterbury swinging through the entrance in a glistening curricle drawn by a pair of matched chestnuts.

"Lud, Miss Fanny, there's the young gentleman who came the night of the fire," Janet said excitedly. "Who'd have thought to see him here!"

"I would," Fanny returned calmly, "because he has kindly promised to drive me to witness a balloon ascension, while you will take the list of errands and return to meet me here."

"No! Oh, Miss Fanny, you won't never drive alone with him! Whatever would the mistress say?"

"Nothing, for she will never know of it. Now, Janet—*dear* Janet," coaxingly, "he thinks me a mere schoolchild, the age of his little sister—and I only want a bit of adventure, I'm so tired of never going anywhere or seeing anything. Where's the harm, for a few hours on a fine sunny day?"

"Oh, dear, I know very well you should not, Miss Fanny," Janet protested piteously, "but I don't know how to stop you."

"Don't try! All you need do is carry out the errands," thrusting the list into her hands together with some shillings, "and meet me here in a few hours. See, there is even a bench on which to sit. Janet, you wouldn't have the heart to refuse me," artfully, "when *you* have the freedom to walk out with Perkins."

The curricle had drawn up beside them while Janet was blushing. She might still have protested, but Lord Waterbury was raising his hat with a broad grin. "What a prompt little conspirator you are," he approved. "Come up quickly, child. My cattle prefer moving to standing." With one strong hand he'd pulled Fanny up beside him and was fumbling in his pocket, withdrawing a coin which he tossed lightly to Janet. "There's something to line your pocket," he smiled. "Mind you meet us right here! Miss Fanny mustn't be kept waiting."

"Y-yes, sir. That is, no, sir—thank you, sir," Janet stammered confusedly as the curricle moved away. Looking over her shoulder while Lord Waterbury neatly feathered the corner, Fanny could see the girl staring bemused at the coin in her hand, and chuckled to herself. That had been a gold piece, she'd seen the glint as it flicked through the air.

"I hope you brought your smelling salts?"

"Why?"

"In preparation for this horrid sight you are determined to witness," Lord Waterbury said. "Only tell me in which pocket to find them, so I need not waste time."

"You would hold them to my nose with one hand and continue to observe the spectacle."

He laughed. "Show more respect for your elders," he advised with mock severity, "or I shall take you back at once."

"You will not," Fanny remarked, "for you would lose a vast amount of time and quite possibly be too late for the balloon."

"Sheer blackmail," he grumbled, and grinned at her boyishly. "Well, how have you gone on since that fire?"

"Excellently, thank you. There was much to freshen before the musicale."

"I collect it was a triumph," he said carelessly. "Such things are not in my line."

"You do not care for music, milord?"

"In moderation—very *much* in moderation." Lord Waterbury winced, "The number of evenings one must endure a flat voice, a strumming of the harp or twiddles on a flute—dismal!"

"Papa called it an 'infernal racket' and went to his club, which was a pity, for Almy has a truly beautiful voice," Fanny said loyally. "She sang after supper at the Duke of Wyvern's particular request, and the professional singers asked permission to join her."

"Hah! Wyvern, eh? What a dull dog!" Lord Waterbury dismissed the Duke. "How did you escape your dragon?"

Fanny crossed her fingers surreptitiously. "Oh, she has not come back. There was illness, you know, and mama gave her leave to stay as long as she was needed."

"So you are having a holiday, or did she set you an immense bundle of lessons to keep you out of mischief?" he teased. "What do you study?"

"French, music, drawing, and dancing."

"What, no sums? No Latin or Greek? No perusal of the globe?"

"No, milord."

"What a magnificently uneducated miss in such a bluestocking age!"

"You cannot be serious! No young lady would admit to education, surely?"

"No, they do not," he agreed, "but they are so accomplished, to hear tell, as to leave no other possible interpretation. All young ladies read the latest improving books, write verses, fabricate screens and footstools. They travel north, south, east, and west, and bring back charming watercolors of the scenery. They always know where they have been, what they have seen, and can bore you for hours with the history of each shire—and now that Boney is gone, I suppose they will expand their travels to the Continent, which will increase the scope of their boring reminiscences."

There was a cynical note in his voice. Fanny murmured tactfully, "Perhaps later it may be found my education is deficient, but at present, of what use are sums? My pocket money is too small to require accounts. And I never travel anywhere, so there seems no particular need for a globe."

"Still," sardonically, "no Latin or Greek?"

"Hardly anyone in London speaks anything but English, milord."

He shouted with laughter. "Damme, what a neat answer! I must remember it."

By the time they'd reached the spot fixed for the ascension, Fanny had completely forgotten her reprehensible behavior. Lord Waterbury was as comfortable as Harry, whom he vaguely recalled as an august upperclassman at Eton. "I fancy Egerton was his fag, it was a different house." On his side, Lord Waterbury teased her and ordered her about like his youngest sister. As they drew into position among the other carriages, Fanny was recalled to dangerous discovery by a vigorous hail from another spectator.

"Who am I?" she hissed agitatedly, as he prepared to toss the reins to a lounger.

"What d'you mean 'who are you'?"

"If we meet your friends—how will you introduce me?"

His face cleared. "You're a country cousin," he decided swiftly. "What's your name again?"

"Fanny."

"Right. I'm your Cousin Charles," he muttered as a positive Tulip sauntered forward.

"Charlie, old boy—thought I'd see you here. Said to myself, 'Give anyone twenty to one old Charlie shows up!' Pity I didn't think to get it covered at White's," the Tulip drawled.

"Lord, you couldn't have found a taker," Waterbury returned scornfully, leaping down from the curricle and straightening his cuffs while the Fashion-plate raised his quizzing glass to Fanny. "Here's my Cousin Fanny—it's Bertie Pakenham, Fanny. Come on, get down and we'll have a look at the balloon."

"Your servant, ma'am," said Bertie automatically. "Never knew you had cousins, too, old man."

"What d'you mean 'too'?"

"Why, you know—all those sisters. My God, the settlements to make in your family with all these females."

"We'll worry about Fanny when we come to her, which won't be for some time," Charles returned austerely, and gave her a prodigious wink as she stepped down.

Controlling her face, Fanny made a demure curtsey and ignored Bertie's audible comment, "You'll get rid of this one without a settlement if she grows up as neat as she is now."

Lord Waterbury frowned. "Mind what you say, she's

only a child in the schoolroom."

"Playin' hooky? Well, she's a better choice than the little ladybird you had last week, and that's a fact! No need to scowl at me, old boy—only statin' the truth. Never saw a chap with such bad taste in women. Where you find 'em, I don't know, and each one worse than the last."

"Hold your tongue, you fool!" Charles growled, while Fanny bit her lips and looked the other way. With a brother like Harry, she was perfectly conversant with "ladybirds." She stole a glance at His Lordship's reddened countenance and smothered a giggle. "Dammit, it's not funny," he told her, harassed, while Bertie was wandering forward to the balloon. "Not the thing to say before a child, can't imagine what Bertie was thinking of—usually the soul of courtesy."

Fanny's shoulders shook slightly. "Courtesy doesn't require thinking, Cousin Charles—and one glance at his face," she gasped. "I'm sorry if he's a particular friend of yours, I'm sure he's very nice, but you can see he was absent when the Lord handed out brains."

Charles' eyebrows rose, startled, but Fanny chuckled, and he suddenly laughed heartily. "Damme, you're right—not but what he's the prince of good fellows, up to every rig and row in town."

"I'm sure he is. Shall we examine the basket? They look nearly ready to leave."

She stuck very close to her escort, avoiding notice and glancing cautiously at the other spectators, but apparently it was not an occasion to interest any of Almina's friends. She saw no one she recognized. More confidently, she ventured to raise her head and look at the great circle of silk to be inflated from the pumps nearby. The carriage basket seemed quite too small and insubstantial to hold the two brawny men who were making ready for the trip. Everyone had questions, but to Fanny it seemed that Charles' inquiries were more intelligent than others. He fell into a long chat with one of the ascensionists, who paid the most flattering attention to his words.

At last everyone was requested to step back. The balloonists entered the basket to a round of hearty applause and scattered cheers. The ropes were cast off, and with a shudder the gas-filled bubble dragged them a few feet this way or that. Fanny held her breath and unconsciously grasped Charles' arm. For a moment she feared an accident. The contraption dipped dangerously; then caught by the wind, the balloon veered about and strained as though unable to lift the men from the ground. She had a horrid vision of the whole thing landing ignominiously in a clump of trees a short way ahead, of the men being overturned and falling with resultant broken bones.

She was not reassured by Charles' absent murmur, "Don't worry, they've two doctors at hand. Ah, *there* it goes!"

A sudden strong breeze lifted the balloon, until it floated higher and higher. All Fanny's fears were forgotten in the thrill of observing that soaring flight. She clung to Charles' arm, conscious only of an inchoate yearning to be aloft. As she watched the erratic wavering path of the balloon with the men waving gaily from their basket, Fanny's lips parted in mingled joy and envy. To be able to see the tops of the trees, leave the little earthbound people behind and drift toward the clouds—how wonderful it must be! Silently she stood until the balloon became a speck and was lost to view. "Oh, wasn't it lovely," she sighed, and was suddenly aware of Charles' hand resting warmly over hers clutching his arm. "Oh, dear, I am so sorry," she apologized with a blush, examining his coat sleeve anxiously. "I didn't think, Cousin Charles, but I do not believe I have crumpled the cloth."

His sherry-brown eyes were lit with little glints of gold excitement. "Did you enjoy the horrid sight, smelling salts not required?" he asked, with a strange half-smile.

"Well—just for a moment until they were safely up,

I had a qualm," she confessed, "which is stupid of me, because if they'd fallen then, it'd be no more than broken bones—but later, when they were dangling far above us, I had no fears at all! Yet an accident then would have meant certain death."

"Very strange."

Under the intensity of his gaze, Fanny was impelled to honesty. "Don't think me mad—but if there were a second balloon, I would now be sitting in it, waiting for the ascent."

"You, too?" he said in a low voice.

Before Fanny could find words, Bertie came wandering back. "Famous sight, eh, Miss Fanny? Not given you the headache, I hope?"

"No, indeed. It was a thrilling experience."

"How far d'you think they'll go?"

"To the moon!"

"No, seriously. Last chaps were blown nearly up to Cumberland. I'm backing this to overreach 'em."

"Don't waste your blunt," Charles advised. "Wind's wrong today."

They entered into a lengthy argument of possibilities and probabilities, not one word of which was comprehensible to Fanny, although she found the interchange absorbing for the differences between the two young men. Lord Waterbury was quick of speech and mind, while Bertie Pakenham simply clung more firmly to his opinion as one point after another was demolished. He was perfectly good-humored, just *stubborn*. When Waterbury strode across to the betting booth, Bertie looked after him admiringly, "Never knew such a fellow for facts and figures. Where he gets 'em, I don't know. Makes your head spin to listen to him, no use to argue; if he can't prove it one way, he'll find another. Safest thing is just to stick to what you said in the first place."

Privately, Fanny thought Mr. Pakenham must lose a good many bets that way, but her eyes were following His Lordship with appreciation. He was infinitely more to her taste than the Duke of Wyvern; there was nothing stolid or pompous about Charles, and as for *handsome* there was no comparison at all. Lord Waterbury had much the best on every point, including the nonchalance with which he allowed the breeze to ruffle his black hair and disarrange his neckcloth. Vaguely, she wondered if he was what was called a Corinthian, or by his handling of the ribbons perhaps he was a Nonpareil. Harry had once explained the nuances of *haut ton,* but she could not precisely recall them.

Lost in her contemplation, she nearly came to grief. Bertie had been standing politely beside her, making an occasional remark suited to a schoolchild. "One of Sally's brood?"

"Yes, sir," she murmured absently.

"Lord, the number of females," Bertie shook his head. "Old Pevency had five, managed to settle 'em all—and what must this one do but have another five! Don't know where it'll end, demmed if I do. Oh, hallo, Duke—you here?"

"Well, of course I'm here—you're lookin' at me, ain't you?" a hearty voice demanded, and added slyly, "Who's the little pigeon? Not goin' to refuse an introduction, I hope?"

Fanny froze with horror after a single side glance. Bertie's friend was Sir Marmaduke Lofton, a heavy contender for Almina's hand, and for all Fanny considered him a touch stupid, she had no dependence on his stupidity extending so far as total lack of recognition after three previous meetings. She swung away, quaking with fright, while Bertie said jovially, "Damme, what a sell! Well, you have put your foot into it and no mistake! Why, that's only Charles' cousin—one of Sally Gresham's brats."

"No!" said Sir Marmaduke incredulously. "Charlie gone paternal on us? I say, old boy," as His Lordship approached, "Ain't you well? What are you about, lugging around a great schoolgirl? Ain't like you at all."

"Taking no chances on your stealing habits,"

Charles replied, his eyes catching Fanny's fearsome grimace. "Off to the carriage with you, child. Have to get you home in time or Louisa'll raise a rumpus."

"Louisa?" Bertie looked confused. "Thought she said she was one of Sally's?"

"So she is, but staying with Louisa," Charles said swiftly. "Got to drive her back, get rid of her and join you. Where'll you be?"

"Might look in at Tatt's—see the race results," Bertie said vaguely, "or toddle along to White's for a look at the betting book, see if there's anything I fancy."

"If that ain't like you, Charlie," Sir Marmaduke protested. "How the devil do we *know* where we'll be an hour from now?"

Hoisted into her seat by the loiterer holding the horses, Fanny bent her head until the bonnet hid her face, while Lord Waterbury swung up to his seat with a laugh and tossed a coin as the man handed over the reins. "I'll catch up to you somewhere—at Tomaston's dinner, if not before." With a slap of leather on the horses, he'd set them moving forward—rather slowly, among the press of other carriages leaving the scene, but at least out of range of his friends. Fanny sighed with unconscious relief.

"I collect you did not wish to encounter Lofton," he chuckled. "I've never seen a more speaking countenance than yours, Fanny! What have you got against old Duke?"

"Only that he has been a particular friend of my sister's any time these two years," she returned. "Not that Almina favors him, but he's met her younger sister both here and in the country."

"Lud, what an escape!"

Safely away from Marmaduke, Fanny giggled, "An escape, certainly—but for me, or Almy?"

Charles' eyes glinted gold again at Fanny's wickedly innocent face, "Oh, lumme," he gasped with laughter, "that's famous!"

"But not for repeating," she warned. "Remember,

Cousin Charles, you mustn't give me away, please?"

"Never!" he said dramatically, flicking his whip to set the team moving smoothly through a space in the traffic that looked only wide enough for a snake. "My lips are sealed until death! And so," while she was recovering her breath, "you enjoyed the 'horrid sight'?"

"Vastly, and thank you, milord. It was immensely kind in you to take me," Fanny looked up at him seriously. "London—well, it is not amusing when one is young. There is so much one may not do."

"Such as?"

Fanny was silent for a moment, looking blindly into space. "Oh, I cannot really be seen, you know, for I am not Out—and while I am without a governess, I can only take walks in the park with a maid. There is only the one carriage, and it is needed for mama and Almina."

"Surely there are other children, you have friends?"

"Not really. There is no one quite my age. Papa did not realize, and now it is too late to send me home to Cherley. I must make the best of it, and later we will go to Bath."

"Bath? Good God, what a dismal place! I wouldn't go there, if I were you, Fanny."

She could not help laughing at his appalled voice. "I'm afraid I've no choice. Cherley is closed, and I must go wherever mama and Almina go, but perhaps in Bath it may be possible for me to ride. They will not need Perkins so often, or we might arrange for me to join a group with a groom."

"You are fond of horses?"

"Yes, but *not* of the stables. Harry did try to teach me, and I know *how* to do everything, but I would rather leave it for the stableboy."

Charles chuckled. "So should I! I collect Harry is your hero?"

Fanny nodded vigorously. "We are oldest and youngest. Almina and I were the wrong age for each other, she was bored when I tagged along, but Harry's old enough not to mind. He was going to teach me to drive, but then his leave was canceled."

"Should you like to be a whip?" Charles asked amusedly.

"Of all things! Almina doesn't care for it, which Harry calls a mercy," Fanny dimpled, "for she does it remarkably ill."

"But you would like it? Let's try your capabilities." With no further ado, he set the reins in her hands, and folded his arms for observation.

Fanny was momentarily frozen in shock that he should entrust his team to a schoolgirl, but Harry's training firmed her hands automatically. With only a tiny hesitation, she was in control. The horses were a delight, what Harry would call "sweet-goers," responding easily to the lightest touch. Fanny could have sung for joy, it set the seal on an already perfect day, and *damn the consequences,* as Harry would have said. All too soon they were reaching more crowded roads, and Charles took back the reins.

"Your brother taught you well," he smiled, "but I fancy I could carry on for him. Shall I teach you the niceties?"

"Please!"

"Then we must contrive to meet again. Shall we visit the Royal Exchange, or are lions and tigers an old story?"

"No, indeed. I am very fond of cats—any sort, except human."

"You have excellent taste," he chuckled. "Wednesday next? I do not think you should try sooner, or it may be remarked."

"Wednesday would be very good, milord. Someone gives a party that day which will occupy mama and Almina."

They were swinging into the park by then, and he eyed her curiously. "Who would ever have thought," he murmured half to himself, "that I should become a mentor for a school chit. Damme, they must breed 'em more knowing these days."

"There is Janet, milord," Fanny said quickly, before he could pursue that train of thought.

"Eh? Oh, yes, I see her." He drew the curricle to a halt, and Fanny descended. On the path, she curtsied in her best nursery manner, and rather thought she had convinced him, because Janet was some inches taller. Lord Waterbury's face seemed cleared of any questions. "Next Wednesday, here, one o'clock!" He grinned at her, "Good day, little conspirator." With a flourish of the whip, he drove away, leaving Fanny stare after his dashing exit at Hyde Park Corner.

"Ooooh, Miss Fanny," Janet sighed in heartfelt relief. "I was that scared, waiting for you. I says to myself, wot if the mistress and Miss Almina should happen to drive by?"

"Silly! You know they were going to Lady Wigmore, I doubt they'll be home before tea." Fanny started sedately for the gates. "Oh, Janet, I would not have missed it for the world!" It was evident the maid did not share her enthusiasm for the reported highlights of the excursion, although she listened with enjoyable shudders. They were turned into Hill Street before Fanny had finished. "Now—quickly, tell me where you went and what you did, Janet. Remember, nobody must know I was not with you."

With a gasp, the maid plunged into a disconnected recital of the errands, and buying new ribbons for herself with His Lordship's guinea, "but I didn't spend it all, Miss Fanny. I've still a few shillings put by, thinking perhaps I might have enough to buy muslin at Grafton House for a new dress."

"I expect you will, if Lord Waterbury continues generous—but," Fanny pointed out anxiously, "how would you explain it, Janet? Cook or Pitcock is sure to ask where you got the money. Please be careful, for my sake."

"I never thought of that. Oh, Lord, Miss Fanny, you're never going off with him again?" Janet protested, equally anxious.

"Yes, I am! Next Wednesday he is going to take me

to the zoo, and he has promised to continue Harry's lessons in driving." Fanny's eyes sparkled, "Oh, Janet—don't refuse me! You know how dull it is for me here. I never go anywhere or do anything, I've no one to visit with. He thinks I'm about thirteen, introduced me to one of his friends as a schoolgirl cousin—he calls me Fanny and treats me as casually as Harry would. Truly, there wasn't a word that would upset mama, Janet. Please let me have a little fun."

"If it's discovered, I'll be turned away, Miss Fanny—not but what we all know it's hard for you," Janet fretted. "Mr. Pitcock says you shouldn't have been brought except that the master wanted to close Cherley. All the servants gone, the horses sold—it's hard on the provisioners to have no orders from the big house, but once Miss Almina's married, it'll change. Oh," she put her hand to her mouth, frightened. "I wasn't supposed to talk of it."

"That's all right, Janet. I already knew," Fanny said as calmly as possible, but once into the house, she ran lightly to her room and set about changing her clothes.

There was not a vast choice in her armoire. The visits to milliners and modistes had been for Almina, "because she is Out, my love, and in any case, the newest fashions would be unsuitable for you," Mrs. Cherill had explained. Fanny had been content to wear what she had—until now . . . but Janet's words were disturbing.

"I wonder if papa could give me just enough to buy fabric at that place Janet mentioned, and I could sew it myself," she thought yearningly. "I'd like a pretty new dress for Charles." Later, she stared at herself in the dressing mirror. "Can it be? Am I in love?"

CHAPTER III

If the truth were known, Lord Waterbury very nearly *had* forgotten his impulsive suggestion to Fanny. It was merely the circumstance of seeing her father engaged at the fifty-guinea hazard table on the previous evening combined with a notice of the balloon ascension in the *Gazette* that reminded him, and since he was a kindly young man, he turned into the park on the chance. At the age of twenty-four and with numerous little sisters, Charles was not too old to remember the excitement of An Outing. "Can't disappoint a child!"

But by the time he was striding into his lodgings, he was both amused and confused. "Damme, she was more fun than her sister or any of the other Belles! I'll warrant she's having a thin time of it, with no little friends to play with," he said to himself, and told his manservant, "Somers, remind me I'm engaged for Wednesday midday."

"Very good, milord—and Her Grace requests your presence at dinner this evening." Somers cleared his throat genteelly. "I ventured to reply that I believed you were bespoke for Mr. Tomaston, but I fear it did not answer."

"Oh, curse it!" Charles groaned. "Nothing ever answers with m'grandmother."

"No, Milord," Somers agreed. "I fancy there is a young lady she wishes to bring to your attention."

"There is *always* a young lady, although why she supposes anyone would have *me* is beyond understanding. Oh, well," Charles sighed, "send word to Mr.

Tomaston that I'll join them later."

"Yes, milord." Somers looked tactfully into space. "I believe Her Grace had already informed Mr. Tomaston, and I have laid out your dress clothes in the event of Almack's."

"Good God, so it is. I'd forgot," Charles groaned again. "Have I a voucher?"

"Certainly, milord." Somers was faintly shocked. "I have placed it in the correct pocket."

His Lordship burst out laughing. "Lud, what would I do without you, Somers!"

Her Grace, the Dowager Duchess of Pevency, said very much the same thing that evening when her grandson bowed gracefully over her hand. "Correct to a shade," she observed. "Your man makes you, Charles."

"Why, so I should hope, ma'am—but I do my own neckcloths," he protested with a grin that caused a twitch of her lips.

"So much is obvious," she remarked austerely, "and if you were not forever in some horrid gaming hall, you might have time to practice for a better result. Does tonight's concoction have a name, or is it a mere flight of fancy?"

"Both, ma'am. This is the Waterbury Fall, greatly admired in many circles, I assure you."

"Cribb's Parlor or Jackson's boxing ring, no doubt." Her Grace sniffed disdainfully, ignoring his chuckle. "Let me present you to Miss Maria Jennings."

"What, *another* one?" Charles asked irrepressibly. "How do you contrive to find so many eligible young ladies no one ever heard of, ma'am?"

"It's more to the point if they have not heard of you," she retorted, "but as it happens, Maria is one of my goddaughters: Sir Bartelmy's youngest girl. You'll find her a sweet creature. Maria, my love, I make known to you my grandson, Lord Charles Waterbury . . . Miss Jennings, Charles, and mind your manners!" Her Grace sailed away to greet other guests, leaving him to marvel mentally at her concept of "a sweet creature."

"Insipid is more accurate," he said to himself while making his bow, but by evening's end he had changed the word to "antidote." Miss Jennings had no conversation of any sort, which he decided was perhaps as well, for her voice was a soprano whine. Her pallid gray eyes were faintly protuberant, as also her teeth. She admitted to no knowledge of anything, exhibited no reaction of genteel interest or ladylike shrinking no matter what he said. She listened, said "Oh?" or "Fancy!" Under his grandmother's eagle eye, Charles persevered manfully throughout dinner, growing more and more desperate.

When at last the company was removing to carriages bound for the assembly, he was sufficiently goaded to tell the Dowager privately, "Good God, ma'am, *how* could you so inflict me? I was used to think you had a kindness for me!"

"Thirty thousand pounds," the Dowager commented tersely.

"It'll take twice that to get rid of her," Charles was equally terse. "Make my excuses, previous engagement, sudden news of a death or something—for God's sake, grandmama, you can't want me shackled that badly!"

"No," she sighed. "I'm sorry, Charles. I hadn't seen Maria since she was a mere child, and at that age—well, one unconsciously makes allowances for even the most repulsive brat. They may grow out of it, you know, but I own she has not. Favors her mother, poor thing."

Charles was so unstrung by his grandmother's doleful face that he capitulated instantly. He could not recall ever to have heard the Dowager Duchess utter the word "sorry," particularly to himself. "Oh, well, I'll accompany you to start her off," he mumbled weakly, "but mind you enlist the patronesses to disengage me, ma'am."

After the first country dance, he bitterly regretted his generosity. Miss Jennings was no Terpsichore. She moved gawkily this way and that, never quite where she should have been when Charles turned around. Once she got into the adjoining set for a full two measures, from which he retrieved her with exasperation. The fact that Bertie Pakenham witnessed his humiliation was infuriating, and only innate good breeding enabled him to return Miss Jennings to his grandmother without slapping the girl's stupid face.

In the anteroom, Bertie hailed him with surprise. "You here tonight, Charles? Thought you was promised to Tomaston."

"I thought you were, also."

Bertie shook his head, "Goin' on later—first here with m'sister, we're popping her off this season. M'mother thinks we'll do it all right and tight—can't see it myself, although she's better than that freak you was capering with. Good God, old boy!"

"Goddaughter of my grandmother's, old Bartelmy Jennings' youngest with thirty thousand pounds," Charles returned succinctly, "but between you and me, not even a gazetted fortune-hunter would have her."

Bertie surveyed Miss Jennings in her seat beside the Dowager Duchess, and pursed his lips. "Ernshire?"

"Not even Rokesby."

"That bad, is she?"

"Worse! I tell you what it is these days, Bertie: the ones you could like haven't a penny, and the fortunes belong to the antidotes. Demmed if I know where we're heading."

Mr. Pakenham's sheep-like countenance brightened faintly. "You're exactly right," he declared, "but that may be what m'mother's counting on. Edie's midway between: not much for looks, but she's got a good temper and fifteen thousand pounds. I say, old boy, why don't you? No one I'd rather have in the family, assure you."

"Good God, are you disguised so early?" Charles retorted scornfully. "I ain't so far in the basket that I need a fifteen thousand pound feather pillow. I'd rather wait until Fanny grows up."

"Fanny? Oh, your cousin," Bertie looked doubtful. "Ain't the thing to marry a cousin, old boy."

His eyes observing the entrance of Miss Almina Cherill, Lord Waterbury gulped and caught himself just in time. "Well, what I'm meaning to say is: wait for another generation, it might be better. God knows, there's nothing in this one."

"Perhaps—but the thing is, they all seem to grow up the same way, and then they change after they're settled," Bertie observed. "It'd be all right if a chap only knew what they'd change *into*. The way it is, you haven't a clue. They hide things until *afterward*. Now *I* know m'sister won't turn into a shrew, she's too lazy—but how the devil would anyone else know it?"

"Yes, by God—and supposing she married a fellow who didn't want a lazy woman?" Charles was much struck by his friend's masterly analysis. "Take Lady Anna Coningsby, for instance, or Miss Soames, and what have you got: pretty faces, who play the harp and dance nicely."

They spent several minutes discussing the young ladies of the *ton*, which was enjoyable but nevertheless a mistake. Lady Jersey bore down on them before they could retreat, and ruthlessly hauled them forth to dance with the two plainest damsels in the room. After that, Charles filled his card as rapidly as possible. He even got a waltz with Miss Cherill, and was emboldened by reason of an unusually clear head (no liquor was served at Almack's) to refer to the balloon ascension. "Should you have liked to witness it?"

"No, I thank you," she shuddered. "What horrid things you find amusing, milord."

"More instructive than amusing, Miss Cherill. Some clever chappie's going to learn how to make the balloon go where he wants, and we won't need three days of coaching to reach Scotland for the grouse shoot."

"Do you seriously expect *ladies* to be blown about in those nasty little baskets?"

"Oh, I expect they'll think up some sort of comfortable closed carriage," Charles conceded, "but compared to jolting for several days, only fancy leaving London in the morning and arriving at Kirkcudbright for tea."

"I can't fancy it," she said flatly. "Besides, I have no acquaintance in Scotland, milord."

"Why, you've only to be seen for an admiring court to form about you rapidly," he smiled. "Astonished at my good fortune in securing a dance with you tonight, assure you I am!"

Almina's eyes flashed dangerously. "As astonished as myself at encountering you, milord. You so rarely grace an assembly that one had a notion you did not care for such mild pursuits."

"Touché," Charles admitted with a wicked grin, "which makes it the more delightful to be dancing with you, Miss Cherill. The highest reward for dutiful obedience to m'grandmother, 'pon my honor."

Under his teasing twinkle, Almina bit her lip and could not suppress a small gurgle of laughter. "Oh, what a whisker!"

They finished the waltz in perfect charity with each other, but when he'd returned her to Mrs. Cherill, made his bows and departed, Charles thought involuntarily of Fanny. Four or five years hence, when she was having her season, would she have changed into just another conventional miss?

Fanny would have been surprised to know how often Lord Waterbury thought of her—fleetingly, to be sure, but events brought her to mind unexpectedly. The balloon had not overreached the earlier attempt, whereby Charles pocketed a handsome sum from his wager; how pleased Fanny would be! Meeting his Aunt Louisa with two of her younger children, Charles startled her by his kindliness in talking to them—but his vague idea of somehow contriving to get playmates for Fanny was useless. She was certainly more than twelve and would only be bored by his Cousin Susan. Observing the Honorable Edgar Cherill at Boodle's, Charles thought of Fanny rather than Almina—and wondered at himself. Last season he'd *almost* felt the Dark Incomparable had captured his heart.

He had certainly been a determined member of her string, springing forward to secure a dance or wangling invitations to as many of the *ton* parties as possible. She'd liked him very well, too, though he was aware her watchful mama hoped for something better. What a difference twelve months could make! Now Charles could not think what he had fancied in Miss Cherill. Had she changed, or was it himself? She was beautiful as ever, willing as ever to flirt lightly. Others of last year's beaux were still pursuing, but somehow—almost without noticing—Charles had dropped out of the running.

In fact, during the intervening months he had subtly become absorbed into the ways of purely masculine *haut ton:* shooting and fishing, racing and hunt parties, snug bachelor dinners and gambling. Such pursuits had always been part of his life; now they engrossed him. An august smile from the Duke of Beaufort, a lazy "Waterbury, ain't it? H'are you?" from Brummell, or acceptance by the Four Horse Club was more exciting these days than the most come-hither glances.

He was in no case to marry, anyway. Even last year he'd not quite come up to scratch despite Almina's beauty, and this year he was even less inclined for shackles. There was fun and to spare with the other free spirits in the *ton,* plenty of ladybirds for lighter moments, and no responsibilities.

"At the pace Cherill's going, there'll be nothing left for Fanny," he told himself disapprovingly. "What ails the man to be playing this deep? He'll never come about, this road." The fact that Charles was following the same path, though at smaller stakes, did not regis-

ter. When his man of business informed him austerely
that Lord Waterbury must either curtail his expendi-
tures or add yet another mortgage to his already encumbered estate, Charles said impatiently, "Did you
haul me down to the City for *this?* For God's sake,
man, increase the mortgage and don't bother me."

"I merely wished to be certain that Your Lordship
was aware no more can be done," the agent returned
primly. "If your requirements continue to exceed income, the next step will be to sell you out of the Funds
or allow foreclosure of Basings."

"Sell my land? Demmed if I will!" Lord Waterbury
roared indignantly. "You must be out of your mind,
Rowbotham."

The agent looked at him impersonally. "I fear Your
Lordship will have no option in the matter. Basings
does not produce more than will satisfy its mortgages,
which leaves you only the funded income for your living expenses. If this were sold," Rowbotham shrugged,
"you would be literally penniless, milord."

"That bad, is it?" Charles frowned. "Well—well, it
won't be necessary. You'll see I shall come about." He
stood up, pulling on his driving gloves and adjusting
the capes of his coat. "Sorry, Rowbotham, I'd no idea I
was this badly dipped. Thank you for telling me."

"Since you are in such an accommodating frame of
mind, and as one who has known you since your first
nankeens," the agent remarked, "I will venture to add
that a six months' repairing lease might well set all to
rights, Lord Waterbury. I fancy there is some irregularity, some laziness at Basings. It should produce more.
It used to do so, but when an owner never visits, never
personally inspects his land," Rowbotham shrugged, "a
staff becomes lax. I will say no more, but," he pulled
himself erect and stepped around the desk to open the
door for his client, "a show of interest works wonders,
milord."

"Good God," Charles stared at him blankly, "d'you
expect me to drop out of everything for *six months?*"

"Not at all! Merely—an unexpected appearance to put the staff on its toes—or perhaps a party of young gentlemen to hold a private race and try the trout stream." Rowbotham pursed his lips, "I believe Basings affords some excellent coverts in the fall, also. Your late grandfather used often to make a party at Basings following the grouse season, and while I recall he termed it 'humbug country' for hunting, there is some modest sport to be found in November."

Lord Waterbury's eyes hardened. "You have it well planned, haven't you?"

The agent straightened his spare figure and met Charles' eyes firmly. "Yes, I rather think I have," he murmured. "I don't say Your Lordship must be mewed up without a week here or there, but I fancy Mr. Pakenham, Mr. Tomaston, and others of your friends will be good-humored enough to keep you company now and then. No doubt the rose gardens are in poor case," he sighed. "They always need a woman's hand."

"If you are insinuating that I should marry for the sake of a rose garden . . ."

"By no means, milord!" Mr. Rowbotham looked shocked. "You are far from ready for parson's mousetrap. No, indeed! It is merely that, when the moment arrives, I should feel I had failed in my duty if Your Lordship were to find himself, er, under the hatches."

Lord Waterbury's jaw tightened. "I shan't," he said tersely. "Good day, Rowbotham."

"And to you, milord," but closing the door behind his client's striding figure, the agent permitted himself a secret smile. "Hunh, you've only to tell 'em they'll lose their land," he chuckled to himself.

He had, in fact, gravely disturbed Charles by the suggestion, and it was only the engagement with Fanny that prevented an immediate inspection of Basings. Driving back from the City, Lord Waterbury was half-minded to change the projected outing to another day—or why not take her to Basings instead of the zoo? Fanny would enjoy a sniff of country air—but then he'd have to return her by teatime, which would limit his investigation. No, leave it for another day when they could plan ahead. Perhaps the governess would be back, and he could figure some way to disclose his friendship with Fanny for an open invitation.

"Yes, that's the ticket," he said to himself, blithely leaving the details for inspiration of a later moment. "Take the child to the zoo today, go to Basings tomorrow when I can really look into things. It might take more than a day. As fa always says, never mix business with pleasure. Get it all cleaned up, take Fanny down for a nice little nuncheon, and ramble around to show her everything at leisure."

It did not occur to His Lordship that he was taking rather a lot of trouble for a mere schoolgirl . . .

On Fanny's side, throughout the week Lord Waterbury had rarely been absent from her mind. She discussed with herself every look, word, chuckle, manly gesture, exactly as Almina was talking to her mama of Wyvern—but was this love? "He is the first man of the *haut ton* I have encountered, for you cannot really count that odious Percy Ribbons who was trying to kiss me in the gardens at Cherley, just because he was a distant cousin. Ugh!" Fanny's nose wrinkled in memory. "And Mr. Cattermole is only a curate who has never entered society, so I've nobody to compare to Charles."

The end product of her reflections was depressing. Charles had to think her a schoolgirl, or nothing could be more improper than taking her to drive—but if Fanny loved him, it was hopeless to dream of engaging his affections in return. Gentlemen do not lose their hearts to little girls. Sometimes she wished she'd never allowed temper to get the best of her, never gone to the balloon ascension as a minor rebellion against the dullness of her life.

Always, looming ahead, was the spectre of what he

would think when he found out. Discovery was inevitable when she finally had her season, and Charles could ruin any chances, even if he thought it merely a famous joke. Fanny could visualize how he'd stare, and throw back his head with a hearty laugh. "Lud, what a little minx!" It was still a devilish coil, and she wondered at herself for courting disgrace, particularly after secretly consulting *Burke's Peerage*. Charles was the younger son of the Duke of Pevency, and he had not only five sisters but an older brother who already had two sons in line for the title. Sadly, Fanny suspected that Lord Charles Waterbury was not what mama would call "an eligible connection."

Yet neither was the Honorable Edgar Cherill; she wondered why mama could not have done better for herself—unless her dowry was small. More and more Fanny was conscious of money. Apparently papa didn't have any, or so he said whenever the bills were presented. "*Another* gown from Madame Fiddle-faddle? Damme, between you, I shall be in the basket within a year."

Once Almina was goaded to reply, "Another few evenings at Watier's, and we shall all be in the basket, sir."

The resultant explosion from her father sent her in tears to take shelter with Fanny, while Mrs. Cherill spent some difficult moments with her husband. Between defending himself from Almina's riposte and requesting that her mama teach her some manners, Mr. Cherill grew hoarse with emotion. When at length he had stamped away, Mrs. Cherill said grimly, "I wish you will guard your tongue, miss!"

"But it is so unfair," Almina sniffled. "It's always you or I that he says cost him money, and you know he throws away more in one night at macao than six new dresses, mama."

"You should know nothing of such things, Almina."

"How can I avoid it? Everyone knows, mama. Do but consider my position: I may be penniless for all we know, and what about Fanny?"

"Nonsense! Your settlements are already made, held in trust. It is simply that papa has had some reverses—I think."

"His reverses are switching from piquet to deep basset," Almina muttered bitterly. "All right, mama—I'm sorry, I will be good, but it is hard."

"I know, my love, but we must be patient," Mrs. Cherill comforted. "Wyvern is not one of your rackety young gentlemen to toss his cap over the windmill, Almina. He has a great position, great responsibilities. One cannot wonder he takes time in choosing his duchess, but all moves most promisingly. Lady Ambrose would never have included you in the dinner party before her ball without Wyvern's direct request."

"Yes," Almina sighed. "I know, mama, but there is still no certainty. I am made known to his relatives, his compliments are graceful, but no more than he might say to anyone. I cannot help but feel anxious. It's some consolation that my portion exists, but it must be pitiful compared to what he has, and I've no title."

"You're the granddaughter of two earls," Fanny reminded her, "and if your portion isn't enough, you can have mine, Almy."

"Pea-goose! Then what will you do when the time comes?"

"Oh, we will 'contrive something,' " Fanny eyed her mother, until Mrs. Cherill smiled ruefully. "There, that's better. Don't be in the glooms, Almy. You're so very beautiful, no man could resist you."

"Hah!" was Almina's comment, but she smiled at Fanny. "Well, *I* must contrive something, or be shockingly late for Lady Wigmore's luncheon."

Wednesday came at last, and Fanny was still undecided what to do. She knew she should go to the park, and if Charles came, she should excuse herself from accompanying him. As matters stood, it was a single incident—a bit larky for a young lady, but possibly quickly forgotten. Why court any risks? Watching Almina, Fanny saw it was obvious there was more to forming an eligible connection than she had thought, and if the Dark Incomparable was having difficulties, how much greater would be Fanny's with her *red* hair?

But all her resolution vanished the instant Charles drew up beside the path. "Hallo," he called cheerfully. "Right to the minute, eh? In a few years, when you're an Incomparable, you'll learn to keep a man cooling his heels."

"My eagerness is shocking, is it not?" Fanny chuckled, quite unable to refuse the hand extended to help her into the curricle. *Oh, once more couldn't matter; they'd never see anyone Charles knew at the Royal Exchange* . . . "But I am not a Belle and dare not depend upon your waiting so I may impress you with my importance," she said demurely, while he dropped a sovereign into Janet's fingers.

"Miss Almina will show you the tricks," he laughed. "Did you know Wyvern waited near an hour at Almack's before she deigned to arrive?"

"It was his own fault," Fanny said before she could stop herself, "and if he had known what a pother he made for everyone, he would never send red roses to an Incomparable again."

"Red roses? Come, tell me the whole!"

Fanny bit her lip, but could not resist his coaxing twinkle. "You solemnly promise not to repeat it?"

He composed his face to stern dignity. "Word of a Pevency."

"Is that any good?" she asked dubiously.

"Sound as Lloyd's—for anything but money—and all in the family, *Cousin* Fanny."

"Oh, what a whisker," she snorted. "Well, Almina was in a flutter that Wyvern meant to engage half her ball card, from something he'd said. Nothing would suit but that mama should promise Fanchette double to finish the new gown in time. Somehow the woman managed it, the dress was delivered together with the bill, and unluckily, papa had *not* quite left for the club. When he saw that bill . . . oh, me!"

"Staggered him, eh?"

"He went up into the boughs! Mama was trying to explain that Almina was engaged to dance with the Duke of Wyvern, and papa said, 'What of it? Damme, d'you mean to buy a new dress every time she's going to dance with a title? God help me if Prinny favors her at one of his dress parties!' " Unconsciously, Fanny was making a good story out of it, encouraged by Charles' amusement. "Then, just as mama had calmed papa and Almina was dressed, Perkins brought up the Duke's flowers. Papa was quite cowed, he said 'Bless my soul,' and conceded Almy was in looks—until the paper was unfolded and there was the nosegay of *red* roses."

"Do not keep me in such suspense: does she have the rose fever?"

"No, but the gown was a vivid bronzed orange. The red flowers were hideous against it. Almy took one look and went into strong hysterics, because she must either change her gown or leave the flowers behind. Then papa went into a second uproar. He said they'd promised him a duke if Almina had a new gown, and now she had it, she could damme well *wear* it."

Charles burst out laughing. "And by the time it was explained that the nosegay was more important than the dress, Miss Almina was so late that Wyvern's consequence was affronted, and he left after two dances. By Jove, that's why her card wasn't filled; she even had a waltz left for me."

Fanny's heart thumped anxiously. "You are acquainted with Almy?"

"Lord, yes," he said. "She's nothing to say to me, you know. I've no money, pockets wholly to let, no expectations unless my uncle remembers me. Your sister wants considerably more than that, although demmed if I know why she's taking so long about it."

"I think she wants someone she can love, not just an eligible connection," Fanny murmured.

"A pipe dream! She ain't likely to get both. By now, she'll choose the best-filled purse."

Fanny was silenced by the cynicism in his voice. The Royal Exchange changed the conversation, and in viewing the beasts, Almina was forgotten. Fanny was sincerely entranced by the lions, tigers, leopards in the flesh. "How beautiful they are. One longs to stroke them—do they purr?"

"I've no idea, and know better than to try to find out."

"Yes, indeed—only look at those great claws!"

At the end of the tour was a milkmaid's stand, which put Charles in mind of Basings. "I must go into Surrey to inspect my land for a few days. Are you fond of the country, Fanny?"

"Yes, indeed. It's all I've ever known until now," she sipped her milk reflectively. "How good this tastes! At Cherley right now the orchards are all pink and white blossoms, and the roses are beginning to flower," she sighed. "I do not know what will become of them. They should be clipped to shape the bushes, and sometimes they need to be watered, but there is no one to care for them."

Impulsively, he asked, "Should you like to drive out to Basings one day, if we can contrive it? Come, let's talk it over and give you a chance to perfect your handling of the ribbons." He pulled out his pocket watch, "There's a good hour before you need be back. Come on!"

She was not proof against that boyish grin, his hand catching hers to swing along beside him like a nursery child. "Are you *sure?*"

"Word of a Pevency!" he said solemnly, and grinned again. "Oh, come on, Fanny—there's time and to spare."

With a laugh, she capitulated. Charles headed swiftly away from the streets until they were across river onto a turnpike. "Hah, I thought I remembered," he turned into a side road and handed over the reins. "Forget which village this serves, but it's all on the way to Basings."

"Basings?"

"My estate, if you can call it that," he grimaced. "All fa can spare for a younger son, but it's a decent small property. I haven't seen it in a while. Old Rowbotham, my man of business, says it's mismanaged. He hauled me down to the City this morning and rang a peal over me. The long and the short of it is, I'm badly dipped—not that I shan't come about, but have to look into it."

"Indeed you must! I trust it is not in too bad case, Charles, but could you not remove there at the end of the season to see for yourself how all goes on? Do you have stock, or crops?"

"Lud, I don't know what I've got," he stared at her. "How come you to be so wise?"

She blushed slightly. "I was used to Cherley, you know."

"It's what Rowbotham advised," he began, and simultaneously a flustered hen burst squawking from the hedge to the road. The horses neighed wildly and under Fanny's inexperienced hands they bolted, nearly pulling her from the carriage. "Oh, the devil!" said Charles, reaching around her to hold her in place while he set his hands over hers on the reins.

The road was deserted, but ahead was a dangerous curve. She fully expected to overturn into the ditch, the pressure of his hands was cruelly strong on her slender fingers, but she had no breath to protest. Slowly, steadily, Charles conquered the beasts until they made the curve with no more than a minor lurch and were halted in a side lane. In the relief of safety, Fanny pulled her hands free with a gulp and burst into tears.

Charles secured the reins and closed her in his arms. "There, there, shhh, Fanny dear. It's all over, shhhh," he said tenderly.

She was so unstrung by his comforting that she merely cried the harder, burrowing against him with as much abandon as if he were Harry—until she suddenly realized that he was not Harry. Not in any way! His voice was deeper, softer; his arms were longer, wrapped completely about her. She'd smelled freshly shaven cheeks and hair pomade before, Harry was extremely nice in such matters—but Charles smelled completely different. With a gasp she controlled herself, wondering confusedly why a masculine scent should be uninteresting in a relative and cause her pulse to leap in a stranger.

She lay trembling against his shoulder, her heart pounding with embarrassment for such shocking behavior. Suddenly, Charles said, "Stay as small and sweet as you are, Fanny dear. Don't let them turn you into a lady of fashion. Promise me!"

"I doubt anything could make me fashionable," she said faintly. "Good God, I never thought to have the vapors in public."

"I had forgot how fresh and clean a girl can be," Charles smiled at her absently. Then with a quick squeeze, he set her free. "What a brave child you are!" and leaning over, he kissed her cheek lightly.

Fanny sat up with a gasp, hiding her involuntary blush by setting her bonnet straight and saying the first thing that came to mind. "I trust the team has suffered no ill effect?"

"Damn the horses! My concern is for you. Should we not stop somewhere for tea, until you regain your composure?"

"Heavens, no! We shall be very late as it is, and Janet will be in a fidget. Pray, let us go back quickly."

Silently, he unwound the reins, turned the curricle, and started for the London road. For some time they drove without talking. Fanny was still shaking inwardly, not from the runaway team but that light kiss. It meant nothing, she knew—merely the consolation he'd have given a sister—but it undermined every scrap of her resolution. She strove valiantly for control, because it was obviously all at an end. He would never wish to be bothered again with a schoolgirl who had upset his horses and spoilt his coat by blubbering like a ninnyhammer. *Don't think of it,* she told herself fiercely, *or you'll start crying. Look at the hedge roses, the birds overhead, the clouds; it's a lovely clear day but I think it may rain tonight . . .*

They were nearly to the bridge when Charles said, "Fanny, you will not let this prevent our plans for the future? You cannot know how much I look forward . . . that is, I swear that fool, Bertie Pakenham, was in the right of it. The Belles and Incomparables are all alike, not a pin to choose between 'em aside from looks and fortune. That's all a man is allowed to see until he's safely bound. Then they show what they really are, which may be anything from stupid to shrewish.

"Damme, but you're a relief, Fanny!" Charles glanced at her with an oddly twisted little smile. "You're not afraid to enjoy something, even if it ain't fashionable. Five or six years hence, when you have London at your feet, let the beaux see your natural self, Fanny." He laughed sardonically, skillfully threading through the increasing traffic. "I can imagine Miss Cherill's shriek of horror if I had suggested a view of wild beasts to *her,* and yet she was probably quite a nice little girl."

"Well, I think she was," Fanny said cautiously, "and I do not think she has really changed—inside, that is. We are not very like, and there is the difference in age."

"You are not at all alike, and it has nothing to do with age."

"No, I expect not. She is so very beautiful, and I shall never have London at my feet—not with my red hair. It will not matter how well I dance or play the piano, which Almy says is all the gentlemen want."

"Hah, does she so?" he snorted. "It just goes to show, don't it? Here I am telling you a man wants considerably more, he wants some clue to what he's getting—and your sister is teaching you the opposite. Don't you believe her, Fanny—and your hair isn't *red*. It's—it's a sort of golden summer sunset." He eyed her appraisingly. "I shouldn't wonder if you took London by storm, Fanny—did better than Miss Almina, and I hope I'm around to witness your triumph."

Under his teasing grin, she clenched her hands desperately together. "Will you beg for my first dance at Almack's?" she asked gaily. "Ten to one you'll be married by then."

"Not I! I'll speak for your entire card for that occasion!"

She frowned dramatically. "Would that not be too particular? You've only my word for it that I can dance at all."

"Then we'll sit them all out," he returned, "but I'll wager you dance like a feather—and as for 'particular,' demmed if I don't wait about for you, Fanny! Meanwhile," coaxingly, "you'll meet me again? We'll devise some way to get you out to Basings, and you shall tell me what to do with those roses?"

"I would it were possible, but I've no idea how to contrive. I might not be missed for a few hours, but a drive into the country . . ."

"When does your governess come back? Could we arrange a casual encounter in the park, or is she a tattling old busybody?"

"No, if Boltie—Miss Bolting—were only here, all would be entirely easy, for she is not at all a dragon. She would understand at once, and think of a way to claim acquaintance, but—but I do not think she will be returning," Fanny murmured. "That is, papa feels we have gone on well enough without her, and—and there is not much more of the season."

"But I say," he protested, "there must be some way to meet, Fanny. I shall have masses of things to tell you about Basings, and I shall need your advice on the roses."

"Your gardener will know better than I."

"Dash it, I haven't got a gardener—at least, I don't think I have. Now, Fanny—dearest Fanny," he cajoled, "I swear I'll never allow the horses to run away with you again! What if I send word to Janet on my return? At the least, you can slip off to the park for an hour some afternoon."

Stronger souls than Fanny had been unable to resist Charles Waterbury when he wheedled. "Y-yes, I should like to hear about Basings. How large is the house and in what style, milord?"

"Lud, *I* don't know," he shrugged. "I've not seen the place since fa gave it to me four years past. He came down for my Come Out, put me up for his clubs and so forth, but he only stayed a few weeks. He detests London, y'know; so does m'mother. As soon as he'd showed me how to go on, he took me down to my property for a few days. Then he went home to Leicestershire, I came up to London, and never went back."

"Four *years?*" she was horrified. "Good heavens, Charles, of course there'll be mismanagement. No matter if the estate is not vast, you cannot let it fall apart. I doubt not it will take a full week for you to inspect everything."

"What? Spend a *week* in that drafty old barn?"

"At this season, the weather is warm enough to be glad of drafts, and you will discover where they are located in order to chink them."

He burst out laughing. "Good God, Fanny, you sound as autocratic as m'grandmother! No, no," as she flushed vividly and hung her head, "I did not mean to discomfit you, child. In fact, 'tis a compliment. My grandmother's as shrewd as she can hold together, and quite my favorite relative."

"Pray, forgive me," Fanny stammered. "I—I forgot myself in speaking so—it was unpardonably rude."

"On the contrary, it was sound sense, and I thank you for it."

They were turning into the park, she could see Janet

wringing her hands anxiously at the side path. Charles brought the curricle to a halt, and Fanny hopped out swiftly. "There was a mishap with the horses, but no harm done aside from delaying us," he called cheerfully to the maid. "Here's something to pay for your worry, Janet," he lightly tossed her another sovereign, "and mind you expect a message next week. My man is Somers. Fanny—take care of yourself."

"Oh," she curtsied formally, "I did not thank you for the excursion. It was most enjoyable, milord."

He eyed her inscrutably for a second. "You are the only female I know who would call runaway horses enjoyable," he remarked. "Your servant, ma'am," and flicking the whip, he drove away rapidly.

CHAPTER IV

It took the entire walk back to Hill Street for Fanny to calm Janet. The maid was torn between apprehension of Mr. Pitcock and the bonanza of sovereigns, but Fanny was sufficiently uplifted that she felt *capable de tout*. The exact events and Charles' words must wait until she was alone in her bedroom, but she had an answer for every hurdle Janet raised. "You have only to stick to it that we walked farther than usual, that I got a pebble in my shoe and we were forced to rest for a while until my foot was able to bear the ground for our return, which was very slow because of my pain—and if that does not satisfy Mr. Pitcock," superbly, "tell him to ask *me*."

"Yes, Miss Fanny, but what about the money?"

"Can you not put it up safely for a few weeks, and when you have bought your muslin, say it was money sent from your mother for your birthday?"

Janet shook her head. "Ain't no place safe, Miss Fanny. Mrs. Hodge inspects our rooms each week to be sure we're cleaning 'em proper, and that Edith is a nasty snoop."

"Give it to me, then. I'll put it in one of my desk drawers."

"Would it be safe, Miss Fanny?"

"Why not?" Fanny still felt competent. "Who is to question it if Miss Fanny has two sovereigns in her desk?"

"Edith. She wouldn't take 'em, but she'll notice they wasn't there yesterday, if you take my meaning, Miss Fanny?"

Fanny stared at her. "Do I understand that Edith inspects the family bedrooms?"

Janet nodded. "She'd never take anything, she's not a thief, but she knows. Every piece of jewelry or clothing, all the billydoos Miss Almina receives," she said calmly, "and she reads the diaries and engagement calendars."

"Good God! Well, I'll lock my desk. You needn't worry about your money, Janet, but even if it were questioned, I'd say papa gave it to me."

"Aye, that'd do it," Janet agreed. "The master's that castaway most nights, he'd not remember."

In any event there were no questions, for Major Harry Cherill had come home! He was just stepping down from a post chaise, with Pitcock hastening forward (in person) to direct Perkins' disposal of luggage as the girls turned the corner into Hill Street. "Harry!" Fanny shrieked, and picking up her skirts, she raced forward like the schoolgirl she was pretending to be. "Oh, *Harry!*"

He swung around at her voice, holding out his arms with a wide grin. "Lud, it's good to see you, puss," he swung her half up from the ground, kissing her heartily as he set her down. "Here's Pitcock saying no one's at home, my letter not received—and here's my kitten to give me the news."

"Oh, it is so good to see you safely back, Harry—we've missed you so!"

"Why, as for that, I've missed you, too," he hugged her. "I'd not know how I'd have gone on without your letters, puss, but all's over now. Boney's on some curst island, chained as fast as one of his demmed eagles. I'm home among the first because of that wound in my arm—not that it bothers me, but I'd a fancy to accept the leave. And how do you go on in London? Enjoying yourself, I'll be bound."

If the butler and footman had not been within earshot, Fanny would instantly have poured out the whole story, for Harry was sure to understand. Instead, she shrugged it aside and asked, "Is Robin come home, too?"

"Not he!" Harry chuckled. "He's still in Bordeaux, casting out lures to a pretty widow. He'll do no good by it, and so I told him. Mrs. Colton wants a husband for her fifty thousand pounds—preferably one with titled connections. Trouble is, she smells too much of the shop. Robin ain't in that bad case, for all he needs a wife with money, but if he would have it he'd make the running in a month. So he refused leave until the next contingent, and we've a wager of fifty guineas on it. Here, I say," Harry looked stricken, "I shouldn't have told you that, kitten! Not at all the thing—forget it, please."

Fanny dimpled demurely. "It is forgotten," she assured him, and giggled irrepressibly. "Oh, don't be formal with me," she begged. "Why should I not know whatever is to be known? How else shall I learn to be a pleasing wife?"

"Good God, wives ain't supposed to know anything," he frowned.

"Perhaps not in the general way," she agreed, "but with my red hair—do admit, Harry: I shall have to have something special in order to get a husband at all, and I think I should strive to be an Original."

By now they were in the entrance hall, with Perkins bearing the luggage upward and Pitcock assisting the Major out of his travel coat. "Thankee, Pitcock," Harry said absently, his eyes on the diminutive form of his sister. "Bring the Madeira, will you."

"Yes, sir." The butler vanished along the rear hall.

"It strikes me," said Harry "you already are an Original. Damme, Fanny, you've grown devilish pretty since I saw you last. How old are you, anyway?"

"Near seventeen."

"Lud, how time flies! You don't look more than twelve, and here you'll be turning up your curls and making your curtsey at Almack's in another year. Damme, I can't get over it!"

Under her brother's appraising blue eyes, Fanny was suddenly shy. "You've changed, too," she said uncertainly. "You look—*commanding,* Harry. I expect it's the war, although Robin was the same as ever when he was invalided home last year."

Harry laughed. "It'd take more than a war to make an impression on Robin, bless his impudence! Vandeleur demmed him up and down for getting himself shot—said Robin did it on purpose in order to be convalescent during the season—because it was not much of a wound, you know." Harry laughed again. "There's Vandeleur stomping back and forth, cursing—and Robin's agreeing to all, saying he has to be in London, there's a dozen females waiting to waltz with him, and Van ain't so hardhearted he wants 'em to go into a decline, does he? You know Robin!"

"He's a complete hand," Fanny agreed, "and you are right, it didn't prevent his dancing attendance on Almy from the moment he came home. He made her mad as fire, supervising her ball cards and telling her who she could or couldn't receive. When mama told him to leave Almy's social acquaintance to her, he said you had instructed him to stand in for a brother."

"Good God, I never said anything of the sort," Harry snorted.

"No, but Robin said you had—and Almy was obviously a pea-goose who needed the guiding hand of an experienced beau," Fanny gurgled in memory. "Oh, it was so funny; I would you could have heard him, Harry! Such a taradiddle the day mama and Almy were leaving Cherley, and Robin rode up saying he'll accompany them—you know how bland he can be? There is mama laughing in spite of herself, and Almina storming that he's not a beau but an experienced rake who'll ruin her reputation, and Robin saying 'That's all you know, my girl, but for Harry's sake I'll look after you until he gets back.'"

Her mimicry was perfect, and Harry shouted with laughter, leaning helplessly on the newel until Pitcock returned to survey them indulgently. "The Madeira is in your room, Major. Perkins has unpacked, the hot water has gone up—you'll wish to change your traveling clothes—and cook has a brace of ducklings, if you fancy dining at home."

"Lud, I don't know," Harry said carelessly. "Yes, if the family's not engaged elsewhere, and no, if I'll be alone. The devil's in it that my letter didn't reach 'em in time."

Pitcock cleared his throat gently. "I believe madam and Miss Almina were to be at home before some evening party. Mr. Cherill was undecided, but I have taken the liberty of sending word to his clubs of your arrival."

"Oh? Then you can tell cook I'll fancy whatever she feels like preparing. It'll be good to get home to decent English food."

"Yes, sir." Pitcock permitted himself to smile slightly. "I apprehend the foreign cooking leaves much to be desired."

"Well, as for that," Harry started up the stairs, "in a war, one's dashed glad to have *anything* to eat, Pitcock. Keep an eye out for Teake, my bâtman. I doubt he'll arrive before midday tomorrow, but he might push straight through and roll in during the night." Harry had gained the upper hall, with Fanny tagging along behind him. "Here," he recoiled slightly, "you can't come in while I'm dressing, kitten. You're too grown."

"I suppose," she sighed, "but couldn't I watch you arrange your neckcloth, Harry."

"If you like," he conceded magnanimously, and grinned at her wickedly innocent murmur, "Oh, thank you, brother dear—it *will* be a treat!"

"Go along with you, miss!"

Fanny dropped him a curtsey and ran away to her room with a giggle. Harry's unexpected return had swept Charles from her mind until her fingers encountered Janet's sovereigns. She tucked them in one of the desk drawers and locked it, but while she set about dressing for dinner, her head was a confused whirl of half thoughts. The memory of Charles' arms holding her safe until the horses were halted, the male scent of his skin, the gentle hugs and soft words of comfort, and finally the touch of his lips on her cheek—all stirred her pulse and brought color to her cheeks . . . for he had not the least idea.

She felt overpowered with shame for so deceiving him. Never would he have behaved so to Almina, for instance—although she would never have been in such a pass. Had Charles taken Miss Cherill to drive, there must have been a groom standing behind. Almina would never have been studying the ribbons, in any case; she had the liveliest distaste for female whips.

"Damme, what a coil," Fanny thought disconsolately. Harry only made it worse, she saw that now. In the tight world of the *ton,* he and Charles were bound to encounter shortly. Even if Charles did not blithely divulge acquaintance with Major Cherill's small sister, Fanny's true age was certain to be discovered to him. "I shall have to tell Harry first . . . ," but in a single evening, she found she could not. Harry was so *very* grown-up.

Fanny sat unobtrusive as a mouse among her family; if she ventured to say anything, she might easily be sent off to bed. It was enough merely to be present and observe. One of Pitcock's messages had caught papa, who had come home for once. Mama was in misty smiles at sight of her first-born. Even Almina was more eager and natural than for many weeks, insisting they should cancel the evening's party in favor of a comfortable coze at home, "for it would not be inadmissable to do so, mama, when Harry is come back unexpectedly. Surely, it would be understood and forgiven?"

"Wyvern?" Mrs. Cherill murmured warningly, but Almy was not to be withstood.

"He'll honor me for putting my brother ahead of a

mere party," she said firmly. "You know he has the liveliest respect for blood ties, mama."

But Fanny *noticed:* Almina cleverly got the conversation back at all points to Robin Elvey, and listened breathlessly to every word of his daredeviltry. "It *is* Robin," she said to herself. "Poor Almy, does he know?" She thought Harry suspected, he eyed Almina's downcast face very sharply when he said he'd arranged to take Robin's lodgings until his return.

"He is not come back with you, then? I suppose Bordeaux is amusing."

"Robin will contrive to amuse himself wherever he is," Harry agreed with a twitch of his lips that nearly overset Fanny, but he did not tell Almina the details.

For a few days there was harmony in Hill Street. Harry was flatteringly impressed by Almina's success, and consented to be lionized while renewing his acquaintance. He was as busy daytime as the rest, but good-humoredly took Fanny with him for various errands which kept her mind from Charles.

"D'you really want to visit the carriagemaker?" or "I'm only going down to the City to see Hale about my Funds, kitten—not very interesting for you."

"Anything's interesting," she said firmly. "Please take me?"

"All right, in half an hour. Mind you're ready!" Fanny's evident delight in such dull outings caused Harry to inquire more closely, and she might have told him about Lord Waterbury, but just as she'd nerved herself, his attention was distracted by encountering an old friend. The opportunity once lost did not arise again, for Harry was gone into his lodgings and she saw him rarely.

Perhaps it was as well, for to her dismay Harry was known to Bertie Pakenham, which argued he must know others of Charles' friends. Sooner or later there'd be an encounter when Fanny was sitting beside her brother, and while Bertie might not recall her two years hence, his memory was probably sound enough to last two weeks. Besides, Harry had emerged from

Hale's office with a black frown and been disinclined for conversation all the way back to Hill Street. Fanny felt half afraid of him in such a mood, as well as worried. Had something happened to his money? She knew only that he was independent of papa, and would inherit Cherley eventually.

Bereft of Harry as a confidant, Fanny let her thoughts return to Charles, which proved dangerous, for twice she was in such a brown study that she failed to hear Almina speaking to her. "In heaven's name, what engrosses you, Fanny? One would think you were in love!"

Fanny flushed involuntarily. "Is that how one behaves?"

"So they say," Almina shrugged. "What is on your mind?"

"The roses at Cherley," Fanny said at random. "They ought to be shaped and watered. I hope the Beadles remember."

"I don't depend on it," Almina sniffed. "If you could attend to me? Have you Miss Bolting's direction by any chance?"

"No," Fanny shook her head, surprised. "She was to visit her family before finding a new situation. I think it was a married sister in Cumberland. Why?"

"The Dowager Duchess of Wyvern needs a governess. I should have been glad to suggest Miss Bolting," Almina fretted. "It would be helpful in every way. Mama had the direction, but she has misplaced it."

"What a pity! The Duchess could not have a better person."

"So I thought, but how to find the woman? You were my last hope."

"She said she would write to me, but she has not. Perhaps the carters at Cherley would know where her boxes were sent."

"She took them with her by post chaise. She had a tiny independence from her father, you know, and could afford such things."

"I didn't know she had any money."

"Fifty pounds a year or some such. I doubt she spent more than a bit for her clothes, which would be covered by her stipend. After ten years, she must have a respectable sum and be in no need of a post, but I wish we could find her," Almina sighed.

Fanny eyed her sister's despondent expression covertly. It would indeed be a feather in Almy's cap if she were able to supply Wyvern's mother with an excellent governess, although if the Duchess were as pompous as her son, Fanny doubted Miss Bolting could endure her. With each peek at His Grace arriving or departing from Hill Street, Fanny was less impressed— particularly by contrast with Sir Robin Elvey. No two men could be less alike.

The more she considered, the more certain she was that Almina's heart was given to her childhood friend. Fanny could see it clearly now, where last year all she knew of her sister's social triumph was from an occasional letter or the reports in the *Gazette*. Miss Almina Cherill had left Cherley, a-tiptoe for presentation to the *ton;* four months later she returned, bright-eyed with anticipation that seemed due to the number of beaux who journeyed into Kent for a glimpse of the Dark Incomparable. In succeeding weeks she grew listless, disinclined for the flattering house-party invitations, and by the disappearance of various gentlemen, Fanny thought their offers had been rejected.

Yes, it was obvious: Robin was at Ullastone, riding over daily: he'd gone up to London and taken the lodgings Harry now had. It was mid-June before he returned to Spain, with no word of him since. Did he think of Almy simply as his friend's younger sister, whom he was helping to launch for auld lang syne? Was he unaware she loved him? Fanny was half angry at Robin for his obtuseness! If only he'd not been at hand, Almina's early preference might have faded and she could have been happy with someone else.

Inextricably mingled with Fanny's silent sympathy for her sister was her own private muddle over Lord

Waterbury. A week, two weeks, passed with no word of him. Could he still be at Basings, or had he forgotten her in the press of his own affairs? She found no mention of him in the *Gazette,* the single clue was a notice that Mr. Bertram Pakenham was spending a se'night in Surrey. Perhaps he was visiting Charles, and if so, there'd be amusement enough to put Fanny out of mind.

It would be the best possible solution all around— after which Fanny burst into tears in the privacy of her bedroom.

So far from forgetting his little friend, Lord Waterbury thought of her almost constantly in his first days at Basings. With the imperturbable Somers sitting primly beside him, Charles drove swiftly into Surrey and arrived unheralded at his property, noting that the journey took no more than an hour if the traffic was thin. It would definitely be possible to entertain Fanny and her governess for a nuncheon.

When he'd reached the modest entrance to Basings, he pulled up involuntarily. "Jove, it's a pretty place, ain't it? I'd forgotten."

The house was of stone, rather low and sprawling, but ivy-hung and shaded by immense oaks. It was pleasantly welcoming, except for a certain atmosphere of neglect. As Charles drove forward, the road was bumpy, the lawn was not well scythed. The shrubs were unpruned, the door brasses were dull, the windows streaked with rain dirt.

The appearance of Lord Waterbury in the stable yard created all the surprise he could wish—on both sides, for if the staff were open-mouthed at sight of him, he found them distinctly unprepossessing. Mrs. Skinner's apron was soiled, her husband's cheeks sported a gray stubble, and the boy dashing from the stable to hold the horses looked like a halfwit. "Good God," said His Lordship, "if the house is no better, you may have to do the cooking, Somers."

"The house will *not* be any better, milord, but you may safely leave it to me," Somers murmured, descending with the light of battle in his eye.

While he took charge of domestic matters, seeing to removal of luggage, Charles discovered a ray of hope. The halfwit was a natural handler of horses. "Eh, ee'm prime cattle, sir, ess ee be!" he crooned, deftly unhitching and disposing the team into stalls. "Gus'll get ee some water first, 'nd wipe ee down well, 'nd some good fresh carrots to chomp till Gus get ee some oats from t'farm. Eh, ee'll be prime again in no time."

"Ah, that's the dandy, Gus. You know your cattle, eh?" Charles leaned against the stable door with a keen eye on the boy, but he was obviously competent and overjoyed to care for the chestnuts. "Where's Mr. Eggleston?"

"He'll be over to Five Oaks. You want ee?" Gus was astonished.

Charles surveyed the unkempt stables that held two broken-down cobs and a farm gig—cast a glance outside to note a missing cobblestone in the yard, a slate fallen from the house roof. "No," he said grimly, "not yet."

Within the house he found subdued frenzy, with Somers reigning supreme. "It appears there is no provisioning of the pantry, milord," the man said disdainfully, "and the condition of the rooms is deplorable. I have ventured to lay out your riding clothes, but I beg you will not sit down anywhere but the dining saloon, which I have dusted temporarily."

"Bread and cheese, some ham and home-brew," Charles said. "They'll have that, or some eggs. I don't care what I eat, Somers. Get some village women to turn out enough rooms for tonight; they can do the rest tomorrow or next day. I doubt there's anything fit to drink in the cellar—never mind, we'll send to the vintner. Get word to the bailiff that I'll see him here after dinner."

"Yes, milord." Somers bowed slightly and suppressed a grin of satisfaction. Time and again he'd staunchly informed his social circle at the Spotted Dog that Lord Charles Waterbury was as sound as a nut. He'd come about in time. By His Lordship's steadfast countenance, that time had come. *Good!* thought Somers, for his cursory inspection of Basings had disclosed definite possibilities of a gentleman's residence.

"We could be well placed here," Somers said to himself, mentally rubbing his hands. "His Lordship could entertain informally—go up to London for occasional amusement, he might even marry suitably. It seems a snug little estate, not unworthy of a young lady with—" he pursed his lips, "say, ten or fifteen thousand pounds."

Lord Waterbury would not have agreed. After only the most casual jog about on one of the cobs, he was appalled by the look of things. There were no more than a few dozen head of cattle in fields that should support a hundred. Other fields held some sheep, "What the devil do I want with them?" Here and there a fence rail was missing, stones were fallen from boundary walls. A good ten fields lay fallow, and another dozen were planted for forage rather than crops.

Little as His Lordship knew of the finer points of management, by the time he'd returned to Basings he knew the truth of Rowbotham's claim of mismanagement. "Good God," he said to himself, "of course the estate should yield more."

The trouble was that Charles hadn't the faintest idea how to set about it. Worse still, when the bailiff arrived in the evening, he swiftly realized his employer's ignorance, and his initial line of nervous ingratiation became an insufferable indulgence. He all but patted Lord Waterbury on the head. That was a *bad* mistake; Charles might be unversed in property, but he was instantly aware when anyone attempted to cozen him. At the outset he found Eggleston unlikable. The man was paunched, faintly seedy, and whatever qualifications he might once have had for his responsibilities were outweighed by indolence.

"My own fault," Charles told himself fairly, "but damme, he'll do no good for me without constant supervision."

The interview then proceeded on unpremeditated lines. Eggleston's irritating paternalism changed to glib excuses and ended in shocked protest when he found himself dismissed by a young aristocrat with a most unnerving glint in his eye. "But, milord," the bailiff gulped, "you know nothing of estate management."

"Neither," said Charles evenly, "do you. Send me the records tomorrow morning, if you please, and arrange to vacate the bailiff's cottage in two days. That is all."

It was, of course, very far from all, as Charles realized as soon as he'd attempted to make sense of the garbled account books. Despite its best efforts, Eton had failed to introduce him to more arithmetic than was needed to lay a bet at White's. By the time the bailiff had departed, Charles was entangled in a morass of incomprehensible details and he became correspondingly stubborn. He made no excuses to himself for the sorry state of affairs. The question was what to do. "Have to get a new man, but if I don't know what's to be done, he'll cheat me, too."

There were certain small encouragements. Under Somers' eagle eye, the house became clean and amazingly comfortable. Mrs. Skinner washed her aprons and proved a better cook than anticipated. Her husband shaved his cheeks, pruned the shrubbery, polished windows, made a number of small repairs, and admitted there was local labor to be had. "What would you want 'em to do, milord?"

"Demmed if I know." The next day Charles pocketed his pride, drove to London and consulted Rowbotham, who concealed satisfaction behind a poker face.

"A new bailiff? I fancy I can put my hands on a very superior man, milord. As for basic information, I suggest you talk with your father's head steward."

"In *Leicestershire?*" Lord Waterbury stared at the agent. "Good God, Rowbotham, I'm missing everything as it is, with all these curst accounts and going out every day to see what else is wrong."

"Hmmm, perhaps Your Lordship might persuade a friend to keep you company for a few days. I believe Fletcher could wait on you within the week, and," the agent finished suavely, "you might occupy the intervening time by making acquaintance in the locality."

"Lud, you're all about in your head! There ain't anyone but farmers and local squires," but driving morosely back to his lodgings, he spied Bertie on Bond Street. "Where are you bound?"

"No place," Bertie said vaguely. "Just on the toddle, y'know . . . might look in at White's, see what's on the book. Where are you bound?"

Charles eyed his friend's ovine countenance and said abruptly, "Come up, will you? Got a notion you could help me, Bertie."

"Oh, shouldn't think so, old boy, but I don't mind joining you for a bit." When he was settled, "Ain't seen you lately, Charlie—was you sick?"

"No, and yes," Charles flicked the team skillfully past a coach. "I've been to Basings. My fa's agent gave me the office last week I'd better look into it. The long and the short of it is, I can get a new bailiff, but demmed if I know what he should do to pull me straight. Fa put m'brother into the way of it at Pevency, but I was at Eton. I suppose he didn't think I'd need it—younger son, y'know."

"Don't follow," Bertie was faintly shocked. "Gives you some land, ought to have given you enough to know how to go on."

"Well, he didn't—he has the gout, you know." Charles dismissed the Duke of Pevency. "Bertie, come back with me, bear me company for a few days until this new man arrives?"

"Rusticate at *this* time of year?" Bertie was astonished. "Oh, I shouldn't think anyone could leave London now, old boy. Lud, there's a dozen engagements for every day—not but what you might have 'em for all of me."

"Exactly! Get away from it all, refresh the spirits, and come back in prime fettle," Charles wheedled. "Say you will, Bertie—we'll get Tomaston and Spenning or some other, make a snug little party for the evenings. I must go back until I put it in hand, and I swear I'll be blue-deviled in twenty-four hours."

It took some persuasion, but eventually Bertie agreed—after being assured the house was comfortable, the cooking edible if simple, and there was a trout stream. The enthusiastic acceptance of Messrs. Tomaston and Spenning (the one admitting he was avoiding certain importunate tradesmen, and the other wishful to hedge off from a young lady whose ideas were rather more permanent than he felt himself competent to face) lent a lift to Bertie's spirits. "Damme, it's the very thing," he said admiringly. "*I* ain't hanging out for a wife, *you* ain't hanging out for a wife, *Spenning* ain't hanging out for a wife—demmed dangerous to stay in London. If that ain't like you, Charlie: to think up a scheme to save us all."

While his friends were packing their portmanteaux, Charles exerted himself to add such ordinary comforts as would be expected: a visit to the vintner, a stock of cigarillos, cards and counters for gaming, trout rods. By teatime, three high-spirited young gentlemen were sweeping out of town in an assortment of curricles and high-perch phaetons, each with a gentleman's gentleman seated beside the driver, and all following Lord Waterbury's curricle. En route to Basings they amused themselves by passing and repassing, grazing wheels, but as Charles had warned, "If you overset me, how will you know where you are bound?" He drove in lonely state at the front of the parade, but felt that on the whole it had been a good day's work.

It did not, of course, occur to him to consider how

many bedchambers Basings afforded, nor whether three extra valets could be housed. Luckily, Somers was prepared for any wild start of his young master. Throughout the day he had supervised provisioning and rooms, procured sufficient forage for a dozen high-bred horses, and by the time carriages were bumping over the drive, Basings was prepared for almost anything. A mere three guests with their servants was, in fact, better than Somers had hoped. He would not have been surprised by ten or a dozen extra people.

So part of Fanny's surmise was correct; Bertie Pakenham was visiting Lord Waterbury, but despite the presence of his friends, Charles had not forgotten her. It was true that she had come to mind more frequently in his first days at Basings. On impulse, he had carefully inspected the rose garden, and although there were roses, it undoubtedly needed attention. "Skinner, do you know how to care for roses?"

"No, milord. I can prune a bit of ivy, but I'm no gardener."

"Well, get one for long enough to do what's needed here."

"Yes, milord." Later he said bewilderedly to his wife, "Whyfor do the young master want roses, with so much else to be done?"

"Eh, there's no accounting for the gentry, Skinner—and I'll thank you to bring up that ham from the cellar."

" 'Tis the last one," Skinner announced gloomily.

"I doubt not, but how's a body to know he'd ever come here? Do we cure more than we'd eat, what'd we do with them? 'Tis not like his grandfa's day, when we'd send up to the townhouse for the season. The young master never asked for anything sent to him, so where's the use in overloading our shelves?"

"Be different in future, I reckon. That Mr. Somers is rare clever at seeing what's to His Lordship's advantage."

In fact, Somers had not enjoyed himself so much in

years, but no more than Skinner could he understand his master's desire for roses. Instinct told Somers there must be a young lady concerned in it, although he had observed no sign of recent partiality in His Lordship. Still, when coupled with setting Basings in order, Somers gave deep consideration to the possibility of a mistress and could not think of anyone he would be happy to welcome. He would have been even more deeply disturbed to know that His Lordship's inamorata was only a schoolgirl.

Not that Charles thought of Fanny that way, but he certainly thought of her every time he was out and about the estate. A dozen times a day he wondered what Fanny would advise him to do. She was astonishingly wise for her age, refreshingly natural in contrast to the Belles. How plucky she'd been when the horses bolted! He could not visualize any other young lady in such a situation. Miss Almina Cherill would have had the vapors and swooned, probably gotten in the way of pulling up the team and caused an overturn.

Occasionally Charles recalled the feel of little Fanny in his arms. What a sweet child she was, he thought tenderly. Some man was going to be lucky to have Fanny to wife.

With the formation of his house party, Charles thought of her less often, although she still came to mind through the town gossip of the other men. "The Dark Incomparable's set her cap for Wyvern," Tomaston remarked. "Shouldn't think she'd get him, but Pendle's hopes are quite cut up, poor devil."

"If she wouldn't have Pendle last season, why should she have him now?"

"The road Cherill's going, she'd better have someone," Spenning said. "Never saw a man with such ill luck."

"Dipped, is he? It's a fool's game to play double when you hit a bad run," Tomaston shook his head. "Hedge off and wait for the wind to change, *I* say, or you'll be rolled up like Illingham."

"Yes, by God, that was a sad thing," Charles agreed, "but surely Cherill's too old to be Greeked?"

"Don't know that," Bertie said. "Harry's home, y'know—saw him at Boodle's one night."

"Didn't know you was acquainted," Charles pricked up his ears.

"Good God, yes—known him any time these twelve years, I was his fag," Bertie explained. "Very sound fellow, did well for himself in the war, medals and commendations and I don't know what all. Thing is, got a notion he ain't pleased with what he's found now he's back. Nothing to be done, of course. Can't prevent your father from staking what's his own, after all."

The conversation switched, but left Lord Waterbury uneasy. It struck him as demmed irresponsible of the Honorable Edgar Cherill to follow his pleasure at the risk of discomfort for his womenfolk, and while Charles was far from contemplating matrimony, the analogy could not be missed. "I'll tell you what it is," he informed the others when the cards were brought out that evening, "I don't mind being close to the wind for a bit of fun before I settle—if I ever do—but I'm not minded to find myself under the hatches. Row-botham, fa's agent, says there's enough to come about with proper management. I mean to draw in for a bit until I can hold household. No more pound points at whist for the present, no more laying a monkey on every race at Newmarket. Wouldn't say this to anyone but you, but you'll not make talk of it. Humor me?"

Such unaccustomed seriousness in their scapegrace crony struck the young gentlemen dumb for a moment. "Lud, yes, of course," Spenning stared glassily at his host. "Wouldn't breathe a word, assure you, old man. Always knew you wasn't too well breeched, honor you for pulling out in time."

"Anything I can do, only to call on me," Tomaston added. "Not plump in the pocket myself, but always happy to raise the wind for a friend."

"It's not that bad. Thing is, I don't mean it to get

that bad," Charles shrugged. "Devilish nuisance being a younger son."

Bertie merely nodded solemnly, but in succeeding days it was he who proved invaluable. "Got to know the locals," he said firmly. "First importance, Charlie! Get 'em behind you, they'll tip you the instant your bailiff ain't doin' his job."

"How the devil do I know which is who, or who lives where?"

"Visit the parson," Bertie said, surprised. "Ask him. Tell him things ain't as they should be, you're looking into it. He'll give you all you need. Go to service Sunday, he'll introduce you to everyone. Next week you ride over to pay your respects to the squires, meet the ladies, drink tea, do the pretty—and there you are."

"Good God, I am indeed!" Charles protested. "What the devil do I say to rural females, Bertie? And drinking *tea?*"

"It ain't so bad, they'll get out the best Bohea, and there's enough time to lose the taste before we dine. I'll come with you, if you like," Bertie offered handsomely. "Once you're known to take an interest, only got to ride out once a year, renew your acquaintance, and you'll be protected. Forget 'em the rest of the time."

"I'll forget 'em in twenty-four hours, I've no head for names."

"Write 'em down, with the children's names," Bertie advised. "That's what I do. Leave the list here, refresh the memory when you come, and either the servants or parson'll tell you when there's been an increase. Makes a dashed big impression when you ask after a man's nursery by name, I can tell you."

Charles stared at his friend's vacuous face and snorted. "It's obvious you can tell me a great deal."

"Oh, I shouldn't think so, old boy. I've not much in the brain box, y'know, but anyone knows how to go on with rustics," Bertie disclaimed modestly. "Make 'em feel comfortable, give a few guineas to the padre, and they'll look after your interests. Simple, really."

Accordingly, Charles presented himself somewhat nervously to the rector, and was astounded to find Mr. Mattison a well-spoken middle-aged Oxford man. In a matter of minutes, Charles was entirely at home and divulging every detail of his perplexities. "The long and the short of it is," he finished ingenuously, "Bertie Pakenham said I couldn't do better than consult you, sir. Pay my pew rent, give you a few guineas for the roof fund, and you'd put me in the way of knowing my neighbors."

Mr. Mattison sternly suppressed his amusement. "*Roof* fund?"

"Well, whatever it is. There's always some sort of fund going with churches, and it's usually for the roof. Can't think why it is, but I notice church roofs don't seem to last as long as other kinds. Happy to know you're not bothered with leaks."

"Not at present. Your father assisted us most generously some six years past. I fancy we were fortunate in our workmen; thus far we appear still weather-tight," the rector observed. "However, it might perhaps be wise to prepare a hedge against the future. I will gladly accept any contribution to hold in reserve, milord."

Charles eyed him suspiciously. "I believe you're roasting me."

"By no means," Mr. Mattison assured him, poker-faced, "although as it happens, what we are principally needing at this moment are new prayer stools—but if Your Lordship prefers roofs, roofs it shall be."

"You *are* roasting me!" Charles burst out laughing, and the rector chuckled gently.

"Well, yes, a very little," he conceded, "for why you should suppose your father's son must wheedle his parson into making introductions to what is, after all, the living of Basings defeats me." When Charles stared at him speechlessly, Mr. Mattison went on *very* gently, "It was your father who appointed me. Reggie and I were at Oxford together."

"Good God, you mean *I* . . ." Charles stuttered,

and looked earnestly at the rector, "I beg you will take the *greatest* care for your health, sir! None of my friends are parsons—wouldn't know how to go on if you was to turn up the toes."

"I am not planning to die for at least twenty years," the rector began and found himself gasping with uncontrollable laughter, "but should God's timetable be different . . . oh, lud, your appalled expression! . . . you have only to apply to the bishop for a replacement. Whooo!" Mr. Mattison wiped his eyes and subdued himself firmly. "And now I will offer you a glass of Madeira, and we will work out the best procedure for you."

Thus, the sojourn at Basings was considerably longer than anticipated, although there was no lack of entertainment. The appearance of Lord Waterbury and three London Tulips at church electrified the assemblage. "I doubt anyone heard a single word of the sermon," Mr. Mattison told his wife sadly, "which is a pity because it was a particularly good one this week."

"Then you can use it again sometime," she consoled. "After all, the congregation can look at you any Sunday. It made a nice change to look at four handsome young men."

The residents of Little Twyford heartily agreed, and exerted themselves to assist Lord Waterbury. "It's late for planting, but you'll still get some crops, and since ours are in, we can spare plowmen for you. Farm horses? Go to Jones, in Upper Twyford. Yes, you do want some sheep; they mow the fallow fields for you—not that Eggleston sheared as he should, for there's always a price for wool, milord."

"Oh, I say," Lord Waterbury protested engagingly, "I'm just Charles, you know. Don't stand on ceremony with me, sir."

"Then I won't," the squire said gruffly, "although I'd not have expected such condescension from your father's son."

"Oh, fa has the gout, you know—makes him starchy, high in the instep, but he's a duke. I'm only a younger son."

Shortly he was *persona grata* everywhere and enjoying himself mightily. So, to their amazement, were Tomaston and Spenning. "Never dreamed there'd be so much to do in the country!" It was only the discovery (via the *Gazette*) that Spenning's determined young lady was affianced and a lucky racing bet would ease Tomaston's creditors, plus the recollection of Lady Pakenham's ball for Bertie's sister ("Have to be there, m'mother would cut me apart!") that led to a dissolution of Charles' house party, but on the final night, all three guests earnestly requested an early return.

"Damme, there's something to be said for ruralizing. Never could understand it before, but if you've a snug house, a decent cook, pleasant acquaintance—a man could be more comfortable than in town, with all the females casting out lures."

"Good God, yes! Thing is, Charlie's in the right spot," said Tomaston. "Close to town, go in when he wants, kick up a lark and come home when he's tired of it. Now, Bertie's too far away; so is Spenning, takes four hours to go and come—and I ain't got anything until my uncle dies, but it'd still be longer than here."

"Keep your rooms in London, live here—that's the dandy," Bertie agreed. "Saves money to live off your land, old boy, which gives you all the more for a bit of fun. Shouldn't wonder but you'd put us all in the basket."

"I doubt it," Charles scoffed, but the approval of his friends was heartening. Even better was the progress under the expert hands of his new bailiff, Fletcher. While he'd half have liked to stay to see how things went on, Charles decided to return to London with the others. "Fanny will like to hear what I've done," he thought, and ordered every rose in bloom to be cut. It made an immense armful for Somers to carry on his lap for the return journey, but to all jests from the other valets, he merely looked down his nose.

"No doubt *you* would feel humiliation, but to one who has *never* worked for other than titled families, such things are quite customary."

The small cortege reached the metropolis at teatime and parted with sincere thanks to the host, a plethora of future engagements, beginning with Lady Pakenham's ball. "Needn't stay long, but m'mother would rake me over the coals if I don't bring you to fill the dance cards," Bertie said. "Got to do it, support a chap *in extremis,* can't let me down, old boys!"

Clambering down at Lord Waterbury's lodgings, Somers asked, "What would you wish me to do with the roses, milord?"

"Bring 'em inside while I write a note," but when His Lordship handed it over with instructions, Somers was more confused than ever. "Go to the servants' entrance, ask for Janet and give her this note. The roses are for *all* the Cherill ladies—say it that way, Somers; she'll understand—but don't let anyone see the note."

"Very good, milord." Somers bowed himself out, but all the way to Hill Street he was perturbed. It was true that last season His Lordship had been dancing attendance on the Dark Incomparable, but Somers had seen no indication that he was wishful to fix an interest this year. Further, from the servants' hall chat at Basings, it appeared she was trying for the Duke of Wyvern. While Mr. Spenning's man said she'd never get him and the Cherills were all to pieces, Somers was deeply worried. Could Lord Waterbury nourish such a *tendresse* as to hope Miss Cherill might accept him if she failed with Wyvern?

CHAPTER V

Miss Cherill was equally at a loss when Janet brought the vase of flowers, "From Lord Waterbury, miss."

"Lord *Waterbury?*" Almina frowned incredulously. "Lud, what possesses him?"

"I can't say, I'm sure, miss," Janet murmured. "I fancy they're country-grown, the scent is lovely—just like Cherley."

"So it is, and will give me the headache. For heaven's sake, take them away."

"Yes, miss. Where shall I put them?" dubiously. "The man brought an armful, saying they were for all the Cherill ladies."

"Well, throw them out. I don't care what you do with them," Almina returned petulantly as Mrs. Cherill came into the room. "Do you see these from Waterbury? What ails the man to be sending me roses, mama?"

"Lud, I don't know. One thought him completely out of society this season, but he was ever a tease," her mother said grimly. "He's sent an immense bouquet for me as well, or so Edith says. I did hear he was gone out of town on a repairing lease. No doubt it amused him to embarrass you at this moment, for he must know of Wyvern's interest. One thing is sure: Wyvern must not learn of it. You cannot be receiving quantities of flowers from ineligibles, Almina. Take them away, Janet, and mine also."

"Yes, madam," the maid carefully removed the vases, but the roses went no farther than to Fanny's room. "From Lord Waterbury, miss, and here's a note," she whispered. "The man brought enough for a dozen vases, but Miss Almina and madam won't accept 'em for fear the Duke'll hear. Oooo, they do smell lovely!"

"Heavenly!" Fanny breathed deeply, closing her eyes with a beating heart. He hadn't forgotten, after all!

"What will I do with the rest?"

"Bring me one more vase, put a few in the schoolroom, and give the rest to Pitcock for the servants," Fanny ordered, "and be *sure* he knows they were rejected."

Janet's eyes widened. "Why, Miss Fanny?"

"He'll report in whatever pub he frequents and it will come to the ears of the Duke's valet."

"His Lordship's man will hear, too."

"Never mind, I'll explain to Lord Waterbury. The roses are really for me. That's why he sent so many, I'd be sure to get some for the nursery."

"Oh, the nursery. Yes, I see," uneasily, "but you won't never go meeting him again, miss. It's too risky, that it is."

"Who's to know if you don't tell? Remember: tell Pitcock the ladies won't have the roses, they're to be thrown out, but it seems a pity. You've put some in the schoolroom for me, could you keep a few for your room, and maybe the staff would like some, too."

"Yes, miss." When Janet had gone, Fanny opened her note with trembling fingers, and chuckled irrepressibly. Good God, Charles' fist was worse than Harry's.

"My dear little Fanny: I have all this while been at Basings, and want to tell you what has been done. There is some business here, I cannot say a time for certain, but if you can walk at one o'clock daily, I will catch up with you before long. Yrs., etc., Chas."

Fanny held the paper to her cheek involuntarily, not that it was a love note, but it was enough he'd remembered her. She sat misty-eyed for a few moments, until

Almina's voice in the hall roused her. Hastily she thrust the note into her desk as Almina entered, asking "Have you a bit of sealing wax, I don't want to go downstairs. Why, where had you those roses?"

"Janet said you and mama didn't want them, so I kept a few and she's to tell Pitcock to give the rest to the servants. I thought it was the surest way to let Wyvern know."

Almina stared for a moment, and slowly smiled. "Very clever! You are learning quickly. May I have some wax?"

"Of course, but I've not much choice."

"I'll take the gold, it's suited for a duke, is it not?" Her glance flicked over the desk, "Lord, a diary? What have you to record?"

"Nothing, but it passes the time," Fanny said simply.

"Poor Fanny, you are finding London *triste,* are you not? I am sorry for it, but it will change before long."

"Wyvern?"

Almina nodded brusquely. "I expect his declaration momentarily, and we will hope papa is sober enough to receive it," she snorted, and left the room.

Belowstairs the roses were received with pleasure to perfume the servants' hall. Janet had been inspired to be explicit that it was *Miss Fanny's* suggestion, "being as madam is afeared the Duke might learn if Miss Almina accepted 'em."

There was a small silence before Mrs. Hodge said ponderously, "Well, for my part, I could wish it settled. Miss Almina's grown so nervy there's no knowing how to go on. I'd scarce believe the change in her from last year if I'd not seen it myself. You'll recall, Mr. Pitcock? The house always open, full of young people—Lord Waterbury among 'em—Miss Almina dancing on air, and on a sudden she changed like. Well," the cook hauled to her feet, "I'll make a pupton of pears for Miss Fanny. Eating alone she'll be again, unless the master comes home."

For once Fanny did not object to solitude. Her mind

was full of Charles. She ate her dinner with relish and crowed with delight over the dessert. "Pray, thank Mrs. Hodge for me."

"Yes, miss. She'll be happy you enjoyed it."

With the house to herself, she said "I'll use the piano for a while. Bring the tea tray to the salon, please."

"Yes, miss," but while Pitcock snuffed candles, the music was vaguely disturbing. Admittedly, she was an excellent pianist; she could compose, make up songs and little sonatas. Tonight the sounds were different. Almost, they were *triumphant*. "Miss Fanny sent her thanks for the pupton, Mrs. Hodge. She wants a tea tray in the salon."

"Later. She forgets time when she's playing," the cook said comfortably. "'Tis good for her, but she's a happy nature."

It was never happier than in the following days, although they passed with no sign of Charles. Still, he had said he would come when he could, and if he had remembered to write and send roses, he would remember to drive into the park. Buoyed by anticipation, she could endure life cheerfully. In the mornings she sewed in the sitting room; punctually at a quarter to one she set out with Janet, and after sauntering back and forth within sight of the rendezvous for fifteen or twenty minutes, they returned to Hill Street. Thereafter, Fanny read the latest novel from Hookham's or practiced in the salon.

She was thus occupied one afternoon when, upon completion of a small improvisation, gentle applause made her whirl to face the Duke of Wyvern, sitting in a chair beside the door. Hastily she slid from the piano stool to curtsey, while he rose and came toward her.

"You will be Miss Cherill's younger sister. Miss . . . ?"

"Fanny, Your Grace."

"Ah, yes—Fanny," he smiled with the effect of a pat on the head. "That was a charming selection, Fanny, but I fancy I have been out of England too long. I cannot put a name to the composer."

"No, sir. That is," she gulped, "it wasn't composed, exactly. I was just—playing, Your Grace."

He stared at her glassily. "You mean, you made it up? How extraordinary! Could you play it again?"

"I don't think so, Your Grace, it never comes out the same way twice. M-may I offer you some hospitality—wine or, uh, some tea? I feel certain Almy—Almina—will return directly. It is not like her to be late for her appointments."

He cut short her stammered apology with a wave of his hand. "No, no, I am in advance of the hour due to an alteration in my schedule," he explained punctiliously. "Did I drive on, I should scarce reach my home before I must return, which would tire the horses to no purpose. Instead, I thought to wait here and perhaps converse with your father, but it appears he is from home."

Fanny's heart dropped into her shoes. Could it be, was it possible that Wyvern had meant to offer for Almina—and papa was not in the house? Of all the curst luck! Pitcock was advancing majestically with a tray. "Brandy, Your Grace," he murmured, "and I have ventured to bring Madeira as well. It is thought to be a particularly good vintage."

"Ah, yes, thank you," the Duke nodded, seating himself beside the piano. "Madeira, if you please, and perhaps Miss Fanny will play for me?"

"With pleasure, Your Grace." Fanny was trembling with nervousness, but she sank onto the stool, surreptitiously wiping her damp hands in the folds of her muslin skirt. Once fairly started, it grew easier. She moved from one piece to another, choosing short selections and alternating Scarlatti with Bach, a bit of Mozart, and finally some popular country dances. The Duke was a good listener, sitting silent and moving only to take an occasional sip of wine.

"By Jove, that was splendid," he observed when at last she paused. "Do you sing also?"

"Not well enough for solos. Almina has the voice—quite glorious, is she not, Your Grace? I do not compare, can only manage an occasional duet for a family evening."

"Does Miss Cherill compose, too?"

"Not really. She plays *very* well," Fanny said loyally, "but mostly to accompany herself. Sometimes she used to find words that would fit a tune, and we would make a song together."

"Ah? Charming, charming," the Duke nodded impassively. "I shall hope to hear you on such an informal occasion."

"Yes, Your Grace," she murmured as the door opened to admit Almina and Mrs. Cherill.

"Your Grace! Did I mistake the hour? I had thought it was for half after four," Almina was softly apologetic, but her eyes were sharply on Fanny.

"Why, so it was, but I arrived in advance due to a trifling change in my appointments." The Duke rose, and bowed to Mrs. Cherill. "Your servant, ma'am."

"Oh, indeed, indeed—so kind in you," Mrs. Cherill fluttered a protest. "Almina, make haste to freshen, my love. Pray, be seated, Your Grace. I see Pitcock has brought wine; I hope it was to your taste . . ."

"Excellent, excellent—and Fanny has kindly entertained me with music. Yours is a most accomplished family, ma'am. I count myself fortunate in the acquaintance." He bowed graciously to Fanny, who was emboldened to reply with a curtsey.

"I am the more fortunate, Your Grace. It is heartening that a superb but impartial critic such as yourself should approve me." Beneath his blank stare, she added, "A family is too apt to think its ducklings are swans, you know. Your commendation means far more to me."

The Duke's eyebrows shifted, his lips twitched ever so slightly. If she had not been looking directly at him, she would not have believed it! "I am happy to be able to encourage you without fear or favor," he said, and his tone was as flat and expressionless as ever, but Fanny's irrepressible ebullience responded to that hint of a smile.

"I feel sure Your Grace is no toady," she breathed earnestly, "so I may thank you sincerely."

"Fanny!" Mrs. Cherill was aghast. "I beg you will not run on in this fashion, it is most unbecoming. Pray, leave us!"

"Yes, mama." Fanny curtsied once more and retreated, to run lightly upstairs. "Can I help you, Almy?"

"No, I'm nearly ready. What were you doing in the salon? How long were you there, what did you say?" Almina demanded.

"Nothing. I was practicing, Pitcock showed him in and brought wine. The Duke asked me to play and I did. We had no conversation."

"Thank heavens!" Almina swiftly tied her bonnet strings and surveyed herself in the cheval glass. "Is anything amiss?"

"No, you're beautiful as ever, Almy." As her sister turned to the door, she added softly, "I—like him, Almy."

"*What?*"

Fanny nodded firmly. "He is mostly inside, I fancy he is shy."

"*Shy?* Good God, what has he to be shy about? One of the oldest titles, one of the greatest fortunes in England. Really, you are too absurd!" With a sardonic laugh, Almina was running hastily downstairs.

Fanny followed more slowly, knowing her mother would demand a full account the instant they were alone, and so it proved. "Lud, was there ever such ill luck!" Mrs. Cherill sighed, sinking onto the chaise longue in her dressing room. "But for some fool attempting to lionize in the middle of Bond Street, we must have been home in good time—not that Wyvern was expected, but what must he think: to be forced to listen to piano practice!"

"I don't know that," Fanny muttered rebelliously. "He likes music, mama, and he enjoyed it. I know he did; besides, he said so."

"What else said he? Every word is important, Fanny. Oh, lud, my head; find the vinaigrette, for pity's sake," Mrs. Cherill moaned.

"Shhh, there is no need for the vapors, mama," Fanny soothed. "All went excellently well." Carefully, she detailed the encounter from start to finish, omitting only the Duke's remark about conversing with papa. Too tantalizing, too titillating, and it might signify nothing at all, would merely increase mama's agitated nerves. Instead, she emphasized Wyvern's hope of being present at an informal family musical—and was instantly sorry, for Mrs. Cherill pounced upon it as a delightful scheme: "Only when can it be contrived? The schedule is so crowded. My love, pray fetch the engagement list."

"I do not think it should be contrived, mama," Fanny objected while she handed over the book. "Would it not appear too obvious? I think the Duke would not quite like such open evidence of pursuit."

"Pooh, nonsense, you know nothing of these things, Fanny. Depend upon it, if we can but find an evening with a very *dull* party, he will be delighted to excuse himself in favor of a snug dinner with us," Mrs. Cherill riffled the pages. "Lady Wigmore's rout is sure to be a dead bore . . . oh, no, it is the same evening as the Cavendish ball. A Sunday, perhaps; there is so little offered on Sundays. Yes, here is the very thing: the Marchioness of Gaites is sponsoring a choral group from an orphanage. Well, one has not great hopes of *that*," she closed the book triumphantly. "We will invite Wyvern to dine, and I miss my guess if he does not find you and Almina more to his taste. Harry should be returned from his ruralizing by then—heaven knows what keeps him so long, his property is no great estate, after all. Then if we contrive to engage your father, I fancy it might be the very thing to tip the scale."

Fanny was far from agreeing, but she said, "Yes, mama," dutifully. She might privately suspect there was more to Wyvern than appeared, but the *haut ton* moved by rules as yet unknown to Fanny. Mama and Almina must know best how to handle matters. "If I were Almy, I should allow myself to be caught singing one day when nothing particular was afoot," she thought, "instead of always being so promptly dressed and ready to leap when he says 'Frog,'" but she dared not say so next morning when Almina came into the sitting room.

"You made an impression on Wyvern, and I wish you will tell me how!"

"I played for him while he was drinking his wine."

"You should not have been there in the first place. Good God, what must he think?"

"I suppose he'll think I'd have been upstairs, but for his inopportune arrival," Fanny said with spirit. "Would you have had me dash out of the room at sight of him? He enjoys music, he asked me to entertain him, Almy, and I did. That's all."

"Oh, he had a deal of questions on your masters and high praise for your performance," her sister admitted, "and you say you *liked* him?"

"If he is apt to be my brother-in-law, should I not?"

"Devoutly to be wished," Almina agreed restlessly. "La, how long d'you mean to keep these roses stinking in the room?"

"They remind me of Cherley. I'll take them away if you like, but you used to be fond of roses."

"That was long ago, now they give me the headache," Almina muttered. "No, keep them—they'll die shortly in any case."

Daringly, Fanny asked, "Who is Lord Waterbury?"

"Last year's beau, before I knew my way about."

"You don't like him?"

Almina looked into space briefly. "Oh, I liked him very well last year," she shrugged, "but it was different then. He's an amusing rascal, well connected, but only a younger son not to be taken seriously."

"Like Robin?"

Almina's lips tightened. "Like Robin," she agreed evenly, "although Waterbury is less in every way from appearance to fortune."

"Are all younger sons ineligible?"

"No, of course not," Almina said. "Sometimes a younger son inherits from other relatives and may end with more than the heir—but that is not the case with Waterbury or Robin. Lord," she swept to the door, "do not be delaying me, Fanny. Mama will put you in the way of it when the time comes."

Via the *Gazette,* Fanny was enabled to learn that Lord Charles Waterbury had been present at Lady Pakenham's ball for Miss Edith. It was described as a triumph, and "an interesting announcement" was shortly expected. With a lump in her throat, Fanny wondered if it might be Charles; nothing would be more likely, considering his friendship with Bertie.

"Well, if it is," she told herself, "I shall get over it. I am not so very much in love with him—yet."

She was steeled for a confidence of his engagement as she set forth decorously for her walks in the next days, but it was nearly three more before he whirled through the entrance and reined in beside her. For a moment she was too breathless for speech; he was so much *more* than she remembered. She stood, lips slightly parted, looking up at his boyish grin and the dancing gold glints in his eyes, while he stretched his hand eagerly to pull her up beside him.

"Hallo, hallo! Janet, here's the usual," dropping a coin into her hand. "Mind you're waiting here in three hours!"

"Yes, milord." Janet curtseyed as the curricle dashed away, feeling the money with excitement. With what she had, there was more than enough to buy a new dress to impress Jem Perkins. All thought of Miss Fanny's impropriety was swept from her mind; Janet was already walking toward the Pantheon Bazaar before the curricle had turned the corner.

"Little conspirator, it is good to see you!"

"And you, milord!"

"Oh, sad stuff! Why the formality?"

"One must be respectful to one's elders; mama says so."

Charles laughed, "She would certainly consider me an exception. Well, how have you gone on these past weeks?"

"Excellently, thank you. Harry is come home, the very day you left. He is now gone into Robin Elvey's lodgings, and inspecting his property to the north."

"Elvey? Aye, I recall him. He was in town last season, cutting everyone out with Miss Cherill," Charles chuckled. "Made Pendle mad as fire! I heard your brother was here, Bertie Pakenham said he'd seen him; it was when he was staying with me. Oh, I've a deal to tell you!"

"I am all ears! I was constantly thinking of you, wondering what you had found and what you were able to accomplish."

"I was constantly thinking of *you*," he said warmly, "for you were absolutely in the right of it: you and Rowbotham. There was gross mismanagement, the bailiff was a lazy rogue who'd let all go, and the devil was: when I'd discharged him, I hadn't a notion how to go on for myself . . . but Bertie put me in the way of things."

"Bertie?"

"I couldn't believe it either, but he's a knowing 'un for what he knows, which is property. Lord, let me begin at the beginning." Forthwith, Charles launched into full recital to which she listened intently, occasionally inserting a question or expressing approval.

"What fun you must have had," she sighed. "Truly, the country is very good living, Charles, and Basings sounds a charming residence, not at all the usual repairing lease. Well, your friends enjoyed themselves mightily and begged to return! After all, the season is only three months, what does one do with the other nine? Why should you not live at Basings? There would always be house parties, family holiday gatherings, the hunting season when you would be away. I do not think you would be bored, with friends to visit you, and the local gentry sound tolerable.

"You need not *do* very much; your mere presence would keep all in hand. You could come and go; if you were moped, there would be your lodgings here—and of course during the season, you would be supplied from Basings. Butter, eggs, cream, milk, your own poultry and hams and bacon—a great saving!"

"So they tell me," he admitted wryly. "I should always have had the produce of my land to reduce London expenses; because I did not think of it, the bailiff raised only for the staff's use. Fletcher, the new man, was shocked at the condition of sties and poultry runs. I suppose I should be grateful Eggleston did not produce a full complement, to sell for his own gain."

Fanny shook her head, "Mr. Mattison would have been aware, he would have written your agent. That would be theft, you see. No, it would be easier to raise only what they needed, and to live well at your expense. If questioned, they would say that since you required nothing, it was in the interests of economy."

Charles eyed her with amusement. "That is exactly what Skinner said!"

She colored faintly. "Well—that *is* the way it is done, Charles; it is all laid out as to how many pigs, poultry, eggs and dairy stuff will be needed throughout the year . . . when to plant the vegetables and how many rows of peas or beans. Then it is despatched regularly when you are in town residence, or sufficient sent for a night or so when you are en route to hunting or a race meeting. Mama has a sort of calendar, to be sure the Cherley bailiff does as he should—if papa should be from home, you know."

"Hmm, I should have the same, but demmed if I

know how to go about it," Charles frowned. "Rowbotham says to ask fa's bailiff, but I doubt it would answer. Leicestershire must be different from Surrey."

"Yes, it will be at least a week later for planting, because it is to the north. You must ask the neighbors, and Fletcher; he will have a list of dates for planting or slaughtering, as well as how much of what, but you must keep your own record, Charles," she said authoritatively. "Write everything down in a diary to consult whenever you go to Basings."

"Together with the names of my neighbors and their children," he chuckled irrepressibly. "I say, you *must* be able to drive out one day; what if I make myself known to your brother? He'd consent to drive you, would he not?"

"I expect so, but," she suppressed a shiver, "he is from town, inspecting his own property."

"I wonder, is your mama known to my sister Louisa, Lady Hazeltine . . . or there is my grandmama," he frowned intently. "If we can but contrive some connection, Fanny, I can arrange that you are asked to make one of a group for a country picnic. Think, child: whom do we know in common? I am grown tired of these secret meetings, Fanny. I would be openly allowed to take you driving, you are better company than the society misses."

"You are better company than anyone," she murmured involuntarily, "but I do not think mama is acquainted with any of your relatives."

"Never mind, my grandmother will know how to contrive it," he said easily, "and how did you like the roses?"

"Oh, what a pother you made! You'll not be displeased? Mama would not allow Almina to accept them for fear Wyvern would hear, so I told Janet to leave some for me and give the rest to Pitcock for the servants," Fanny chuckled. "She worried that your man might learn as well as the Duke's, but I knew you would understand."

Charles looked blank for a moment, then laughed heartily. "Oh, famous!"

"It's the nature of the female," she agreed sadly, "but *thank* you for sending them, Charles. I collect the garden is not in too bad case? If ever I get home to Cherley, I shall beg cuttings from you. There were two deep red roses that I know we do not have."

"You shall have anything and everything you wish," he promised. In talking of Basings and its future, they had been driving to the outskirts of London and were suddenly approaching a group of tents interspersed with brightly decorated booths. "I say," he pulled the horses to a walk, "St. Bartholomew's Fair! Shall we go, Fanny?"

"By all means! How gay it looks."

"I've no business to take you," he muttered dubiously. "Even for a child it is improper, Fanny. We shall be surrounded by Cits in all their finery; your sister would swoon at the mere suggestion. Damme, I think we should not—I'm sorry I mentioned it."

"No, please!" she begged. "It would be good to stretch our legs after the drive. Besides, if I could not come here when I am Out, you cannot deprive me of this chance to broaden my knowledge."

He laughed at her mischievous coaxing. "Well, I won't then." He pulled the curricle into a field already crowded with gigs and wagons. "I swear, Fanny, every time I see you I think what a pity it is that little girls must grow up to be fine ladies. I hate to think of you buried in missish propriety."

"I doubt it is possible," she said demurely. "Besides, I have already decided that since it is in the highest degree improbable I shall be an Incomparable, I shall strive to be an Original. My brother thinks it would be a good thing."

"So do I," Charles tossed the reins to one of the idlers and jumped down, extending his hands to assist Fanny. "Stay as you are! You have not far to go to achieve your decision," he said with an odd little smile.

The fair was the greatest fun. It was thronged with shopgirls, tradesmen with their wives, country folk from outlying farms, but while they were boisterous, at this hour there was no drunken rowdyism. "Keep tight hold of my hand," Charles ordered. "You are so little that if we were separated, it would be hard to find you."

"I would make my way back to the curricle and wait for you," she said absently. "What is a Penny Pool, Charles?"

"You pay a penny and fish for a prize," he dragged her forward, hauling out pennies. They had three tries each with the scoops, laughing helplessly over the silly fairings in the packets. Subsequently they visited the Booth of Knowledge where an Educated Pig displayed its acquaintance with the alphabet, and they wandered on to buy cakes, comfits, glasses of milk. "I shall never eat my dinner," Fanny protested.

"You've plenty of time to regain an appetite."

Behind them a deep grating voice said, "Come, little lady, and know what's in store for you. Old Kate can tell your fortune. Come away in, and hear the future, eh?"

Startled, Fanny whirled to face a grinning crone in grimy gypsy rags at the entrance to a tent. She was nodding and beckoning Fanny to follow her into darkness lit only by a flickering candle. Involuntarily Fanny tightened her grasp on Charles, who laughed indulgently. "By all means, hear what the granny has to say." He thrust a shilling into her hand and led her to the tent. "Be sure you make it a *good* fortune," he warned the gypsy. "Nothing less than happiness and roses!"

"That's as may be," the woman shrugged. "I cannot change what is in the hands. Come you in, little lady, and let me look."

Hesitantly, Fanny entered and extended the shilling to cross the dirty palm held out to her. "Sit ye down, little miss." The gypsy swiftly secreted the coin beneath her gaudy skirt and lit a second candle while Fanny slowly sank onto the stool. She was not so much frightened as repelled by the fug of mingled musky scent and airlessness.

Leaning across the small table, the gypsy seized Fanny's hands and pored over them, muttering to herself with a show of mounting excitement. "Aha, I knew it—I felt it in you, little lady."

"W-what?" Fanny quavered uneasily. "I don't think I want to know, after all," but the gypsy would not release her hands.

"He wanted happiness and roses for you? Ah, you'll have all the happiness there is, little miss, though it may not seem so to others. There's true love till death, which is more than money to *you*. You'll never be rich in money, but you'll never be poor. I see a dark sweetheart, and a trip across river. Tears will follow you, and if you go, you may find it hard to return."

"Do you mean I may not go? But how shall I know?"

"You will know," the old crone nodded cryptically, "and you will go, for your heart rules your head. The moment is sooner than you think. If you followed my advice, you would go straight away from here, back to your home—and if you did, your fortune would still be the same. Remember that, little lady: it cannot change, it would only be delayed and the tears would be different. But you will be impulsive, you will court the trouble, for there are dark clouds ahead." She shook her head ominously, gripping Fanny's trembling hands and staring at her. "The clouds are black and all about your head, little lady," she rasped menacingly. "You could avoid them, you won't—but never despair! Remember: there'll be tears and sorrow, but it will end the same either way. Never despair!"

Wordlessly, Fanny pulled her hands free and fled from the tent to cling to Charles' arm. "Why, what is this?" he raised his eyebrows laughingly. "Did she discover some dark nursery secret? Come, don't believe her, child!"

"N-no," she strove for control, "it was only—the place *smelled*."

The gypsy's voice came ingratiatingly, "A fine young gentleman! Come, my bonny boy, and old Kate will tell your future."

"Don't go! The stench . . . don't go, Charles!"

The gypsy had surged forward to grab his hand, "Ah, it's a long life and a merry one," she cackled. "You'll know laughter and the truest love, if you're quick to see people are not always what they seem. For a shilling, I could tell you more, young gentleman."

"I've heard enough," he pulled his hand away, found a shilling. "There's for your trouble."

She snatched it from him and in a flash it was secreted as he turned away with Fanny beside him. "Ah," she crooned, "it is as close as your doorstep, my bonny boy, and you'll wish you'd listened this day. It'll come to you within a two—days, weeks, months, or years—but remember: people are not always what they seem, and love comes in small packets as well as big."

"What a hum!" Charles said disgustedly. "Did she fright you, child? These gypsies are all alike."

In the fresh air of daylight, Fanny regained her composure to some extent. "She said I should go straight away home, but she knew I wouldn't."

"But there's a deal to see yet, and a full half hour before we need leave," he frowned. "Do you really want to go, Fanny? We will, if you wish it, but it seems a pity."

She hesitated, with a prescience that the gypsy was right and some danger lurked ahead. She had opened her mouth to say, "Yes, please let us go," when a voice said, "Hallo, Charlie. You *here?* Thought you was off to the horse auctions with Spenning?"

"Well, I'm not," Charles said automatically. "Oh, the devil! What are you doing here, Bertie?"

"Just having a look," Mr. Pakenham began, and raised his eyebrows in surprise. "Still dragging your cousin around?" he inquired. "Your servant, ma'am." Fanny curtseyed, and clung to Charles' hand tremulously. "How long's she staying in town? Ain't like you, playing nursemaid to an infant."

"Fanny's a deal more fun than most infants," Charles said. "Mind your tongue, Bertie!"

It was a useless admonition, and if Fanny had not been so anxious at the unexpected encounter, she would have been giggling to herself at Bertie's censorious tone. "Can't think what you're about, Charlie. Not the thing to bring a lady here—only come here to see what's new among the Cyprians. Well, you know that yourself; it's where you got that freak you was beauing last year." Bertie shook his head in disapproval. "Louisa won't like your larking about with Fanny."

"Bottle it, will you?" Charles growled irately. "Where's the harm in broad sunshine? I'm here, ain't I?"

"Come to think of it, so am I." Bertie's blank face was suddenly illumined by A Thought. "Demmed if I don't come with you, old boy. Look after her together, eh? All right and tight, get her home for tea, and keep the chaffer close, eh?" Mr. Pakenham turned and gallantly drew Fanny's other hand through his arm. "Beg you'll allow me to escort you, ma'am. Safe enough with two of us."

"I really think we should . . ." she began desperately, but he merely patted her hand.

"Mum's the word," he assured her, "and you'll enjoy the swinging boats, eh, Charlie? Well, I do myself, if it comes to that. Can't think why it is, but never lost my taste for 'em. Come along, Miss Fanny."

She was not proof against Charles' agreement. "Do you take her first, Bertie; I'll replace you for the second swing. There's just time enough. You'll be back with no one wiser, Fanny."

Weakly, she allowed herself to be lifted to the seat and securely fastened. With a strong pull, the brawny attendant set the boat moving, swaying at first, then moving higher and higher until she caught her breath in delight. They were at the very edge of the fair, flying out above the palings and parallel to the carriage road running beside the river. At the top of each swing, all London seemed spread before her in tantalizing glimpses. She felt again that exhilaration of the balloon ascension, not that they went so high, but it was an approximation.

When at last the boat slowed to a halt, she was breathless. "It was wonderful! Thank you so much, Mr. Pakenham."

"Well, you are a good little sport, and that's a fact," he said admiringly. "Damme, old boy: cool as a cucumber, never turned a hair," he told Charles as he clambered out.

"Lud, yes, I told you so," Charles returned scornfully. "Fanny don't get the vapors, they ain't trained her to 'em yet. Here," to the swinger, "I'm secure, set us going."

"Aye, sir."

Once more the boat shivered, began to move, went higher and higher at each tug of the sweaty man on the ground. Fanny's eyes met Charles', alight with the dancing golden glints, and unconsciously she stretched out her hand to be warmly grasped between his own. For a moment they were lost in each other, until at last they were reaching the top of the swing and she cried out, "Isn't it glorious? It is almost like flying."

Involuntarily, they were both craning this way and that, looking across the river for glimpses of town, and comparing notes excitedly. The swing was ending, the boat going more and more slowly, and with a sigh of satisfaction, Fanny turned from side to side for a final glance at the fair. She caught sight of Bertie, unmistakable in exquisite lavender pantaloons and molded coat of purple superfine, leaning against the palings. Hat in hand, he was talking to the occupants of a carriage drawn up on the river drive beyond: Almina, with the Duke of Wyvern and a starchy groom standing behind!

As quick as might be, Fanny averted her face. She was not quick enough, Almina, the Duke, Bertie, and the groom had already looked up. Even frozen with horror, Fanny was swept with a furious impatience at her sister's starting eyes and shriek of recognition, while Charles was saying, "Devil take it, now we *are* in the basket!"

The boat was still swaying when he loosed the buckle and leapt to the ground, heedless of the attendant's protests. "Quickly, Fanny: jump into my arms, I'm braced to catch you."

Somehow she managed it, and they hastened toward the exit, gaining the curricle almost at a run. In a twinkling, they were turning out of the carriage field into a side road away from the river drive. "With luck, we may outstrip Wyvern and get you to Hill Street before Miss Cherill," he flicked the team with his whip. "That fool, Bertie! Damme, how can a man have so little brains?"

"It is the unluckiest mischance," Fanny murmured, clinging to her seat as the horses picked up speed. "If only—but do you not see the gypsy was right? She said there was trouble very close to me, black clouds around my head, and I should go away at once," catching her breath in a sob, "and now it is all over. Oh, Charles!"

"No, it is not," he said firmly. "We'll come about, never fear. Miss Cherill has only to hold her tongue. Wyvern don't know you, after all."

"But he does!" Her eyes filled with tears. "It's only five days past that he arrived early. I was practicing in the salon and he asked me to entertain him until Almy arrived. He might not have been *certain* if she had not recognized me; now he can have no doubt. Oh, Charles!"

"Devil take the silly chit," he muttered, biting his lip, "not that she'll get Wyvern. You must know the betting runs six to two against her at White's. Wyvern don't need money, but he takes himself very seriously. Catched or not, he'll listen when his sister and the Dowager say Miss Cherill ain't grand enough."

"So much the worse for me," she sighed. "You cannot know, Charles; I don't myself, exactly, except that all depends on Almina and she depends on Wyvern . . . and I think perhaps it might be more possible than you know, for when he sat with me in the salon, he said he had come betimes because it would tire the horses to drive home when he must straightway return—and he had thought to talk with papa."

"Good God, did he so? That is certainly a horse of a different color."

"Yes, but do you not see the position I have created? If it was touch and go, as you surmise, and if he does not offer because of her hey-go-mad younger sister," the tears spilled silently down her cheeks, "there will be an uproar. Oh, Charles!"

"Dash it, I will not have them mistreat you, Fanny. Suppose I lay the whole matter before your father? What is there to disclose, after all? A balloon ascension, a visit to the zoo, and a drive today—nothing so shocking about it, but I am wholly to blame. Surely, your parents would understand. You are too young to realize, I should have been wise for you, Fanny."

"No, no, it is far worse then you know," she shook her head, clenching her hands together for courage. "I—have deceived you, Charles," she said in a very small voice.

He was so startled that he nearly dropped the reins. "I beg your pardon?"

"Yes," she nodded dolefully. "I allowed you to think me a little girl, because I was so tired of never going anywhere or doing anything. In reality," she caught her breath in a sob, "I shall be seventeen next month, and should make my curtsey next season."

CHAPTER VI

Charles slowed the horses to a stand. "Good God," he said blankly.

"Yes," Fanny's shoulders drooped and she pulled a handkerchief from her reticule to wipe her eyes. "I knew very well I should not be jauntering about with no chaperone, Charles, but I could not resist. I think I must have admitted today in any case; you would have learned shortly from Harry, or in arranging the scheme to visit Basings." She sighed, "I am sorry, Charles. I cannot even ask your pardon, because it affects your reputation as well as mine."

"Be demmed to it," he said roughly, staring at her. "So that is why . . . I should have guessed," he muttered. "I nearly did; for all your tiny size, you talked so wisely. Well," he drew a deep breath, starting the horses forward, "it *is* serious. If we can gain Hill Street and you change your frock, could you insist it was not you whom your sister saw?"

"I doubt it, I am a poor liar. She will be in a taking, you know, and the servants are bound to say how long Janet and I were gone, or notice I am wearing a different gown."

"Harry! What if I tell him the whole? Would he not understand, and come to your aid?"

"Perhaps. I don't know, he is grown so mature and authoritative from the war. He was used to be fit to go, he and Robin. Now I'm not sure. I don't even know if he's returned from his property."

"Still, it's worth trying. Give me his direction."

"It is 23 North Audley."

For a space, they drove silently. "We must have a plan for communicating," he said suddenly. "Can you remember my direction: number 3, Holton Square . . . not too far from you. Perhaps Janet could bring a note, or I might send Somers at an agreed time each day."

"Midafternoon when the staff is resting—but do you not think he may be known to our butler, Pitcock?"

"So much the better! Somers will know how to get news of you without arousing suspicion for Janet."

"I hope so, for that is the worst of it. She might be turned away for her share in this, and she has a sweetheart among the footmen. Somehow I must protect her. If there is an uproar, I shall insist she had no idea whom I met. I don't know, I hope it will answer."

"We are too gloomy," he remarked. "Almina has only to hold her tongue . . ."

"She will not," Fanny prophesied.

"She may be persuaded. Wyvern cannot be certain after a single meeting with you . . ."

"I was wearing this very gown . . ."

"Nevertheless, let Almina say she was mistaken; looking up at such an angle in the sunlight made her dizzy and caused her to cry out," Charles countered hopefully, "and as it happens, I do have a Cousin Fanny. At least I think I do, although it may be a niece; there's no keeping up with our family nurseries. In any case, she'll serve for authenticity. I don't doubt your sister will ring a peal over you, I wish I could think of any way out—but surely she can be brought to see the advantage in denying the whole thing."

"That is where we started: all depends on Wyvern, and if Almina does not attach him, she will lay it at my door, whether or not you are right that he would not offer anyway," Fanny returned distractedly. "We were never very sisterly, but in London I cannot understand her at all. I am positive she loves . . . well, no matter who . . . but she is determined to have Wyvern, and I do not think she even likes him above half. He is simply an 'eligible connection'."

"Highly eligible, and I wish her joy of him!" They were dashing into the park toward the waiting figure of Janet, and he slowed the horses, turning to Fanny. "I cannot quite take it in that I shall not see you again for a while," he muttered. "Fanny—Fanny, you are already such a woman. All spirit and heart beyond all the simpering Belles in the *ton,* a true Incomparable."

"You do me too much credit. I've been willful and deceitful, and placed us both in an awkward predicament, but you cannot know how much I have anticipated our meetings. It was more than a mere break of dull routine. Whatever befalls, it will seem worth it to me."

"A high compliment, if undeserved," he laid his hand over hers. "Mind you let me know what occurs? I shall be desperate with worry," he said urgently. "I will do my possible with your brother, and whatever else comes to mind, but *promise* you will send word."

"Yes," she said faintly, "and thank you, Charles. If it were not for the ending, today would have been the greatest treat of all. Goodbye."

"Until we meet again," he corrected, as she descended to the path. With a final smile, he drove away.

"Oh, miss, what has happened?" Janet asked fearfully. "Lord save us—was you seen?"

"I fear so, but it may yet turn out all right," Fanny said with a confidence she was far from feeling. "Janet, say nothing unless you are directly questioned. Then you must say you have no idea whom I met, you thought it was a party of young ladies. Do you understand?"

"Y-yes, Miss Fanny."

"One more thing: be alert for a message from His Lordship's man, Somers."

"Oooo, I can't never be talking to *him!* Mr. Pitcock'd notice."

"Well, it may not be necessary," Fanny soothed as they approached the house.

There was no sign of Wyvern's carriage, and by good luck the door was opened by Jem Perkins, who looked more at the maid than her mistress. Hastening upstairs, Fanny thought the man would be unable to say what dress she'd been wearing. With desperate speed, she bundled the sprigged muslin into Janet's arms. "Set it in the laundry tub at once," she whispered, "and say it has been there for hours."

"Y-yes, miss. Oh, Lord, what's to become of us!" Janet scuttled off to the back stairs, and not a second too soon. Fanny had just time to pretend to be arranging her hair at the dressing table before Almina crashed open the door.

"Well, Miss Innocence—be good enough to explain!"

Fanny suppressed a shiver at her sister's harsh voice. "Explain what, Almy?"

"Don't try to lie," Almina sniffed. "I see you've changed your gown, but if you think to be unrecognized, it is useless with that red hair. There cannot be two such flaming mops in all London, let alone coupled with the name Fanny."

Fanny wilted at once, she had forgotten her brilliant hair. "I'm sorry, Almy. Indeed I have done nothing so very bad."

"Bad? You have disgraced the family and made a laughing stock of me, particularly with that fool, Bertie Pakenham, to spread the news that Miss Cherill's sister behaves like a serving wench!"

"He doesn't know I am your sister. Charles said I was a nursery cousin come up from the country to visit Lady Hazeltine."

Almina closed her eyes with a faint shriek. "Good God—one of the starchiest females in London! Oh, what have you done, you wicked girl? It must surely come to her ears, what will she think?"

"That Charles has a new ladybird," Fanny quavered, "but he would never tell her it was I, Almy, and Bertie Pakenham doesn't know. Do but listen, Almina: you have only to hold fast that it was *not* your sister after all. You could not see clearly in the strong sunlight, the resemblance was strong, but on your return home you found I'd been here all the while."

Almina laughed sardonically. "Useless! Wyvern recognized you instantly, and if Bertie didn't know, he does now, for Wyvern said, 'Ah, little Fanny—what a charming child your sister is, Miss Cherill!' "

"Well—but then he must not have thought it so improper, Almy. After all, anyone may take a little girl to drive. I might have known Lord Waterbury any time these ten years and been considered as a younger sister—like Robin. There was never a question of my going anywhere at all with him for a treat."

"In the country, and a long-standing family acquaintance," Almina said scornfully. "This is London, and you have *not* known Waterbury for ten years. God knows how you ever met him, but I'll assure you you'd not be allowed to go so far as the corner with *him*. Forever in the gambling hells, a notorious rakehell!"

"He treated me with the most perfect consideration," Fanny cried. "He meant to rescue me the night of the fire, and he thought I was only a child."

"But you are not," Almina flared, "and when I receive an offer from Wyvern, how are you to be explained? A grown girl for all your wispiness, careening about with a man who'll think it a famous joke for every club in town . . ."

"No, he will *not*," Fanny muttered rebelliously, but Almina ignored her.

"You can never have a season after this, you've ruined yourself forever," her voice soared hysterically, "but you shall *not* ruin me! You'll have to be sent from town, hidden away, d'you hear? Good God, after all the care and planning, to have it destroyed by a stupid little marplot at the most crucial moment . . . I might have hoped for some consideration, some assistance from my sister. Wyvern was well pleased with you. He spoke most warmly of your music, and predicted a great success for your entrance into society, but you must need ruin all with your backstairs intrigue."

"It was *not!*" Fanny returned indignantly. "Could you have kept your head this afternoon instead of screaming like a ninnyhammer, all would have passed off easily enough—and if it does not, do not blame me! Charles told me the betting at White's has been six to two for the past month against your ever getting a declaration from Wyvern."

"Girls, what is this?" Mrs. Cherill stood in the doorway. "For shame, control yourselves!"

But Almina was beside herself. "Mama, Fanny's been sneaking out alone to meet Charles Waterbury . . . for weeks and *weeks,* mama . . . and Bertie Pakenham says he's pretended she was his cousin. She admits it! And today we saw them in the swing boats at St. Bartholomew's Fair, like a kitchen slut! With Wyvern present! Oh, I shall die of the shame—and now she says they are betting at White's he will never offer for me at all."

Turning on her sister, Almina seized her shoulders and shook her until Fanny's teeth chattered. "You heartless snip! You don't care what happens so long as you can have your vulgar romances," she panted. "I'll make you care, I'll marry Wyvern in spite of you, and when the time comes, we'll see who helps you to get a husband. You'll be fortunate if we can contrive to get Mr. Cattermole for you!"

Mrs. Cherill came out of her lethargy and speedily pulled her daughters apart. Simultaneously Mr. Cherill appeared unsteadily in the hall, demanding, "What's to do here? Good God, can a man have no peace in his own home?"

Between his booming voice, Almina's mounting soprano, Mrs. Cherill's attempts to quiet the turmoil, Fanny massaged the bruises of her sister's vicious grasp and sobbed in a pitiful undertone, protesting earnestly, "It isn't true—I didn't—I am *not* depraved! Mama, papa, don't believe her, she's imagining the whole."

"Well, you must have done something, miss," Mr.

Cherill rounded on her angrily. "Damme, what a set-to."

"I only said they've been betting for a month at White's against an offer from Wyvern," she said tremulously.

"That's true enough," he agreed, and recoiled from Almina's fury.

"I suppose you were betting against me too, sir? Well, but for Fanny's exploits, I'd have proved everyone wrong. You'd have lost that bet like all the others that are putting a bailiff in the house."

"Hold your tongue, miss," Mr. Cherill thundered, and the uproar recommenced. With every recital, the tale of Fanny's enormities grew, until at last her mother managed to push Almina from the room.

"I will talk to you later, Fanny," she drew the door closed. "Indeed, I am shocked. You are far too old to be so witless."

With a click, the key turned. Fanny's knees buckled and she sank down exhaustedly beside the bed. She had not even any tears left, it was all so much worse than expected. In the hall, the voices died away. She could hear her father stomping down the stairs, Almina retreating to her bedroom, where Mrs. Cherill endeavored to quiet the hysterical weeping. Finally Fanny fell asleep. The room was dark when she waked to the unlocking of her door. Mrs. Cherill came in, followed by Perkins carrying a tray.

"Merciful heavens, why have you not lit the candles?"

Fanny scrambled to her feet. "I think I must have dozed."

"How you could *sleep!*" Mrs. Cherill's voice was exasperated. "Perkins, light the candles and make up the fire. Then you may go."

She sat down in silence while he obeyed. He was looking sullen, from which Fanny deduced Janet might have been dismissed, and her heart sank. When he had gone, her mother said, "Well, Fanny, I scarce know what to say to this start. I have been all this time talking with your father, and it is only by a miracle that you are not sent away to a convent school. However, papa agrees it were better to send you to Cherley."

"But—you said the house was closed with only the Beadles, no servants. Couldn't I go to Aunt Maria?"

"We do not choose to make explanations to family members. It was hard enough to get your father to consent to Cherley, while as for Almina—how you contrive to vex your sister! I vow I do not know how I came to have such a daughter; to look at you, miss, you seem all sweetness and tractability—and you are forever involved in some mischief. Everything done to rear you becomingly, but you seem bent on depravity: kissing Mr. Ribbons in the garden, and receiving poems from Mr. Cattermole under the guise of lessons in Biblical history!"

Fanny's eyes flashed indignantly. "I did *not* kiss Percy Ribbons, nor receive poems. You are unjust, mama: you *know* Mr. Cattermole had slipped them into my Bible, I never knew they were there. You found them before I had reached those chapters."

Mrs. Cherill sighed. "It don't signify, Fanny. You must see that to be putting yourself in a position where these things happen is as bad as outright encouragement. I do not—cannot—believe you so lost to your situation as to be inviting these events, but the result is the same."

"But you would not really marry me to Mr. Cattermole?" Fanny pleaded. "Surely he cannot have *offered* for me, mama? Oh, please . . ."

"As to that, nothing is decided yet," Mrs. Cherill said repressively. "Eat your dinner, Fanny, and tell me the whole."

Listlessly Fanny took a spoonful of soup. "It was the night of the fire," she began, holding her voice steady by main force. Mrs. Cherill sat silent until Fanny concluded, "So you see it was not so very bad, mama. Almina is making a big to-do over nothing."

Mrs. Cherill regarded her daughter with irritation. "No, she is not. To be seen even once alone with a man like Waterbury could ruin any chance for your presentation to the *ton*. I will concede that your meetings have been innocent in themselves, for which I am as much amazed as thankful. From thinking you a child, he appears to have behaved as a gentleman. Nevertheless, Waterbury is a gamester, forever in a scrape. Half the scandals in town include him, one of the sharpest young devils in London, accepted only because of his lineage and the very man to think it a famous joke when he learns the truth."

"He knows already," Fanny whispered. "I—confessed, and he does not think it a joke, mama."

Mrs. Cherill closed her eyes faintly. "You *told* him? Good God, have you *no* sense at all?"

"He would be bound to learn, I thought better to admit," Fanny hung her head, "and first he wanted to visit you and papa to assume all blame. Then he meant to visit Harry and ask him to intercede. Truly, he is most concerned for my reputation, mama."

"It will not answer," Mrs. Cherill returned grimly. "In fact, the less he does, the better. That were only to impress the incident on other minds. The real damage is to Almina, she cannot be blamed for her anger, nor can your thoughtlessness be overlooked. You knew she must be settled this season, you knew the Duke to be exceedingly high in the instep. Without title and fortune, Almina has only her beauty and breeding to cause his capitulation. It has been touch and go as to whether it would succeed, whether his attraction would outweigh his sense of what was due to his consequence. If your hoydenish desire for adventure causes him to think before allying himself to our family, you will have done your sister incalculable harm."

"Yes, mama," Fanny sighed, "although I do not think she cares a fig for him."

"You are not to be the judge of that, miss! *Almina* knows her duty to contract an eligible connection."

"Yes, mama." Silently Fanny finished her dinner. "When must I leave?"

"As soon as may be. Set about packing the portmanteaux, and meanwhile you will stay in your room as much to prevent another uproar as to reflect on your stupidity." Mrs. Cherill arose with decision and rang the bell. When the dishes were removed, she said "Pitcock will bring a tea tray later. Good night, Fanny."

Left alone, Fanny stared dully at the fire. She did, indeed, reflect on her stupidity and in retrospect, she was quite as appalled as her mother and sister. "How came I to do such a thing, I must have been mad! I did know, I did consider every objection they raised. To be taking such risks was sheer folly. If it were only myself—but now it involves everyone. I do believe Charles will keep silent, and I do not really mind being sent home . . . or at least, not so *very* much." Her eyes filled with tears; she knew that to be a lie, "Although what does it matter? If I were here, I should still never be allowed to see Charles again, and Almina's temper would be worse than ever."

It was already in no good mood. Dimly, she could hear Almy complaining querulously in a voice not far from weeping. There was a slit in the gown she wished to wear, and no time for it to be mended. One pair of gloves was slightly soiled; another was missing a button. The curling tongs were too hot; she would have the headache. Mrs. Cherill soothed and cajoled distractedly, while her maid silently assisted Almina's toilette. When at last they descended, it was to encounter Mr. Cherill in the lower hall, from which an apoplectic roar soared upward, causing Fanny to droop even lower in her chair.

"It is all my fault," she thought shakily. "We were not a very happy family at the outset, but I have undone us completely. I have been a willful, selfish girl, and all for nothing. If Charles ever might have loved me, it would never be allowed. He is definitely not an eligible connection. Oh, why did I?"

The gypsy's prophecy was fatally true. "Your heart rules your head, but never despair. Remember it will end the same whatever you do, but never despair, little lady."

"I would I could believe that," Fanny sighed disconsolately and jumped as her door was unlocked for Pitcock with the tea tray.

"Madam directed me to bring this, and cook has sent some small cakes with a glass of orgeat she thought you might fancy later."

"Thank you, Pitcock—and thank Mrs. Hodge. It was kind in her."

"Yes, miss." The butler cast an eye to the fire and unbent to the point of mending it personally. "If there is anything further, please ring for me, Miss Fanny." He withdrew, locking the door behind him, while Fanny poured her tea and listlessly nibbled a petit four.

She was not to know that following Pitcock's explanation of the initial uproar, Mrs. Hodge had ruthlessly quelled all pleasurable shock in the servants' hall. "We'll have no gossip, if you please! You'll not get *me* to believe Miss Fanny's done anything she shouldn't!"

"Oooo-er, Mrs. Hodge," Edith breathed avidly, "to be driving *alone* with a young gentleman? Coo, 'ow came you to allow it, Janet? Very sly you've been!"

"How could I tell who she was meeting? I thought it was a party of young ladies to walk with while I was doing the errands."

"That will do," Mrs. Hodge stated. "It is not for Janet to say who Miss Fanny may or may not meet—not but what she should have given *me* a word of it," severely. "Howsoever, what's done is done, and for my part, Miss Almina is behaving very badly. A whiskey-frisky young gentleman, perhaps, but you'll recall, Mr. Pitcock: *last* season His Lordship was quite one of the preferred beaux."

"Very true," the butler nodded gravely, "but entirely ineligible, Mrs. Hodge. To the best of my belief, he was not among those who offered for Miss Almina, knowing himself ineligible, I presume. *This* season he has not appeared on our visiting list at all."

"Eh, 'tis all different now," Mrs. Hodge conceded, "but to be locking Miss Fanny in her room is what I cannot approve . . . and I'll thank you to delay the tea tray until I've time to add a titbit to cheer the little darling, Mr. Pitcock."

Unaware of the championship belowstairs, Fanny drank her tea and felt more depressed than ever by the silent house. If only she might be released to play the piano for an hour, but she could not bring herself to suggest it. Pitcock must have had his instructions; he would greatly dislike to refuse her, yet be obliged to do so. Better not to embarrass him. Fanny continued to sit in unhappiness, until a quick tap made her turn to the door, where a white envelope was sliding over the sill.

Fanny caught her breath and dashed to pull it free, hearing soft footsteps darting away to the rear. "Charles!" she whispered thankfully, tearing open the message with trembling fingers.

It was even harder to decipher than the former note. Lord Waterbury had evidently written in considerable agitation of mind, and along with its failure to instruct him in arithmetic, Eton had not succeeded with penmanship. Fanny set all the candles in a semicircle on her desk, and bent determinedly over the letter.

"My dear Fanny: Your brother is returned to London but from home. I have left urgent word for him to meet me as soon as may be. Meanwhile I have set a seal on Pakenham's tongue; he will say nothing to anyone and asks your pardon for the coil we are in. You may rely upon him for any assistance, only tell us how best to help. Somers will expect a note from Janet's hand at ten tonight. Pray send me a line to say how you go on? I depend upon you to throw all blame to me! You were too young to consider, I should have been wiser, and the thought that you may suffer unkindness for my rackety ways is agony to me. Dear

Fanny, I must be allowed to protect you! Your obedient servant, Charles."

With a dry sob, she pressed the paper to her cheek. Ten o'clock? It was already nine-thirty. Pushing the candles aside, she drew out a sheet of writing paper, picked up a pen, and wrote quickly.

"Dear Charles: There is nothing you can do aside from telling Harry, and I pray he will understand. I am to be sent to Cherley as soon as possible, in the hope that Wyvern may not discover my age before offering for Almina. All must be silence! I dare not ask your forgiveness for my shocking behavior, but your kindness and gentle courtesy to one you believed a child have taught me much of the world, and I shall forever be grateful to you. If possible, please let me have a word that you do not think me entirely depraved? Yrs, etc."

She had no sooner sealed her note than there was a timid tap at the door. "Miss Fanny?"

"Yes! Dear Janet, how does it go with you?" Fanny whispered, sliding the envelope over the sill.

"I said what you told me, but I doubt it was believed."

"But you are not dismissed? Thank God for that!"

"I'm forbidden to be abovestairs, and I'm to go to Cherley with you. Tonight it's to be, when the madam comes home with Miss Cherill; there's moonlight, and the carriage can return in time for tomorrow's engagements," Janet's voice trembled forlornly, "but Mr. Pitcock and Mrs. Hodge say as how they'll see I get me character. No one don't believe you done *anything* wrong, Miss Fanny."

Watching the envelope disappear, Fanny drew a long breath. "Never despair!" she said softly. "Well, I won't. I'll believe it will end satisfactorily for everyone—but I wish Harry were here, or Robin come back . . ."

Lord Waterbury was not so hopeful. Rackety he might be, but better versed in the *haut ton* than Fanny, and once her deception was confessed, he was well aware of all the possible ramifications and correspondingly anxious. When she had left the curricle, he drove directly to Major Cherill's lodgings, where Teake admitted his master was returned to town, "but he's gone out again, saying as he'd not be home for dinner. Nor he didn't say where he *would* be, milord, which might be anywhere," Teake explained earnestly in response to a nuance he observed in Lord Waterbury's expression—or as Teake put it to himself, "Wot's eatin' *'im,* I wonder?"

"Devil take it," Charles muttered, slapping his driving gloves against his thigh. "You'd give him a message: I need to speak with him most urgently. It concerns his sister Fanny. If he should chance to come home before setting out for the evening, tell him to send me word, or say where I may catch him later. It really is vital." He flashed a rueful smile that instantly enlisted the bâtman to his case.

"Yes, milord, I'll make sure he gets your message." Closing the door behind His Lordship, Teake frowned. *"Now* wot's afoot? Miss Fanny's the little 'un," he stumped away to the salon, where after a slight hesitation he delicately inspected the drift of papers and invitation cards on his master's side table. There might be some indication of this evening's engagement. He found nothing. "Write a note for the Major," he decided, "and step around to see old Pitcock. The Major'll need to know wot's 'appened, particular with Miss Fanny. She's the only one who ever troubled to write 'im when we was on the Peninsula."

While Teake was laboriously penning a screed for Major Harry Cherill, Lord Waterbury was moving on to Bertie Pakenham's lodgings, where Bertie (for once) was wide awake. When Charles was ushered in, Bertie stared at him very hard. "Oh, it's you, is it? Said to myself, 'Lay a monkey Charlie'll be here within the hour.'" Bertie consulted his watch and shook his head sadly. "I'd have lost."

"Of course you'd have lost," Charles returned

wrathfully. "I stopped to see Harry Cherill first—and I wish you will tell me *why* you cannot keep a close mouth! In God's name, why must you draw attention to Fanny?"

"Sorry, old boy. Didn't know she wasn't your cousin, y'know," Bertie apologized feebly. "Don't understand any of it, to tell you the truth. Wish you'd explain? Nice little gel—well, I know she's not a new ladybird . . ."

"Good *God,* no!"

"No need to take a pucker at me, Charlie. Thing is, thought you was doing the pretty for a country relative. Not the place to take her; well, I told you that to begin with, but no harm done with two of us. Hadn't a notion but you was merely being kind to the child," Bertie said earnestly. "Stands to reason she couldn't be enjoying herself with Louisa—if she was staying there, that is; never knew such a Sunday-faced woman—but when Wyvern pulls up and asks what I'm doing there, I'd no idea you didn't wish it known.

"Told him the truth: we was taking Charlie's cousin to see the sights. At least," Bertie floundered, *"thought* it was the truth. Knew you didn't want Louisa to hear, but not likely she would; no reason for Wyvern or Miss Cherill to mention it. And *then* I find she ain't a cousin but Miss Cherill's sister. Wish you'd explain, old boy."

"Oh, dash it," Charles groaned, "you say Wyvern recognized her?" At Bertie's solemn nod, "Well, now we *are* in the basket."

"Sorry, Charles—can only beg your pardon and Miss Fanny's," Bertie said abjectly. "Know I'm not brainy, but wouldn't hurt the child for the world. Anything I can do, you've only to tell me."

"Demmed if I know *what* to do," Charles muttered, absently pouring himself a glass of wine. "Oh, not your fault; I don't blame you, Bertie. You couldn't know. Well, I didn't myself, if it comes to that."

"Didn't know she wasn't your cousin?"

"No, no, I knew she was Miss Cherill's sister, but I thought she was a schoolgirl. Now it turns out she's seventeen, only waiting until they've settled Miss Almina before making her own curtsey. Listen," Charles flung himself into a chair and rapidly outlined the story. "That's it," he finished, tossing off the remainder of his wine, "and no more than a lark if she were the age we thought her."

"Don't see that," Bertie observed. "Worse, if she was that devious in the nursery; expectable from an older one."

"Fanny is *not* devious," Charles fired back, refilling his glass. "She's as honest and natural as the daylight. Lud, you can talk to her, Bertie! She enjoys things, without simpering or swooning. All it is: I took her for a little girl, and because she was having a dull time of it, she did not correct me." He sprang to his feet, pacing back and forth nervously. "She will have it that if Wyvern don't offer she'll be blamed."

"Odds are six to two against."

"And so I told Fanny, but here's an odd thing: the reason Wyvern recognized her was that he was early for an engagement with her sister. He was shown in while she was practicing her music, and she says he told her he had thought to talk to Mr. Cherill while waiting for Miss Almina."

Mr. Pakenham's vacuous expression took on a spark of interest. "Think it means anything?"

"Lord, how should I know? Fanny says her sister loves someone else, but is determined to catch Wyvern."

"Shouldn't think she'd do it, but might be as well to hedge my bet," Bertie reflected.

"Oh, the devil with your bets! What's to be done about Fanny?"

"Hmmmm." Mr. Pakenham pondered, sipping his own wine. "Consult the Dowager," he said suddenly. "She'll know how to bring it off."

"My *grandmother?*" Charles expostulated. "Good God, she'll only read me a long lecture and have the vapors."

"Don't think so," Bertie said stubbornly. "Mothers

have the vapors; grandmothers are mightily tickled by your scrapes. Always noticed, it's the old ladies who can't be beat on any suit. She'll start by pretending shock and washing her hands of you—but she'll come around, you'll see."

Charles rumpled his hair wildly. "But what could she do?"

"I don't know precisely," Bertie looked vague, "but ten to one, she's an old friend of the child's grandmother or aunts or someone. She invites little Fanny to tea, takes her driving in the Promenade, makes it clear she's accepted by the Dowager Duchess of Pevency. Girl ain't out, but no reason she shouldn't companion an old lady for a turn about the park."

"What good will that do?"

"You ain't thinking," Bertie told him severely. "Got to make it appear Fanny's always known your grandmother—nothing more logical than your taking her to drive. Ought to have been a groom, of course, but if the Dowager don't see the harm, you'll find the *ton* don't dare say a word. She'll poker up and stare 'em down for suggesting her grandson ain't a fit escort of the young relative of an old friend—and I was there, as well.

"Don't say that's as good as a governess," Bertie admitted, "but better than nothing. Damme, we may be fit to go, Charlie, but we're no Peep-o'-Day boys. You put it to your grandmama, see what she says. I'll back you. Well, if it comes to that, I *was* with you except for the zoo."

"That's so," Charles agreed slowly. "I doubt it will answer, but it's worth a try. I mean to see Major Cherill if I can find him, and I wanted to speak to her parents, but Fanny forbade it. She says they will only be in an uproar, and the less said the better." He bit his lip unhappily, "I would go direct to Wyvern, but that I know him too slightly—and what could I say? To be attempting an explanation to him must imply I think his interest in Miss Cherill entitles him to it . . . and if he has not such a firmed interest, might it not frighten him away? That would be to cause even more anger against Fanny, and if I know Miss Cherill, she has already created a thunderstorm over the poor child.

"Well," Charles shrugged into his coat, "I'll be off. If you should encounter Harry Cherill during the evening, tell him I desperately need to meet him."

Bertie nodded. "Spenning expects you for dinner."

"Make my excuses, I'm in no frame for it this night," Charles said restlessly, "but for God's sake, don't explain! Say nothing to anyone, Bertie. I rely on you."

Mr. Pakenham nodded again. "My word on it, old boy," he said solemnly, "but go see the old lady. You'll find she can help."

He continued to sit staring into space when Lord Waterbury had gone, and did not move when his manservant entered with a tray of fresh glasses and decanters. Mr. Tilson silently tidied the room with no more than a slight *clink* in replacing wine with brandy. He was quite aware that Mr. Pakenham was *thinking,* and equally aware that this was a process requiring undivided attention. As quietly as possible, he mended the fire and was removing the used glasses when his master suddenly said, "God bless me—I think Charles is in love!"

CHAPTER VII

Somers was somewhat of the same opinion when Lord Waterbury flung into his lodgings a short while later. "Are you acquainted with the Cherill's butler?" he demanded abruptly. "Pit-pet-something."

"Mr. Pitcock," Somers replied blankly. "I see him occasionally at the Spotted Dog, milord."

"What sort of man is he: reliable, or stiff-rumped?"

Somers gulped, "I should call him most reliable, milord. Uh, he is not one to gossip unduly, although it would appear the household is not an easy one."

"I'll wager it isn't," Charles muttered, rummaging for paper and pen, "but you know him well enough to get news? Could you contrive to have a note delivered to Miss Fanny—either through the butler, or the maid, Janet?"

"Miss *Fanny?*" Somers gulped again, totally at a loss. "Uh, I could try, milord, but I am not sure . . . That is, I am not closely acquainted with Mr. Pitcock."

"Well, do your best, but it must *not* come to the ears of the family," Lord Waterbury was scribbling rapidly. "There's trouble enough already." He sanded, sealed his note. "There—try to deliver it, Somers, and return for an answer at ten."

"Y-yes, milord," Somers stuttered slightly, accepting the letter. "Does Your Lordship recall an engagement to dine with Mr. Spenning? I have laid out the rose pantaloons and wine velvet coat, or would Your Lordship prefer the gold with bronzed twill?"

"No, I've canceled Spenning. Put out formal evening

dress," Charles directed tersely.

"Y-yes, milord. Uh, would you wish to dine at home?"

Lord Waterbury shook his head, "I've no appetite." An hour later, after dressing in a most unaccustomed silence, he strode away without a word, leaving Somers more shaken than ever in his life.

"If I were not above the use of vulgarisms," Somers said to himself, "I should have to say I'm regularly betwattled!" Only the sternest rectitude prevented him from instantly repairing to the Cherill's staff door, but from experience he was aware that Mr. Pitcock would not set forth for the Spotted Dog before half after eight. Futhermore, His Lordship's words strongly indicated some personal connection with this trouble that was already enough. If so, the appearance of His Lordship's man might be interpreted as nasty curiosity. On the whole, Somers thought better to wait for the usual gathering.

Mr. Teake, however, was not so nice in his manners. When he wished to know something, he had no hesitation in asking. "Wot's the worst that can happen? Someone looks down his nose and tells yer to buzz orf." Accordingly, he slouched around to Hill Street with the tireless lope that had carried the Light Bobs up and down Iberia and over the Pyrenees. He arrived nicely timed to accept a glass of port, and observe the existence of A Situation. One of the maids had a tear-blotched face; the rest of the staff were quivering with excitement, carefully subdued by the butler's cold eyes.

"Wot's afoot?" Teake inquired bluntly, "and don't mince words. The Major's gone out for the evening or he'd be here himself, seeing as how a certain young gentleman has left an urgent message to meet him in a matter concerning Miss Fanny."

Pitcock attempted no denial. "It appears that Miss Fanny has been meeting Lord Waterbury on numerous occasions when she was thought to be walking in the park with Janet. I could scarcely credit such a thing,

Mr. Teake, but today Miss Cherill saw her: in the swing boats at St. Bartholomew's Fair, Mr. Teake!" Mr. Pitcock shuddered. "But that is not the worst. Miss Cherill had been driving with the Duke of Wyvern, and his grace also recognized Miss Fanny—with Lord Waterbury and without a chaperone." Pitcock closed his eyes faintly.

"Coo-er," Mr. Teake muttered. "I'll bet there was a rare *revoltillo* over that."

"I do not understand Spanish, as you know, Mr. Teake, but if you mean there was an uproar to set the household on its ears, I must admit that nothing has ever equaled it," Pitcock moaned. "I think—I *pray*—that not all of it could be clearly heard belowstairs. Indeed, I had the forethought to close the service doors as quickly as possible, and personally linger at the foot of the stairs to prevent any vulgar eavesdropping."

"Very wise," Mr. Teake approved with a straight face.

"Thank you," the butler accepted the compliment with a slight bow, "but I fear it may not answer, being as Miss Almina is of a nervous temperament as well as a *carrying* voice."

"Screamed in high C, did she?"

"Yes, Mr. Teake, she did, and when Miss Fanny was goaded into telling her the betting odds," Pitcock said mournfully, "I regret to say Miss Almina hit her sister."

"Gave her a *bofetado*, eh?" Teake inquired with interest. "Nothing like a mill between two females, and why they call 'em the weaker sex is a wonder."

But this was straining Pitcock too far. "Mrs. Cherill arrived to take charge at that moment," he said, "but unluckily, the master was at home and he substantiated Miss Fanny's statement."

"Whew!" Teake was awed. "That put the cat among the pigeons!"

"Yes, Mr. Teake, it did, and now Miss Fanny is locked in her room with instructions that she is to have whatever she wants: food, tea, fresh candles, fire-wood—but no visitors. I'll not say it's not a blessing," the butler confided, "for Miss Almina—well I was *shocked,* Mr. Teake. Really, almost unstrung! When it was finished I had to calm myself with a small glass of sherry, which is a thing I do not permit myself in the usual way."

"In course not," Teake said absently. "What's the maid say?"

Pitcock shrugged, "That on three occasions Miss Fanny told her to do errands, she understood Miss Fanny was to meet some young ladies for a walk. She is lying, of course, but cook and me think better to ac-cept the story. Miss Fanny means to protect the girl; it would be her way. She's a true aristocrat, Mr. Teake, which makes it the more incredible that she would be so lost to propriety."

"Hmmm, the Major won't like this *caldera de pez,*" Teake frowned, "and a kettle of fish is all it sounds like to me, aside from Miss Cherill making a stew out of it."

"Exactly—although I must agree there is justifica-tion. Miss Fanny has behaved disgracefully at a critical moment," Pitcock said fairly, "for I do not scruple to tell *you,* Mr. Teake, that we are not in good frame these days. There is an insistence on economy that is distressing," he shook his head gloomily, "very distress-ing."

Teake chewed his lip thoughtfully. "What's to hap-pen now? Can't keep the little girl locked in her room forever . . ."

Pitcock coughed genteelly. "I believe—that is, I chanced to bring Mr. Cherill a fresh decanter of port when madam was discussing . . . and from what was said, they mean to send Miss Fanny home to Cherley. That is the crux of it, you see: she is not a little girl, Mr. Teake."

"How old is she?" Teake was startled.

"She will be seventeen next month."

"Cooo-errr!"

"Yes," Pitcock nodded regally, and there was a short silence.

"Thought Cherley was closed," Teake said suddenly.

"It is."

There was another silence, while the men looked at each other impassively. "Well," said Teake at last, "the Major won't like it. I'll tell you what it is, Mr. Pitcock: we've to put our heads together over this, so's I can tell him everything. He's fond of Miss Fanny, he'll think of something."

"I had it in mind to discuss the matter with Somers," Pitcock looked into space expressionlessly. "He is Lord Waterbury's gentleman, we occasionally encounter at the Spotted Dog of an evening. Perhaps you would care to accompany me, Mr. Teake?"

"I should consider it a privilege, Mr. Pitcock."

It took no more than three pints of the best for a full meeting of minds between the butler, the bâtman, and the gentleman's gentleman.

"His Lordship charged me with a note for Miss Fanny," Somers pursed his lips. So did Pitcock.

"Here, give it to me," said Teake. "I'll step down, hand it to the maid, and you'll be none the wiser, Mr. P. But," warningly, "mind you don't go too far too fast before I come back, or it'll be all to tell over again."

Obediently, the matter was not advanced during Teake's absence; nevertheless much was accomplished. By the time the bâtman sank into his seat and thrust Fanny's envelope into Somers' hand under cover of the table ("Look the other way for a moment, Mr. P."), the two men were greatly calmed in spirit. There was no longer doubt in Mr. Pitcock's mind that Lord Waterbury's apparently wild escapades were merely the normal frisk of a blue blood sowing some wild oats before setting up his nursery.

"I assure you, Mr. Pitcock," Somers said earnestly, "if you could see His Lordship's interest in Basings—a most respectable property, complete in every way! Mr. Pakenham's gentleman conceded that despite its limited extent, the placement with respect to town made it the equal of properties twice the size that are located to the north. I may say that I found *nothing*," impressively, "to deplore. The house is a charming residence, the local gentry are above average. Indeed, there were two gentlemen's gentlemen whom I found entirely conversable."

"You relieve my mind, Mr. Somers—not that I doubted Lord Waterbury's soundness, for we received him frequently last season, but occasionally one may be deceived," Mr. Pitcock returned. "However, *you* would not remain with him were there any irregularity."

"Lord, no one remains with an out-and-outer," Teake inserted scornfully, "let alone one of us. Come back to the question: what's to be done?"

But on this point they could not entirely agree. Beyond a full report to Lord Waterbury and Major Cherill, they were at a loss, "for the less said to our acquaintance, the better," Somers stated. "We only know gentlemen's gentlemen. What's wanted is a few dressers and maids to well-placed ladies of the *ton*, although I'm not sure . . ."

"I am!" Teake said flatly. "Never tell a female anything unless you want it spread from John o' Groats to Land's End in a day! I say leave this to the masters; keep our eyes and ears open, exchange every detail, but keep all safely between us."

Unaware of the concern on her behalf, Fanny had hauled out her portmanteaux and set about emptying the bureau drawers. She made slow work of her packing, her mind was too full of extraneous details. She recalled the gypsy's prophecy, but could not find it consoling. Thus far the prediction seemed eerily correct: the clouds were certainly here, together with tears, but the rest was impossible to interpret. To reach Cherley, she would certainly have to cross a river—but once at home, would she be unable ever to return to London? A dark sweetheart and true love . . . could that be Charles?

Meanwhile, Lord Waterbury was ranging about town in search of his grandmother as well as Major Cherill. He had no success in either quest. Her Grace was gone to a private dinner party with elderly friends, meaning an evening of whist before the tea tray and gossip. "Oh, the devil!" said Charles moodily. The Dowager would certainly not return before midnight, and would then be too anxious for her bed to attend to his problem. "I'll wait on her in the morning," he decided, "when she's rested and ready for the day. Aye, that's the dandy: give her a titillation at the outset, something to chuckle over."

For on considering Bertie's words, Charles found them sensible. "A very knowing 'un," he told himself astonished. "Look how he gave me the office to consult Mattison at Basings; I'd never have thought of that."

Abandoning his grandmother for the moment, he went from club to club but found no trace of the Major, although gaining the information that the Honorable Edgar Cherill was trying his luck at the Cocoa Tree. "How does it go for him?" Charles asked the door steward.

"Poorly, milord—as always. Would you wish me to inform him of your arrival?"

"Good God, no!" Charles retreated hastily, and continued his canvass of the gambling spots. It was a fatiguing course, slowed at several points by friendly recognition and insistence on his joining someone for a hand of piquet. When he had finished the *ton* clubs, Charles bethought him of the various private establishments and groaned inwardly. So much walking had not merely wearied his feet, but aroused his missing appetite. The buffet at Watier's caused an unmistakable flow of saliva, although the display of cakes and jellies was insubstantial. He ordered a bird and a bottle, "or an omelette—whatever's quickest to serve," and as luck would have it, found Bertie Pakenham with Spenning and some others playing basset in an inner room.

"Hallo, Charlie—you here?" they chorused jovially. "Slipped the leash, eh? Come, take a hand."

"Well, I don't mind if I do," Lord Waterbury sank down wearily, beckoning to the basket boy, who hastened forward with the roulades. "Fill the time until they bring my order."

"You ain't dined, Charlie? Thought you was bespoke for a gala. Well, full rig and all that," Tomaston eyed the formal knee breeches and buckled evening slippers with a faint frown. "Not Almack's tonight, is it?"

"No, no, merely escorting m'grandmother to a private party."

"They didn't feed you?" Spenning was shocked.

"Would have," Charles invented rapidly, "but I didn't stay long enough. Deal out, will you?" He was a hundred pounds to the good by the time he'd finished the meal set on a small table beside him, and between repletion of both stomach and purse, he was obscurely cheered. He very nearly settled down to make a night of it, but Bertie's silent stare unnerved him. "Must excuse myself, give you a return another night," Charles consulted his watch. "Have to collect the Dowager, see her safe home, y'know."

Bertie came out of his silence abruptly. "Walk out with you," he thrust away from the table. "Stretch my legs, be back for the hand after this." In the entry hall, "Well?"

"M'grandmother's playing whist with her cronies," Charles said tersely. "See her tomorrow after breakfast. I'm trailing Major Cherill, not found him so far—last hope is the gambling hells."

Bertie rubbed his nose thoughtfully. "Doubt you'll find him, he don't gamble beyond a flutter now and then. His meat's sport: racing, a cockfight, or a mill. Lay you a hundred to one he's gone out of town to a match somewhere; be home tomorrow, you'll catch him then. Give it up for tonight, Charlie. Only start the tongues wagging if you're going everywhere, asking for a man you don't know!"

"Damme, you're right! I left word for him in any case; he'll either answer or I'll send Somers tomorrow," Charles exclaimed. "May as well come back with you . . ."

"No," said Mr. Pakenham firmly. "Can't. At least, not for an hour. Said you was escorting your grand-mother. Got to allow enough time for it to look right. Better know where she was, too," Bertie warned. "Can't afford a slip, old boy: you say she was one place, the *Gazette* tomorrow says she was somewhere else."

"Good God, never thought of that! As it happens, I know she's at Lady Gilmartin's. The butler said I'd just missed her, curse it."

"Don't think so," Bertie murmured. "No time to dis-close your budget when you're delaying her for an en-gagement. She'd fly into the boughs, refuse to hear a word. No, catch her tomorrow morning and you'll see." Mr. Pakenham's amiably ovine expression was earnest. "Set her up for the whole day. Assure you I'm right, Charlie."

"Well, I think you are," Charles conceded admir-ingly. "Demmed if I know what to make of you, Bertie. Always say you've got no brains, doing the modest, but I'll tell you what it is: you're a *fraud*. Put me in the way of it at Basings, putting me in the way of it now . . . dashed if I know what I'd do without you."

Mr. Pakenham looked embarrassed. "Too good of you, Charlie," he disclaimed awkwardly. "Thing is—I ain't got brains, but I notice things, y'know. Now, you're so busy *thinking* that your mind is crowded. Easy to miss something; with me, there's so little in the cockloft, a detail stands out—and you can't be playing with us when you said the Dowager was waiting for you. Come back in an hour, happy to see you; go away now."

"Yes, but don't wait for me," Charles said restlessly. "I sent Fanny a note by Somers. There may be an answer. In any case, I can't keep my mind on the game."

"Did well enough to gain a monkey," Bertie observed.

"Yes, but I was hungry," Charles said simply. "No, I can't be castaway tonight, Bertie. Not if I'm to visit m'grandmother in the morning. Besides, I'm in no frame," he sighed. "Keep worrying about Fanny: what's happened, are they mistreating her. She's such a sweet nature, Bertie—gentle, but spirited."

Mr. Pakenham felt himself at a loss for words. "Uh, bound to come about shortly," he murmured, but when Charles had trotted down to the street entrance and disappeared, Bertie said to himself, "Damme, he *is* in love. Never known him use such words about another female!"

Returned to Holton Square, Lord Waterbury pounced on the letter Somers handed him. Covertly observing His Lordship's expression, the man ventured to murmur, "I was privileged to make the acquaintance of Major Cherill's bâtman this evening, milord."

"Did you so?" Charles looked up sharply, and flung himself into a chair. "I collect you also saw Pitcock? What's the news?"

Somers had been rehearsing his report for the past hour, he brought it forth smoothly. "Miss Cherill went into hysterics and made a disgraceful scene. Unluckily this was overheard by her father. Miss Fanny is now locked in her room, although whatever she wants is to be brought her," Somers inserted hastily as Lord Waterbury's eyes blazed. "Mr. Pitcock believes the incarceration is wise; it appears Miss Cherill so far forgot herself as to hit her sister in the height of the scene, when Miss Fanny revealed the betting odds."

"Good God!" Charles murmured, stunned.

"Yes, milord," Somers cleared his throat, "and matters were not eased when Mr. Cherill agreed Miss Fanny was correct. However, it is hoped Miss Cherill's nervous disposition will be calmed in time."

"Hah, I don't depend on it! But what of Fanny? Is she to stay locked in her room for the rest of the season?"

"She is to be sent away to Cherley, milord."

"Oh, that's not too bad. She loves the place."

"So I apprehend, milord, but it appears the house is closed aside from a subsistence staff." Somers flicked an imaginary drift of dust from the table and looked innocently into space.

"Still, it's better than pulling caps with Miss Cherill," Charles said slowly. "There must be friends, neighbors, acquaintances near Cherley. Here, she knew no one and could go nowhere for lack of proper escort. It is why I took her to drive. Ought to have had a governess, of course, but I thought she was about twelve, and where's the harm in taking a child to the zoo? Or to watch a balloon ascension? Lord, if you could have seen her pleasure in any simple outing, Somers!"

"Yes, milord. I collect Miss Fanny's life has been much restricted, being as she is not Out. Mr. Pitcock passed the observation that, aside from the unfortunate circumstances, the staff would have been happy to think she had a little enjoyment," Somers murmured, quivering with suppressed eagerness—for the one thing Pitcock was unable to say with certainty was the frequency of meetings or what they comprised.

"I wonder who was the unfortunate circumstance: Wyvern, Mr. Pakenham, or myself?" Charles remarked ruefully. "Perhaps the most unfortunate circumstance is Miss Cherill, screaming like a silly chit—for you must know there was nothing in it, Somers. I ain't such a loose screw."

"H'indeed *not*, milord!" Somers was shocked out of his grammar. "Nor it ain't thought by the staff, Mr. Pitcock even saying you was quite a regular last season and praising my polish to your boots."

His Lordship nodded absently. "Never saw two girls less like! Fanny loved the balloon ascension; that same evening Miss Cherill near swoons at the mere mention. Can't imagine taking *her* to the zoo, but Fanny loved the wild beasts. Said she'd like to stroke the big cats. Never turned a hair later when the horses bolted—I was teaching her to drive, she's got the hands for it, and telling her I had to inspect Basings when a chicken startled the team—but aside from a few tears, Fanny was fit to go in a trice. What d'you think of *that?*"

"A most redoubtable young lady, milord," Somers agreed blankly.

"All of that and more! Put me in the way of what to look for at Basings, knew she'd be interested to hear how I'd gone on, today was the first chance, and the devil's in it we were seen."

Somers was genuinely startled. "Do I apprehend Your Lordship has only met Miss Fanny on three occasions?"

"That's all, but we'd just devised a way to come into the open. Meant to get m'grandmother to make up a nursery party to include Fanny, and drive to Basings for a picnic so she could see all for herself," Charles sighed. "All at an end, if they're sending her away. Meant to tell the Dowager, wheedle her into taking Fanny to drive in the Promenade . . . put a good face on it, y'see. Mr. Pakenham's suggestion: make it appear I'd always known Fanny, she's related to an old friend of m'grandmother."

"A very sound suggestion, if I may say so, and if I may venture an opinion . . ."

"Anything, Somers. Got to protect Miss Fanny first!"

"Well, me and Mr. Pitcock and Mr. Teake, that's Major Cherill's man, has put our heads together this evening, being as we're all concerned in a manner of speaking, and we're agreed it may pass over without comment. With your permission, I will step around to inform Mr. Teake of the details to be given to the Major. Mr. Pitcock was under the impression, from Miss Cherill's outburst, that the meetings were far more frequent. I believe she was overheard to say that it had been going on for many weeks and you had been seen all over town . . ."

"Good God!"

"Yes, milord. Of course, I was able to inform Mr. Pitcock at once that we had been out of London for a number of days during the period in question . . . and Mr. Pitcock passed the remark that Miss Cherill was inclined to exaggeration, being as she is of a hysterical nature, but I believe it would be wise also to set his mind at rest with the truth. He was naturally unable to learn this, being as her mama spoke private with Miss Fanny."

Lord Waterbury stared at his servant for a moment. "You have my permission. Do I collect the three of you have settled the matter?"

Somers eyed his employer indulgently. "Not precisely, but the lines have been loosely agreed, milord. Mr. Teake will apprise the Major and form the liaison between myself and Mr. Pitcock, should an unexpected development arise. Mr. Pitcock has the intention of speaking to the Duke of Wyvern's man: innocent-like, to discover if His Grace may have made any comment. We think it wiser to keep the matter to ourselves, and will consult together each evening."

"You *will* inform me of progress?" Charles asked dryly.

"Certainly, milord." Somers permitted himself a smirk. "Mr. Teake is of the opinion that the Major will take decisive action; he observed that Miss Fanny might well be happier at their property, where she would have the advantages of novel surroundings as well as her brother's company. It appears Major Cherill plans to remove there shortly. However, there is the disadvantage of distance; it is to the north, in the general vicinity of Mr. Pakenham's estate. On the other hand, Cherley is no more than two hours from town," Somers finished, his eyes fixed saint-like on the ceiling. "I took the opportunity of inquiring the turnpikes and roads from Mr. Pitcock, and while the cross-country directions are not entirely certain, we are of the opinion Cherley may prove about an hour's drive from Basings."

Lord Waterbury stared thoughtfully at the fire. "Well, it seems you have left nothing for me to do," he remarked, hauling to his feet. "I'll change this infernal court rig, and go back to join Mr. Pakenham."

Once into the street, though, Lord Waterbury hesitated. Nearly midnight, Fanny would long since be abed, but Hill Street was only a block off his way. Unconsciously his feet turned in that direction. At the house, the flambeaux were lit, there were a few candles in salon and entrance hall, but no sign of occupancy or entertaining. Charles made his way to the side garden, where a faint gleam in Fanny's windows was all that broke the dark stillness. It was somehow disturbing: was she unable to sleep, perhaps weeping? Automatically his fingers scrabbled in the shrubbery dirt, found pebbles, and tossed them upward.

For a moment there was no response, then the curtains swayed, the window opened, and Fanny was peering down.

"Sssst, it's me," he called inelegantly. "Fanny, are you all right? Why aren't you asleep?"

"I'm to be sent to Cherley tonight when the carriage brings mama and Almy home," she called back softly. "I was packing my portmanteaux."

"Tonight? Good God! Fanny, I must talk to you. I'm coming up."

"No!" she hissed urgently. "I'm locked in, you can't get down again."

"Phoo, nonsense!" Charles seized the thick ivy stems and hauled himself up with determination, suppressing a few oaths as the side shoots occasionally tore apart under his weight, but at last he was throwing a leg over the windowsill and facing Fanny. They were both a bit breathless, but unconsciously grinning at each other. "Hah! 'Never Say Die': it's the Pevency motto, y'know."

She chuckled infectiously. "Charles, what a card you are!"

"Ain't I?" he agreed proudly, and sank into the slipper chair, grabbing her hand to pull her onto the stool before the dressing table. "Now, tell me—or no, I'll tell you first." Swiftly he outlined everything, "So you see it may pass over without notice, and once you are settled, I will drive out to see you."

"I would it were possible, but you dare not," Fanny said shakily. "You do not understand, Charles. Indeed, it is now inflamed out of all proportion, for you must know that Pitcock did not witness the whole. I suppose he may already have gone out to meet his friends, and the rest of the staff would have been abed."

"What happened?" he asked, tightening his hold on her hand. "Tell me the whole, what have they done to you, Fanny?"

"Nothing, really—but that Almina came home in midevening to change her gown, someone had spilled punch over it. There was a note from Wyvern excusing himself from the next day's engagements on the score of family affairs calling him from London," Fanny gulped. "Almy—well, she is certain he is withdrawing because of me, and the things she said . . . Well, it is better for me to leave at once, luckily there is moonlight, and by midnight Pitcock will be home—for he had the key, you know, and Almy could not open the door."

"Good God!" Charles was appalled. "What did she say?"

Fanny colored faintly and looked at the floor. "Nothing of importance. That is, Almy is like papa and they both often say more than they mean when there is a crisis, but however, I said it was *not* so, and mama believed me. I had told her the whole, you see."

Lord Waterbury's face whitened, his eyes blazed with fury. "Did she accuse me—me—of being a libertine?"

"N-not precisely, but even mama says you're a scapegrace with a reputation for wild starts, and to be seen even once in your company unchaperoned might ruin my future," Fanny said earnestly. "She did not doubt me, but she says no one else would believe it, Charles."

"Dash it, Fanny, I'm no worse than any other man, I swear!" His Lordship was aggrieved, "Pockets to let, estate encumbered, and so on—but I ain't blacklisted anywhere, when I play I pay. I don't live by my wits, nor by marrying a daughter to a duke."

"Charles, I wish you will tell me something. I do not perfectly understand the—unguarded words but," she brought it out in a rush, "is papa rolled up and I may never have a season anyway?"

Pinned by her honest blue gaze, Charles could not equivocate. "I don't know," he said uncomfortably. "Your father has dropped large sums, but perhaps no more than he can spare, Fanny. To be honest, there have been rumors."

She nodded soberly. "Mama said our portions were in trust, but I doubt there's enough to satisfy a duke."

He was still impelled to honesty. "Perhaps they're safe, but as your legal guardian, your father might be able to use those funds. Lud, Fanny—how can *I* tell? Don't take it to heart, he'll come about."

"That's what they all say," she remarked, "but it never happens." Fanny drew a long breath, "So now I understand: I am a grave encumbrance, and they would be rid of me quickly to anyone who will have me."

"What *are* you talking about?"

"Mr. Cattermole."

"Good God, *is* there such a name? Sounds like a demmed sniveling parson."

"He does not really snivel, but actually he is only a curate. Of course he might become a bishop in time, he is extremely well connected," Fanny said with great fairness.

"Good God!" Charles said again under his breath. "That is—beg pardon, Fanny—shall you like to marry this Catter-whatsit?"

"Well, it is not a case of liking. It is probably what I

must do, although they are not sure he will have me, in spite of the love poems he slipped into my Bible."

"Love poems—in your *Bible?*"

"They were not very good poems, either," she sighed pensively.

Lord Waterbury's eyes widened with incredulous anger, he took several strides this way and that before the fireplace. "Fanny, you cannot be serious, they would never marry you off so ruthlessly! Damme, I've a mind to tell Wyvern the whole; I'll not allow them to hustle you out of sight in favor of your sister."

"No, you must *not,* Charles," she cried. "No good could come of it. To ruin Almy's chances cannot help me, and it may not come to anything in any case. Once I am gone, all will grow calm, and perhaps Wyvern will offer . . . then there would be no need of Mr. Cattermole."

"There's no need of him anyway," Charles said slowly, looking down at her. "I've an alternative to put Miss Cherill neatly in her place. That is, if you could like it, Fanny? She might stomach your marriage before her own if it were beneath her notice, but how if—after two seasons—she is beaten to the altar by a sister who is not Out, and if that sister should marry into the same rank of society she aspires to gain?" When Fanny stared at him in bewilderment, he threw his head back with a roar of malicious laughter. "Little pea-goose," he finished affectionately, "how if *you* should marry *me?*"

Fanny blinked. "You're bamming me!" she protested.

"Not a bit of it," he assured her, his laughter subsiding to chuckles. "Damme, I said I'd sooner wait about for you than take this year's society miss . . . told Bertie so weeks back at Almack's, told you so yourself when the team bolted," he caught her hands and pulled her to her feet, his dark eyes dancing with deviltry. "Why wait?" His arms drew her against him, his mouth caressed hers softly, grew more firm as her lips shaped involuntarily to return his kiss. After a moment, "Why wait?" he repeated huskily. "Fanny—darling Fanny—will you marry me?"

"Yes, please, Charles. I should like it of all things," she said simply, raising her lips again.

"It will have to be over the anvil," he muttered when they'd drawn apart. "Curse it, it's not fair to you."

"Nor to you," she said tremulously. "I shall not have a cent, it will be a hideous scandal. You might even be blackballed in your clubs. For you to be tying yourself up in quixotic gallantry, snubbed by the *ton,* cast beyond the pale—in time you will regret it."

"No, but perhaps you might, Fanny. I've no great expectations. There's Basings, a certain amount in the Funds, but our only hope of bettering things would lie in m'grandmother taking a fancy to you—which ain't likely, if you run off with me." He released her with a deep sigh and turned to stare moodily from the window. "You deserve more than a rakehelly man-about-town, Fanny. I don't know; it *sounds* better to be Lady Waterbury than Mrs. Catter-thing, but I've not the name nor fortune to guarantee your acceptance. You might never be able to take your proper place in society, Fanny."

"I don't know that I care," she said clearly. "I expect it would be pleasant to dance at Almack's or promenade in the park, but for the rest of . . . Well, I should never be a Belle, even if papa has enough money to give me a season. I think I could go on very well at Basings, and if I am unacceptable, it will not matter provided you can go back and forth to see your friends."

"Fanny—*Fanny,*" he caught her against him once more, staring down at her shining blue eyes. "God, you've all to lose and I've all to gain," he muttered, "but I swear I'll do my possible to care for you."

"That will be all that's needed," she murmured. A sudden tap at the door made them spring apart. "W-who is it?" she asked shakily.

"Janet, miss. I've packed me bag, and Mr. Pitcock says as he'll open your door so's I can help you, if you need me."

"I'm already packed, Janet, and for God's sake, don't let Pitcock open the door!"

"He'll have to, miss, to get the portmanteaux."

"To the devil with them, we'll throw them from the window," said His Lordship forcefully. "Janet?"

"Y-yes, sir? Oh, Lord, what're you doing *here?*"

"I'm taking your mistress off to marry me this instant. Can you contrive to smuggle your bag from the house to join us? Miss Fanny must have an abigail; would you like the position?"

"Oh, milord . . . oh, Miss Fanny, you won't never?"

"Yes, I will," Fanny said firmly. "Janet, tell Pitcock I need no assistance. Get your valise out to the shrubbery and hide in the shadows. We'll be down in a few minutes."

"But *how,* miss? Mr. Pitcock has the key."

"Don't waste time on silly questions," Lord Waterbury commanded. "If you want to come with us, get yourself out of the house with your bag in five minutes. I shan't wait for you, understand?"

"Y-yes, sir," Janet squeaked. "I'm coming, indeed I am . . ."

As her footsteps died away, "What about your portmanteaux?" Charles asked. "Have you everything, can we close them up? We're running it a bit fine. There's still the question of getting you out of here, Fanny."

For answer, she secured the catches on her bags, tugged them to the window, and cast them forth into the night. While His Lordship stood transfixed by the dull crashes below, Fanny peered down to the garden. "I expect the Denmark cucumber lotion has broken into my unmentionables," she remarked casually, "but they can be laundered, and that lotion has never removed any of my freckles. I hope you can become accustomed, Charles; there seems nothing to be done about them."

"Good," said Lord Waterbury. "I am extremely fond of freckles." He had a sense that this was not happening, it was only a dream—and an equal sense that he did not wish to wake up. He strode to the window. "I'll descend to retrieve the luggage, but what about you, Fanny?"

"I will come after you, provided you have not torn away all the ivy," she said calmly, and giggled at his expression. "Silly! I've climbed up and down the ivy at Cherley for years, Harry taught me."

Charles threw one leg over the windowsill and paused. "Good God, what a fool I am," he said suddenly.

Fanny caught her breath. "W-would you rather not marry me after all?" she asked in a very small voice. "It doesn't matter, Charles. I quite see it might not answer for you."

He looked up at her gallant little figure, sternly controlling a quiver of her lips. "I want to marry you more than anything ever in my life," he said slowly. "Never doubt, Fanny! No, it's not that, but I've just recollected: I came here on foot, the curricle's at the stable, and even did I have it, we can't go to Scotland in a curricle. I'll have to hire a post chaise, but what the devil shall I do with you and Janet while I'm about the arrangements?"

"Well, we cannot go back, so we must go forward," Fanny said after a second. "I'd forgot about needing a carriage, too, but could we not wait at your lodgings? I shall have Janet with me for propriety."

"I've a better idea—I think; talk it over later. The first thing is to get down to the ground." He swung round with decision, found toe and hand holds, shortly disappeared while Fanny reconnoitered anxiously above. It was true she'd often scrambled among the ivy at Cherley, but only in daylight and never so long a climb. For a moment, her courage faltered. Then she could see Charles' face turned up to her, Janet silently stealing into the garden from the kitchen door, and hear the unmistakable sounds of a carriage: mama and Almy returning? It was now or never, Cherley or Charles, but with disgrace either way, she'd prefer Charles.

She pulled up her skirts and crawled cautiously over the sill, while the carriage was stopping before the front entrance. Clenching her teeth grimly and heedless of torn flounces or bruised fingers, she went down from one handhold to another, until just as she feared she had no more strength but must fall, Charles' strong arms were bracing her, picking her from the ivy like a fly. "Shhhh!" he hissed. "It's your mother and sister. Janet's taken the bags to the end of the mews. Quickly! Can you walk, or shall I carry you?"

"I can walk."

Silently they fled past the darkened kitchen and turned along the mews to find Janet hovering over the portmanteaux. "We must get away before they discover you're gone, they'll search the vicinity first." Charles seized Fanny's bags, "Janet, can you manage yours? Follow me." He strode forward, with the girls trotting behind him, until he ducked sideways into a garden and dropped the bags. "Here!" Breathlessly, they sheltered under an immense tree, while Charles said, "You're safe enough to wait here, Fanny. The owners are from home."

"Yes, Charles." She was overcome by a shiver in the cool night air, and he rumpled his hair ruefully.

"Lud, what a dunce I am: you have no cloak, you must be shaking with the ague."

"Well, at least it proves you are not well versed in elopements," she said irrepressibly, "but if Janet will put her arm about me, her cape will cover us both. Where are you going?"

"To get the curricle. Listen," he seized her hands urgently, "you have Janet to bear you company. I mean to take you to Basings for a good night's rest, Fanny. Tomorrow, when they are not looking for us here, we will post up to Scotland! D'you see? It is the first thing they will surmise, your father will send out the Runners to intercept us tonight, and instead we will proceed at our leisure by a circuitous route!" He peered at her anxiously through the gloom, "You would not object if it were delayed for several days, Fanny? You will have Janet for propriety, you know, and it occurred to me: if we are not bang up to the mark, your father might well have the marriage set aside because of your age."

"Yes," she agreed, horrified. *"Nothing* would be worse than an abortive elopment, Charles! Only *think* how foolish we should look! No, Basings is an excellent idea. By all means let us go there for the night. Papa will never think of it. I doubt he knows it is your estate, and before he has time to learn we shall be away."

In the event, however, the Honorable Edgar Cherill never knew his younger daughter had fled her home. Following a disastrous evening at the Cocoa Tree, he was stricken with an apoplectic fit at the top of the stairs, and ended on the pavement with a broken neck.

CHAPTER VIII

At Basings, Fanny slept dreamlessly with Janet on a trundle bed beside her. Lord Waterbury was roused at ten from his room at the opposite end of the house. "Miss is having her breakfast in the kitchen," said Skinner. "She wants to talk to me missus."

"Eh? Good Lord, I'd forgot." Stricken, His Lordship rolled from the bed and flung himself into his clothes. When he was finally downstairs (with a remarkably ill-tied cravat), it was to learn that Miss had gone for a walk with her abigail.

"Wild strawberries she's after. Gus says there's a plenty in the far lots," Mrs. Skinner reported, setting ham and eggs before His Lordship. "I've the pots and sugar. Like old times it'll be to make jam again. Miss says me recipe for marmalade is the best she's ever tasted," she finished with unconcealed pride. "Very knowing she is for such a little girl, and that Janet's a real treasure, milord! Quick, neat-fingered, well trained, but not too lah-di-dah to lend a hand, seeing I've no chambermaids nor tweeny. And how long will Miss be staying, milord?"

"Uh, I'm not certain," Charles choked over his muffin.

"I've a mind to do up some of the curtains and coverlets, if I had that Janet to help," Mrs. Skinner explained, "but I'd not like to start if we haven't three or four days."

"No! That is, don't begin anything for the moment. I'll, uh, know better later on," he said wildly, "uh, don't bother me at the moment."

"No, milord; sorry, milord," she curtseyed respectfully and whisked away to the kitchen. "Whooo!" she said to her husband. "Very touchy he is this morning."

"Not enough sleep," Skinner opined, "but it queers me, it do. Whyfor is he driving in at near two of the morning, with little Miss and her maid? Where'd they come from, where be they going at such an hour?"

"Eh, there's no accounting for the gentry—and I'll thank you to bring up that basket of jam pots from the side cellar."

Absently applying marmalade to his muffin, Lord Waterbury was equally at a loss on where he was going. In daylight, sober counsel prevailed, and he realized a number of fine points that had escaped him last evening. It was not that he wavered; he was committed to this elopement and the discovery that Fanny was already bestirring herself for his comfort with wild strawberry jam rather reinforced his decision to marry her.

On the other hand, he had only the clothes he was wearing; the shortest road to Scotland would require two full days, if they stopped only to eat, change horses, and take on a fresh driver. A more circuitous route to avoid interception would take twice as long. Was he to be married in travel-stained clothing? There was the further question of money: he had last night's winnings and perhaps another sixty pounds. It was not enough for such a journey; once married, there was still the return trip. "Damme, what a fool I am!" Charles chomped his muffin moodily, wishing Fanny were here for consultation, but on second thoughts, it was as well she wasn't. As matters stood, Janet and the Skinners could swear that Lord Waterbury had not so much as spoken to Miss Fanny since their arrival.

"Leave her a note," he decided. "Go up to London for the necessaries, come back for her—that's the ticket. Skinner, have the horses put to."

By ruthlessly springing the team, Charles reached

town in an hour. He went first to his bank and reached his stable mews without seeing anyone of his acquaintance. Thence he entered his lodgings through the rear door, to find the kitchen temporarily deserted. He had gained his chamber and stripped off his rumpled clothes before ringing the bell. "Pack enough for a week," he began, and stopped to stare at Somers' ashen face. "Good God, what is it, man?"

"Mr. Cherill," the servant's voice trembled. "He was taken with a fit last night, milord, and Miss Fanny—she's run away. I felt sure she was with you, milord. Whatever can have become of her?"

"She and her maid are at Basings," Charles said slowly. "Are you saying Cherill's—dead?"

"Yes, milord, and the Major's not returned as yet. The household's in a turmoil, with madam taken to her bed in a swoon and Miss Cherill in hysterics. Mr. Pitcock's fair beside himself with no one to take charge. They'd but just discovered Miss Fanny's absence when Mr. Cherill was brought home," Somers reported shakily. "Mr. Pitcock sent Mr. Teake around to me, milord, but I was unable to say more than that you had gone to join Mr. Pakenham. Nor they didn't think to notice the curricle was gone, milord, and I saw no reason to mention the fact. Mr. Teake did suggest the Runners, but I pointed out that Mr. Pitcock could not take it on himself to call them, with which Mr. Pitcock agreed. Would you wish me to reassure him on Miss Fanny's safety, milord?"

"Not yet," Charles shook his head, sinking into a chair. "Then no one *knows* I was out of London but yourself?"

"No, milord—not that either Mr. Teake or Mr. Pitcock wished to know more than I told them. Mr. Teake did pass the comment as how Miss Fanny might be gone to Scotland, and he couldn't say how the Major would take it, but Mr. Pitcock pointed out that it was more probable Miss Fanny had gone to relatives. He was able to name several families closer to London, whom Miss Fanny would prefer to the closed house at Cherley, and from the circumstance of Janet's absence too, he surmised Miss Fanny was not alone, which was a consolation to us all." Somers coughed genteelly. "It was left we would await the return of Major Cherill, but should Mr. Pitcock learn of your presence, milord, I fear I would not have the heart to withhold some information. The poor man is distraught as it is."

"Good God, what a devilish coil! Where the deuce can Harry Cherill be?"

"Mr. Teake believes in the vicinity of Oxford, milord; he understands there was to be a mill, which would attract the Major, being as he is a sporting gentleman."

"Aye, Bertie said the same," Charles recalled, "but damme, what to do? Miss Fanny must be at home at this moment, and how to explain last night? There has to be a watertight story to silence Pitcock's staff, Somers. For all the maid has been with her every minute since we left Hill Street last night, you know it will not suffice." He looked defenselessly at the servant, "I mean to marry her, Somers. If not now, as soon as may be."

"Yes, milord," Somers squinted reflectively. "If I might suggest: the Dowager Duchess, milord."

Ushered into his grandmother's morning room, Lord Waterbury was instantly unstrung by her piercing glance. "Heard you was here yesterday, thought you was to wait on me for breakfast," she remarked. "In a scrape again? Don't come to *me* for money, I've none to give you. Hmph, you'll only throw good coin after bad with your foolish wagers and vulgar Cyprians! Hmph! Well, how much is it this time?"

"It ain't money, ma'am," he bowed over her hand nervously.

"Not?" Her eyebrows rose in astonishment. "Then what is it? Don't say you ain't in some sort of trouble—never visit me otherwise," she snorted, but the faded blue eyes were alarmed. "Well, sit down and open your budget—not that it'll help, but I like to be abreast of the news."

"Y-yes, ma'am," Charles stammered. "It ain't really me, but Fanny Cherill."

The Dowager looked startled. "Thought her name was Alice . . . Albinia . . . whatever it is? Father dropped dead last night, heard he was all to pieces . . ."

"Very probably, but it ain't the Dark Incomparable," Charles said desperately. "That's Almina; Fanny's her younger sister, and I've got her at Basings with her maid. We were going to elope, but now we can't until after the funeral. I'll have to bring her back, and how's her absence to be explained?"

"God bless my soul!" Her Grace fumbled for her vinaigrette and inhaled, blinking at him dazedly. *"Elope, My* grandson? Never heard anything so shocking!"

"I'd no choice, ma'am. They were going to marry her to some miserable curate, to keep Fanny out of Miss Cherill's path until *she'd* got the Duke of Wyvern."

"A curate? Good God!"

"Fanny says he will probably become a bishop, he's very well connected, but that's neither here nor there, ma'am. I want her myself."

The Dowager shook herself erect in her chair. "Begin at the beginning," she commanded. It took him an hour, interspersed with her comments "Lud! Mercy on me! Bless my soul!" and frequent recourse to the vinaigrette, but when he was finished, she stared at him fixedly for a minute. "Hmph, sounds like a minx. Shall I like her?"

"Yes," said Charles simply.

Her Grace continued to stare at him unnervingly for another endless minute. "Lineage is good, for all the father was on the edge of ruin," she admitted grudgingly, "but you're in no case to wed a penniless girl,

Charles. She only agreed as the alternative to a curate, poor child. Don't say she mightn't do her best for you out of gratitude, but Cherill's death alters things. No need to elope, the family's bound to retire, reopen the house. She'll be safe enough, can't marry her to anyone for a twelvemonth of mourning. Sister can't marry either, if it comes to that. Plenty of time to think it over, see how the land lies . . ."

The Dowager pursed her lips, her fingers tapping the chair arm. "What's wanted is to get her home with an acceptable alibi," she finished. "I don't mind helping you that far, though I don't know if it will answer. Do you return to Basings, drive her and the maid to the nearest posting inn, where my coach shall pick them up as though they had been staying with a relative and were coming home because of the father's death. I'd not know what could be said to the mother and sister," the old lady shook her head dubiously, "but at least it should stop the servants' chatter."

"Do we accomplish that, it will be enough," Charles sprang to his feet. "Ma'am—grandmama—I swear you're the prince of good fellows! No, no, I don't mean that precisely . . ."

"I trust you do not," she returned austerely, but was not proof against his brilliant smile and hearty kiss on her cheek. "Go along with you, do," she said crossly. "As it happens, her grandmother, Laura MacLeod that was the Countess of Aranshire, made her curtsey in my season, and a dear sweet creature she was. I'm happy to do a kindness to her granddaughter—and your fertile imagination will embroider the rest."

His Lordship strode swiftly back to the stable mews, calling for the horses to be put to and plunging unceremoniously through the rear door, where he found Somers and a military type with bristling mustaches who could only be a bâtman. "Teake!" said Lord Waterbury cordially, while they were standing up in confusion. "The very man I need! The Major's not back?"

"No, nor I don't expect him until dinner," Teake replied gloomily, "being as how, *if* he's where I think he is, there'd have been a snug dinner with friends in the locality, milord."

"Excellent!" Charles rubbed his hands together. "Here's the plan: you'll drive out with me to pick up Miss Fanny and her maid. We'll take 'em to Maidstone, where you will appear to be a relative's groom until the Dowager Duchess of Pevency's carriage arrives. You will then transfer the young lady to the coachman's care and return to town with me. How does it strike you?"

"Very good, milord; no one won't recognize *me*. I'll just step along to inform Mr. Pitcock, and he'll do the rest."

"I," said Somers regally, "will set it about in the Spotted Dog that Miss Fanny had just set out to visit in the country, and had to be summoned by an express on this sad occasion."

"Good! That should do it, I think," His Lordship grinned engagingly at the two men. "It don't matter about me, have to protect Miss Fanny."

"Aye, she'll have enough to face when we get her home," Teake muttered. "By what Pitcock says, that sister is fair creating. Hear her all over the house, even with the service door closed, but do the Major get home, he'll take care of all." Clapping his hat on his head, Teake strode to the rear door. "Back in twenty minutes, milord."

Fortified by a luncheon hastily put together by Somers ("I thought best to send the Robinsons on errands, milord, so they'll know nothing but you sent for hot water at the usual time this morning"), Lord Waterbury set out once more for Basings with Teake setting stolidly beside him. Conversation was minimal, for it had suddenly occurred to Charles that he was going to have to break the news of Mr. Cherill's death to Fanny. He had not the faintest idea of what words to use, nor how she might react. Might she swoon from the shock? Perhaps she would be too unnerved to carry through the plan of driving her to Maidstone; might it be better to tell her nothing until she was safely transferred to his grandmother's carriage?

All the way to Basings he pondered, but found his fears unnecessary. The news of a female visitor at His Lordship's bachelor establishment had reachêd the vicarage together with the fish at eleven that morning. "Oh, dear," said Mrs. Mattison resignedly. "You'll have to look into it, Cedric, although I can't believe . . . Such a nice young gentleman, but one never knows, does one? And we cannot be having muslin company in Little Twyford."

"No," Mr. Mattison agreed.

His wife eyed him suspiciously. "Then why are you sighing?"

"Because I had hoped to work up the parish accounts for the vestry meeting," he returned mildly, "and now I must use the time to investigate something I would much rather know nothing about, my dear."

However, the path of duty was clear. Mr. Mattison allowed himself a perusal of the *Gazette* and a cat nap following the midday meal, but by half after two, he was driving into the stable yard at Basings, to be received with unclouded faces by the Skinners. "Eh, His Lordship's gone off to London," Skinner tweaked his forelock respectfully, while his wife curtseyed and added, "There's only little miss, down in the rose garden."

"Ah? Well, I'm sorry to have missed Lord Waterbury, but since I'm here," he tossed the reins to Skinner, "I'll just stretch my legs before I finish my visiting round." Climbing down from the gig, he asked, "Does His Lordship have a house party?"

Mrs. Skinner shook her head. " 'Tis just a little girl with her maid—a relative, I suppose, but I disremember the name."

Greatly reassured, the vicar made his way along the

path toward the small figure at the far end and introduced himself with a smile. "I am Mr. Mattison, the rector. Are you a niece or a cousin of Charles?"

What a pretty child, he was thinking as she curtseyed, but his practiced eye recognized her blush as alarmed confusion rather than youthful bashfulness. *What is this?* "I had thought myself tolerably well acquainted with the family and all its branches," he went on smoothly, "although I cannot recall anyone with such beautiful hair."

She gasped faintly. "I—I am not a relative, sir."

"Not?" Mr. Mattison raised inquiring eyebrows.

"No."

She left it there, and for once the vicar found himself at a loss. By voice and appearance, she was no bit of fluff, "far too young, in any case," said his mind. Yet, if not a relative, who was she and why so uneasy to be found here? In the face of her pleading blue eyes, Mr. Mattison felt unable to ask. "Ah?" he said warily. "Do you make a long visit?"

"N-no," she murmured hurriedly. "That is, I fancy we shall be gone as soon as Charles returns from London."

"Gone? He is escorting you to your school perhaps?"

"N-not precisely. Oh," she drew a long breath and sank onto the garden bench in an attitude of despair, "it's useless, you will have to know. What a *curst* mischance for you to arrive today, although I expect Mr. Cattermole would have done the same upon learning of a female visitor to a bachelor establishment . . . but one might have *hoped* for a—a christening or a deathbed to delay you until the morrow." She sighed deeply, and Mr. Mattison sat down beside her hastily. Indeed he felt his legs might not continue to support him.

"My dear young lady, I beg you to believe I had no wish to distress you, and if I had known . . . That is, there is not at the moment anyone in the parish who requires my services for either door of life," he floundered, "and I should infinitely prefer to be making up the accounts for the vestry meeting, but . . ."

"I know," she nodded dolefully, "Mrs. Mattison directed you to investigate at once. If I had to be Mrs. Cattermole, I expect I should do the same."

The rector felt his head reeling gently. "Mrs. Cattermole? I do not wish to press for confidences, but I fear I do not perfectly comprehend. What is it that I shall have to know?"

She debated briefly. "The details are too long," she decided, "not that there was anything disgraceful!" Her blue eyes fixed him sternly; involuntarily he nodded agreement. "Well—Charles and I are in a scrape. It could have blown over, but Almina insisted I must be sent to Cherley and marry Mr. Cattermole so that she could marry the Duke of Wyvern, and the long and the short of it is: I have run away from home, and as soon as Charles returns we will set out for Scotland to be married," she finished valiantly. "If only you had not come here today and seen me—because *nobody* would ever forget my red hair—you need never know that the new Lady Waterbury was m-married over the anvil."

Her breath caught in a suppressed sob, and instinctively the rector put his arm about her shoulders. "God bless my soul," he muttered.

"I knew you'd be shocked," she said in a muffled voice, "but you do see we couldn't set out at midnight for Scotland in a curricle? It was horridly cramped as it was, with Janet squeezed beside me, and that was no more than an hour. In any case, Charles had no change of clothing nor enough money, for it was all on the spur of the moment when he learned they meant to marry me to the curate."

Mr. Mattison pulled himself together. "Mr. Cattermole is a curate?"

"Yes," she nodded, drawing out a handkerchief to wipe her eyes, "And as Charles said, *anybody* would rather be Lady Waterbury than plain Mrs. Cattermole, but now—how can I make any place for myself in local society?" She blew her nose firmly and sat up, "For I could, you know," she told him earnestly. "It may seem a foolish match for Charles because I've no money, but I'm the granddaughter of *two* earls, and I know very well how to go on in the country, Mr. Mattison. Already I can see that Basings wants only proper management to provide Charles with all he needs. He would go back and forth to town, you know, and after watching Almina, I do not really want a season even if it were possible, which apparently it isn't, for papa has lost too much in the clubs."

"God bless my soul," the rector said again, and removed his arm with a final pat on her shoulder. "Well! Now we must think what best to do, my dear, for even if I say nothing, it is bound to be known through the *Gazette*. May I ask: why is it not possible for Lord Waterbury to gain your father's permission in the usual way?"

"His formal offer would not be entertained," she shook her head, "because of the scrape. I see I must tell you the whole, for climbing down the ivy from one's window and eloping at midnight is not what one would normally do."

"It is not customary," Mr. Mattison agreed, "and perhaps you should start by telling me your name."

"I am Fanny Cherill. My sister Almina is known as the Dark Incomparable. She has the liveliest hopes of attaching Wyvern, although Charles says it is six to two against her at White's," Fanny explained trustfully. "However, she insists I have ruined her chances by being seen unchaperoned with Charles in the swing boats at St. Bartholomew's Fair. I do not believe Wyvern would refuse to offer because of such a mild prank, in broad daylight with Bertie Pakenham at hand. Even if one does not usually have a young gentleman for a duenna, nothing could have been more innocent. I feel sure Wyvern would have understood and overlooked the whole, Mr. Mattison, for he is really a great gun, you know."

She blushed faintly. "Oh, pray—I should not have said that; I sometimes forget because of my brother Harry who was a major in the Light Bobs. What I mean to say is that the Duke is a very pleasant gentleman, we went on most comfortably together when he asked me to play the piano. He is reputed to be extremely stiff and high in the instep, but for my part, I fancy he is shy. Almina says that is absurd, why should he be shy with so much money?" Fanny's words were tumbling over themselves, "But I think it is only that he is a very eligible connection, Mr. Mattison, and she would far rather marry Robin Elvey who is Harry's closest friend—except that he is only a younger son, like Charles, and has no money.

"Then mama locked me in my room, so Almina should not come to cuffs with me, and papa agreed I should go to Cherley instead of a convent school," Fanny finished breathlessly. "So you see, if Charles were to offer for me formally, I should not be let. The only solution was to elope."

Mr. Mattison looked at her pleading expression and swallowed—*hard*. "My dear Fanny, you cannot do this," he said gently. "No," holding up his hand as she opened her mouth for passionate protest, "it is not as you think. There is something more. You must go home, your mother will need you."

"Why? It will only make a new uproar."

"She will need you in an hour of desolation," Mr. Mattison clasped Fanny's hand between his. "Dear child, it was in the *Gazette* this day. I had but just finished reading it when I drove here. Your father died last night of an apoplectic fit."

"Papa—is *dead?*" she whispered after a moment, and at his nod, "What happened, please?"

"He was taken ill on leaving a club, lost his footing, and fell."

She sat silent, her hand trembling slightly in his, closing her eyes to suppress tears. At length she stood up, "If you would excuse me, sir. I will tell Janet to

pack." With a curtsey, she went away to the house.
The vicar followed more slowly, and had just gained
the edge of the garden when Lord Waterbury's curricle
dashed past to the stable. "Mr. Mattison, thank God
you are here, sir," His Lordship said, harassed. "We
are in such a coil, and not time to tell you of it . . ."

"Miss Fanny has already done so, and I have told
her of her father's death. She has gone to supervise the
packing. What mean you to do now, Charles?"

"Take her to the Three Pigeons, where m'grandmother's carriage is to pick her up for the return to
London," Charles said tersely. "It's to appear she was
with relatives last night. By good luck, only my man
and the Skinners know I was not in London . . . and
yourself, of course." He eyed the rector militantly.

"As well as the rest of Little Twyford by now," Mr.
Mattison observed, "but I fancy I can turn aside any
curiosity. The Skinners believe her to be a young
cousin, and are uncertain of her name. Best to leave it
that way for the moment, although—did you indeed
mean to marry that child, milord?"

"I did—and I do," Lord Waterbury's eyes flashed
even more militantly. "I don't say I liked doing it under
a cloud, but when they were planning to marry her off
to some puling parson, what else was there to do? For
tuppence, I'd still take her to Scotland, so I could stand
behind her. You don't know her sister," he snorted.
"She may be the toast of London, but she's a demmed
shrew, sir, who'll make Fanny's life miserable—and I
won't have that."

"No, of course not," Mr. Mattison agreed, "but to
continue an elopement under these circumstances
would indeed create a scandal, for which I see no
necessity." When Charles stared at him blankly, "Mr.
Cherill's death alters everything. I believe, when the
obsequies are over and tempers are more rational, you
should consult the brother: Harry, is it? You realize
that he is now Miss Fanny's legal guardian? He may
well be better disposed to accept your formal offer for

his sister, which would permit a proper wedding in due course."

"By Jove, I shouldn't wonder if you're right," Charles muttered. "M'grandmother said much the same: have to retire from society, can't have any weddings for a year, gives me a bit of time to see how the land lies. Major Cherill's bound to think Lady Waterbury's better than Mrs. Cattermole for his sister. If only they don't tease her," he frowned. "I won't stand for Fanny to be made unhappy. She's such a sweet gentle little thing, Mattison, and at the same time she's so gallant, so sensible. We deal excessively well together, she enjoys everything, never has the vapors . . ."

Mr. Mattison listened, entranced, to His Lordship's catalog of virtues in his intended, but on the whole, by the time he had seen them on their way with Teake hanging precariously to the groom's step, the rector felt satisfied. "In time it will be a love match like our own, my dear," he smiled to his wife over the tea table. "Meanwhile we must protect them. The Skinners think her a little girl. I fancy we might imply she is a distant family member being escorted by Lord Waterbury due to a death in that branch. We will not be expected to know the exact relationship, and later—if all goes well—it will not cause question if His Lordship should marry a distant relative."

Mrs. Mattison looked at him affectionately. "How cleverly you have worked it out, Cedric. For if she is to be the first lady of the neighborhood, one would not wish the slightest whisper to cause difficulty. Luckily the Skinners are too stupid to gossip, and I shall tell Mrs. Morton—who will be the *first* to inquire—that you do not know which branch it may be, for there must be dozens. So many females, and one does not know who they married, after all," she widened her eyes innocently, "but you found her a most charming young girl." Mrs. Mattison sighed, "If only they do not ill-treat her . . ."

"I devoutly hope so," her husband replied soberly,

"for otherwise His Lordship will be neither to hold nor to bind, and will run off with her again."

Covertly observing the entrance of Miss Fanny Cherill and her maid into the carriage of the Dowager Duchess of Pevency, assisted by Teake whose wooden countenance discouraged any questions from Her Grace's coachman, Lord Charles Waterbury very nearly snatched away that drooping figure forthwith. When the bâtman lounged up beside him, "They've gone, and saving your presence, I'd be glad to do likewise in case the Major's returned," Lord Waterbury downed the remainder of his pint and said, "By all means."

Driving to the inch, His Lordship swept along some byroads and joined the London turnpike some miles ahead of his grandmother's heavy coach. Teake sat taciturn, his arms folded, while Charles reflected upon his abortive elopement. He'd had no more than ten minutes alone with Fanny, in which to explain the plans for her return to London.

"How *very* kind of your grandmother," Fanny's voice trembled. "Pray, convey my deepest thanks. I would I might deliver them personally, for what must she think of such misconduct in the granddaughter of her old friend?"

"She thinks nothing bad," he said quickly. "I told her the whole, she perfectly understands, and is glad to do you any kindness in her power. You have only to let me know; Pitcock will get a message to Somers or Teake."

"I must suppose we shall be returning to Cherley for—for the burial, and I shall not be in Hill Street again." She made a valiant effort to smile, "So this is goodbye, Charles, and I thank you for trying to help. It was most kind in you."

"Be demmed to that," he said roughly. "I don't say I liked being havey-cavey, but all's changed now. I mean to wait on your brother as soon as decency allows, explain all, and gain his permission to drive to Cherley. I would I might be at your side these next days, Fanny, but we'll come about before long. You'll see."

"I hope you may be right, but I fear it will not answer. All is at an end for Almina as well as myself."

"I don't know that. If Almina does not attach Wyvern, there are others—and as for yourself, there is me," he shrugged, "such as I am. Let it wait for the moment, Fanny. We must start for London; what mean you to say? Teake has reassured Pitcock of your safety, but it was agreed he'd say nothing to your family. He'd no idea what story you would tell, didn't wish to interfere, perhaps make matters worse for you."

"What can I say but the truth, Charles?"

He rumpled his hair wildly. "Will that not inflame matters? Could you not say I had taken you to a Pevency relative? It would explain returning in my grandmother's carriage."

Fanny shook her head. "No, the truth is better, Charles. It will not go beyond the family, but it is pointless to lie."

Similarly, Fanny's homeward journey was silent. It was quite clear to her that Lord Waterbury had offered to elope because he felt himself obligated as a gentleman. Now that papa was dead, all would be changed; he'd said so himself. There would be no need for marriage, Charles would feel his duty discharged. He would wait on Harry merely for propriety, and Harry might give him permission to visit Cherley, but Charles would not avail himself of it. She could not suppress a few tears at thought of never seeing him again, and it was a very woebegone young lady who presently ascended the steps in Hill Street.

Pitcock's strained face cleared with a sigh of relief, observing the traveling coach drawn up, the unmistakable Dowager's lozenge on the door, the liveried groom unlashing bags from its rear. He said only, "Good evening, Miss Fanny. The Major has but just arrived and gone into the study."

"My mother?"

"Resting, Miss Fanny. Her nerves have been greatly overset, but Sir Henry Halford thinks there is no permanent damage."

Fanny drew a long breath, squared her shoulders. "Thank you, Pitcock. I'll see my brother first."

The voice calling "Come!" in response to her timid knock did not inspire courage, but when she entered, Harry sprang to his feet from the desk chair with a heartfelt cry. "Fanny, thank God! Almy would have it you'd eloped with Waterbury over some demmed uproar yesterday. She was half out of her mind in anxiety and here's m'mother laid on her bed with the vapors." He strode around the desk to fold Fanny in his arms. "Kitten, you'll never know the worry!"

Fanny thrust her arms about his neck, clinging tightly and weeping. "I'm so sorry, forgive me—Harry, say you forgive me?"

"Of course, but where the devil have you been?"

Behind her the study door burst open. "Pitcock said . . ." Almina leaned panting against the jamb, her dark eyes wild with hope. Then she ran forward with a sob, "It's true! Fanny, oh, thank God!" Major Cherill stood aside, looking more and more harassed as his sisters embraced in a display of female emotion interspersed with kisses.

"Almy, I can never forgive myself—what you must have suffered!"

"*No,* all *my* fault for the things I said. I drove you to it. Dearest Fanny, forgive *me!*"

At length, Harry interposed firmly, "Well, you can forgive each other later. What I want to know is: what the deuce is this all about and where has Fanny been? A straight tale, mind; no roundaboutation!"

Fanny hung her head, mopping her eyes and collecting her courage. "I went driving with Lord Waterbury without a chaperone—only three times, Harry, but yesterday Almy and Wyvern saw us. Papa said I must go to Cherley and marry Mr. Cattermole—but I would really rather not, Harry."

"Good God, I should think so," he muttered aghast.

Almina wept with abandon. "I never meant it, truly I didn't."

"I think perhaps papa did, in order to be rid of me," Fanny said soberly, "because he was all to pieces, wasn't he, Harry?"

"Within an inch of being rolled up," Harry nodded grimly. "Hale tipped me when I first came home, but what could I do? Apparently, papa lost heavily in some East Indian venture and began plunging at the tables, hoping to recoup. The once I tried to talk to him, tell him to hedge off a bit," Harry shook his head, "he demmed me to hell, told me to mind my own business. God knows what's left, aside from mama's jointure. He couldn't have touched that, she's safe in any case. Never mind about it, I'll see Hale tomorrow and learn the facts. Go on, Fanny."

"When Charles learned I was being sent away with Janet last night, he said he would take us to Scotland and marry me, so I threw my portmanteaux from the window and climbed down the ivy," she said tremulously, "but we couldn't start out at midnight in a curricle, so he took us to Basings. That is his property in Surrey."

"Fanny, *no!*" Almina protested. "Oh, God, how could you?"

"Janet was with me every second after leaving Hill Street," Fanny said evenly, "and nobody knows Charles was not in London last night. He came up to town this morning for money and fresh clothing, learned about papa, and arranged that his grandmother would send her carriage to fetch me home."

"But what are we to *say?*" Almina wailed.

"Nothing. I was going to visit a relative, had to be recalled because of papa. The Dowager Duchess sent her carriage for me. It appears she was a close friend of grandmother Aranshire, Almy. Leave it there, and Pitcock will do the rest."

"He knows it is not true."

"No one else knows. Charles had the forethought to

bring Teake to pose as a groom during the exchange from curricle to carriage," Fanny turned to Harry pleadingly, "and you know Teake would never breathe a word."

"So that's where he was," Harry said, relieved. "No, he'll say nothing, kitten. Then Waterbury was not seen at all? Hmmm," at her nod, "demmed if I don't think he's been clever at it, Almy. Stop fluttering, will you? You've only to keep your mouth closed, and who's to know?"

"*We* know," Almina sniffled.

There was a short silence. "Call Janet," Fanny said quietly. "She will tell you I am as much a maid as ever I was."

"Good God, I'd not so insult you!" Harry's eyes flashed. "Almy, how could you?"

"I'm sorry, I didn't mean . . ." Almina mopped her eyes. "That is, I don't know what I'm saying. Forgive me, Fanny."

"Shhh, come away upstairs and rest." Fanny gently turned her sister to the door. "What has been said to mama, shall I visit her?"

"No, she is sleeping. Sir Henry gave her a potion," Almina sighed, but she made no objection to being led from the study. "It was every way dreadful, Fanny. You were gone, we knew not where, although of course mama suspected at once. She was entirely unnerved, one moment charging Pitcock to strict silence and the next, bidding him go to find papa . . . all the while lamenting that *we* had driven you to this desperate act, upbraiding me for a harsh unnatural sister," she shivered, "which indeed I was.

"So all was in a turmoil, with mama wringing her hands and weeping, Pitcock endeavoring to calm her by saying Janet must be with you, and then," Almina caught her breath in a sob, "just as Pitcock was about to set forth, there was the knocker—and the men bringing papa . . ."

"Shhh, don't think of it, Almy dear. Indeed I cannot

forgive myself for causing you such anguish, but I am safely come home, it is all over."

Almina sank onto her chaise longue and closed her eyes. "Yes," she said drearily, "It is all over . . ."

CHAPTER IX

In the summer heat of Cherley, it was truly all over for everyone, although Fanny had never expected anything better. Harry was back and forth to town, salvaging what he could of their father's affairs. In the first weeks, Fanny busied herself in the gardens while Almina acknowledged the pile of condolence letters. Among them was one from the Duke of Wyvern; it had been dispatched from Wyvern Castle in Gloucestershire and not only extended the sympathy "of myself and my family," but specifically explained that His Grace had left London that very evening on family affairs "which have ever since detained me or I should not have failed to wait upon you personally at this moment."

"There!" said Fanny with mingled relief and satisfaction. "You see he is *not* withdrawing, Almy, for he need have done no more than a formal note by the hand of his secretary, and he has certainly writ this personally."

"Yes," her sister agreed, "but it don't signify. All is ended. 'Out of sight, out of mind,' you know—and if he had ever thought to offer for me, how could he do so now? I am not merely penniless, but under a cloud."

"I don't know that," Fanny returned valiantly. "Papa lost too much trying to come about, but there is no question of dishonor. He never failed to settle his vowels or club accounts promptly."

"It don't signify," Almina repeated with a shrug. "He—died before he was completely rolled up, and if

Wyvern was cautious then—for he must have known the situation far more accurately than we—he would be doubly cautious now. No, I do not expect it."

After a moment, Fanny asked timidly, "Shall you mind, Almy? Forgive me—sometimes I felt you did not care for him, he was just the most eligible connection, but Charles said there were many others who wanted you."

Almina shook her head. "Wyvern was the only one who could afford a penniless wife *and* her relatives," she said briefly. "You do not understand these things, Fanny."

"Well, no, I don't," Fanny admitted, "for if he cared for you, why should your family matter? Apparently there will be—would always have been—enough that we need not hang upon your husband's sleeve, whoever you married. Do you not think Wyvern loved you?"

"No."

"But why else should he be so attentive as to cause speculation?"

"It would suit his consequence to marry the outstanding beauty of the season, to display me in jewels as his hostess. The more I spent for clothes, the more lavish my entertainments, the better pleased he'd be." Almina dismissed Wyvern. "What d'you mean that there'll be enough?" she asked fretfully. "I take it very ill of Harry to be making confidences to you. I am the older, after all."

"He does not," Fanny said quickly. "At least, he tells me how to go on for him here. He is so often away, someone must supervise until he gets a bailiff, and I am better versed in the land than you."

"No, I am not at all in the way of it," Almina agreed with a sigh. "It was always expected I would form an eligible connection and have no need of such learning. Now I am useless, and with mama laid on her bed, thank heavens one of us knows something!" she finished tartly, rising to her feet at the tinkling of a bell. "Yes, mama?"

"What is that noise? To whom do you talk? I thought you were writing letters," Mrs. Cherill complained, "and you have waked me. Oh, my head, my nerves! How could you be so thoughtless!"

"I was only talking to Fanny," Almina moved into her mother's bedroom. "It is time for your medicine, mama."

"Oh, don't bother. It does me no good."

To Fanny's surprise, Almina appeared to mind their altered circumstances far less than Mrs. Cherill. Almost, she seemed glad to be free of the London schedule in which she dressed, redressed, and re-redressed between engagements for every minute until at last she reached bed at two or three of the morning . . . only to rise at ten next day and start all over again. The fashionable gowns and bonnets were swathed in muslin, hung away in a disused armoire; she wore the country clothes left at Cherley when they'd removed to town. As time passed and local friends came to visit, Almina willingly described Almack's and the *ton* parties for the other girls' titillation, but with no sign of regret.

It was an acceptance of Fate devoutly to be wished! Conversely, Mrs. Cherill did more than enough repining for both of them. She had instantly taken to her bed, vinaigrette in hand, and never ceased mourning the vanished glories or recounting the details of particular balls and routs to her friends, whom she received from her chaise longue. In between, she cheered her children by animadverting viciously against the Honorable Edgar's stupidity, and inquiring plaintively when she was to be removed to the poor house.

Almina bore it with the patience of perfect indifference, but Harry was exasperated to the explosion point. "Damme, kitten," he complained to Fanny, "we're not in good case, admittedly, but there's no question of being thrown out of Cherley. I wish you will do your possible to get m'mother to stop this constant dolor."

"She will not, she is enjoying it."

"Well, I do *not,* curse it! I'm doing my best to set all straight, and at the cost of my own land," he fumed. "I can't be there when I'm here, and if it were not for m'mother, I wouldn't *have* to be here. I could have let Cherley wait until I'd time for it. Dash it, Fanny, I don't expect any mawkish gratitude, but some sensibility for my efforts."

"I know. It is very hard on you, Harry, but I fancy mama is not in the way of understanding financial matters or how much time is involved. Well, I do not myself, aside from observing you at this moment. I wish there were any way I could help."

"You're already the greatest possible help!" he assured her heartily. "If it weren't for you, I'd be put to the expense and trouble of finding an estate man at once, on top of everything else I've to do. As it stands, I'll wait till Fall—unless it's too burdensome for you?"

"No, indeed! I like to learn how to go on; I think I ought to, you know, for it might be a useful accomplishment if I ever get a husband with some property."

"Oh, you will," Harry grinned. "I've already had an offer for you, puss; Waterbury waited on me most formally a few weeks back, said all that was proper to regularize matters."

"And?" Fanny's lips parted breathlessly. "Did you consent, Harry?"

"For what do you take me?" her brother scoffed. "Admits he's all to pieces, means to put his place in order and trim sails for a while, but he's in no case for a wife. I don't say I wouldn't rather have him for m'brother-in-law than a nobody—very likable chap—but it's not in question."

"But—what did you *say?*"

"Oh, the usual things," Harry shrugged. "You're too young, time enough to consider when the mourning year's up, honor him for stepping in to protect you but unnecessary, and so forth and so on. He agreed to all, of course. Thing is: you were both too impulsive, kitten. If you'd come out here with Janet, it'd all have died down in a few days. You don't suppose *I* would have let you be married to anyone you didn't l.e! The devil's in it I was from town at that moment, or I'd have taken you up to my place; you'd not have had to mope here. Waterbury did the best he could under the circumstances, but you're well out of it, Fanny." As an afterthought, "Asked if I'd permit him to drive over. Naturally said I'd no objection at all, but Almina might be awkward.

"Anyway," Harry hugged her affectionately, "you'll not be left to wear the willow, puss. Damme, you're just seventeen, and you've already had an offer from a titled gentleman, even if it was only to put all in order! Almina never did as well at your age, and we'll do better for you when you make your curtsey. You'll see."

"I—hope you may be right," Fanny murmured in a strangled voice, although Harry's words only confirmed what she had long since deduced for herself: Charles did not really want to marry her, useless to think of him longer. "Harry, can you say how we stand?" she asked timidly. "I know it is not usual to discuss financial affairs with females, but in this instance, I think we should know, do not you?"

"I don't mind telling you, but will you understand?"

"Not everything, perhaps, but at least we should know how much should be spent for what."

"As little as possible for anything but servants and household," he said. "The sale of Hill Street will satisfy house mortgages, but most of Cherley land is still encumbered. Hale is going into the matter of how much I can afford to retrieve at once."

"Well, that is not so bad, after all," she said with relief, "for the land is yours. In time you will get it back, and for at least a year, the household expenses will be at a minimum. We cannot entertain but in the most informal fashion; tea and cakes for the ladies, a glass of wine for the gentlemen, but no lavish dinners, no need for green peas."

"Green peas?" Harry looked bewildered.

Fanny chuckled irrepressibly. "Their cost was exorbitant, but apparently one had to have them for party suppers or be thought a squeeze-penny. However, we will not be having party suppers, so that is an immediate saving—and none of us will need any clothes aside from an occasional fresh muslin which I can make at home. I collect mama has her jointure, but is there anything left of our dowries?"

"Demmed little," Harry muttered grimly. "They were twenty thousand pounds each originally. He'd left twelve of Almina's, thinking she'd go off first, I suppose, but there's only five left for you, puss. God knows how I'll replace it, but you're only seventeen. With luck, I can pull all square in two years; you'd not object to wait that long for your curtsey? We won't have Hill Street, but we'll hire a suitable house for the season."

"I don't really want one," she said. "Not after watching Almy. It costs a great deal of money, and one simply develops the headache from so much rushing about."

"Yes," he agreed, "I can't think how they stand it, but all the same, you must be presented, Fanny. I am determined on it, and somehow I shall find the money to plump up your portion. That's settled! I could wish Almy had found someone, instead of setting her sights on this duke. God knows what will become of her, *I* can't afford to send her back again, and by the time you come out, she'll be on the shelf. I never would have believed it!" He shook his head incredulously.

"She did not really want Wyvern, he was simply an eligible connection, but her heart wasn't in it," Fanny said in a small voice. "I think she loves Robin, Harry, and I wish to heaven he hadn't been here last season. She couldn't settle to anyone else while he was at hand, and I know he hasn't any money besides being a younger son, but if he didn't mean to offer for her, I think it was very unkind of him."

Harry stared at her, astounded. *"Robin?* Good God, what ails the silly chit? I'd never in the world allow her to tie up with him! Yes, I know he's my close friend, but a man may have intimates he don't choose to call brother. What's more, I'll swear Almy was never in his mind."

"So it seems. How goes the wager over the widow in Bordeaux?" she asked after a moment.

"We've both won," Harry chuckled wickedly.

"What d'you mean?"

"It took him longer than a month," Harry caught himself. "Here—you were to forget that!"

"I will," she assured him demurely, "and I suppose he got the fifty guineas for his wager out of her?"

Harry's shoulders shook with laughter, "Of course he did, the rascal!"

Fanny laughed, too, but alone in her room she gave way to unhappiness. "How sad it is for everyone. At least I know there is no hope for me, but Almina—I shouldn't wonder if she is the better able to be placid from a secret hope that Robin will soon come home and all might be as it used."

Her suspicion was confirmed by her sister's animation when Lord Ullastone duly paid his condolence visit. To Mrs. Cherill's querulous astonishment, she found herself ruthlessly dressed and pushed down to the salon by Almina's determined hand, "for you must receive papa's closest friend in person, mama, and you cannot ask Lord Ullastone to attend you in your bed-chamber."

"No, but there is no need to receive him at all," Mrs. Cherill protested a bit resentfully. "He would perfectly understand that I am unwell . . . my nerves do not permit . . . seclusion is necessary . . . Depend upon it, he will be very surprised that I should make such an effort, Almina, for it is not true that he was papa's closest friend. I could name you at least four who were more intimate."

Almina was not to be withstood, however, although the results were far from happy. Once dragged from her chamber, Mrs. Cherill showed no disposition to return. "Since I am come down, I may as well remain down until after dinner." When Lord Ullastone had departed, she made a tour of the rooms and disliked all she saw. The silver and fire brasses were ill-polished; the ornaments were not in their proper places, the wrong vases had been used for flowers, chairs and tables had been rearranged, "and *where* is the silver épergne for the dining table?"

"Harry had it taken away," Fanny said pacifically. "He did not care for it, mama."

"Indeed?" Mrs. Cherill stared, affronted. "And what has *that* to say to anything? Upon my word, a pretty state of affairs that I cannot take my eye from household management for five minutes without discovering my home is topsy-turvy!"

"But it is *not* your home," Almina pointed out. "It is Harry's home now, mama, and if he does not like the épergne, he has the right to order its removal. I must say that I never cared for it, either."

Mrs. Cherill gasped and had recourse to the vinaigrette. "That I should live to hear such words! That épergne was presented to your papa on the occasion of our marriage by the members of the Hudson's Bay Company, he had ever a great fondness for it, it has *always* stood on the dining table. Tell Pitcock to put it back at once."

"He cannot, mama," Fanny inserted. "Do not so embarrass him. He must obey Harry's orders, but if you are fond of the épergne, I am sure Harry would give it to you."

"Nonsense! What should I do with it? Set it in my dressing room? It *belongs* here. Ring for Pitcock!"

"No," Almina said firmly. "Fanny is right that he must obey Harry. It is pointless to countermand anything, mama. If it comes to that, you couldn't countermand papa's orders—not that he troubled himself to give any, and I suppose you may have known what he would like without asking—but Harry is entirely different."

There ensued an uproar. It was a pallid imitation of the former, lacking the Honorable Edgar's thundering bass, but upon walking into it, Major Cherill contributed respectably. His voice was not so deep, but it held a parade ground bark that cut across feminine hysterics and swiftly reduced them to resentful sobs. "If you are attached to the épergne, ma'am, by all means accept it," Harry stated. "Pitcock, see to it!"

"Yes, sir," the butler vanished thankfully into the kitchen, where Teake was enjoying a pint of home-brewed.

"Sounds like the good old days," he observed. "Thought it wouldn't be long before an *escaramuza*. Wot's it about?"

"A silver épergne: madam wants it replaced, the Major won't have it on his table. He's told me to give it to her if she likes it so much," Pitcock looked harassed. "Mrs. Hodge, where did we put it?"

" 'Tis under me bed, being as there weren't no closet big enough," the cook said comfortably, "and a hidjus great 'orror it is. Well, it's hard on the poor lady, it is that, but I'll not say we don't go on better when she keeps her bed with meals brought up."

Out in the salon, whither his mama's faltering footsteps had led her to a sofa, Major Cherill had an even better idea. "I regret you do not approve the trifling changes I have made for *my* comfort in *my* house, ma'am," he said, spitting out the words like so many cherry pits, "but since you find them so distressing, by all means remove elsewhere, and leave me in peace to salvage what I can for your future comfort."

"Harry! How *can* you speak to our mother *so!*" Almina flared.

"Very easily, miss," Major Cherill returned icily, "and while we're about it, you may go with her. You're not a bit of use to me here."

"You would cast us out, penniless in the streets?" Mrs. Cherill moaned. "Oh, never did I think to be so used by my own son!"

"Penniless, ma'am? Hah, you're the only one of us who *has* any money," Harry retorted. "Your jointure is worth two thousand pounds a year, which is more than enough to insure your comfort. You may live in London lodgings, go to Bath if you choose. I will make you a draft at once, and you may set about your packing."

He strode from the room, ignoring Mrs. Cherill's wails and closing the door *forcefully* behind him. Fanny left Almina to deal with her mother and swiftly followed him to his study. "Harry," she said timidly, peeking around the half-open door.

"Well? What is it *now?*"

"Nothing. That is, I did not come to tease you, Harry, and I think you are right that mama should remove for a while until her nerves are more the thing," Fanny soothed, "but—where shall she go? It must take time to find suitable lodgings for her anywhere. Could she not visit Aunt Eliza or Cousin Maria for the interim?"

"Of course. She can go where she likes, so long as she *goes!*"

"Oh, Harry, if that is not exactly like all men," Fanny sighed resignedly. "She can scarce arrive unheralded at a relative's house, together with Almy and all their bags and boxes. An express must be sent, plans must be made. Is she to go by post chaise, or will you let her have the carriage? Shall they take all their belongings and never return, or is it to be merely a temporary visit? And what about me, am I to go, too?"

"Good God, no. I've need of you here." Harry scratched his head, and grinned at her ruefully. "Like all Cherills, I've said more than I meant! All the same, I'll not put up with any more of wiffle-waffling invalidism, Fanny. There's naught wrong with mama but chagrin. Let her go visiting and tell her troubles to someone else. See to it, puss?"

"I'll do my possible, but you must reinforce me, Harry!"

"Anything! You have only to command and I shall

obey," he swept her a mocking bow of humility that made her giggle, but she was already pondering the strategy.

It was no easy task to dislodge Mrs. Cherill, and even more difficult to send Almina with her, but somehow Fanny managed it. Within two days, or the time required for return expresses to various relatives, Mrs. Cherill was positively looking forward to a sojourn with her sister in Warwickshire. "A very pretty letter she has writ me! I declare Harry was clever to suggest it, I shall enjoy it of all things, for you must know I have not seen her in some years. She and papa did not care for each other, and after the last visit—well, we simply corresponded."

Almina was reluctant and sulky. "Why must *I* go with her? She can perfectly well go alone with a maid, it is only one night on the road," Almina complained, "and *I* am not fussing at Harry. What in God's name shall I do with myself in Warwickshire?"

"Well, you don't do anything here," Fanny countered, "so what difference does it make where you are?"

"Here, I have acquaintance, at least. I might ride over to see friends or—or receive them for tea. And who is to chaperone you?"

"Harry has sent for Miss Bolting, not that there is any real need when my brother is here."

Almina's lips tightened viciously. "Oh, I'm aware you're his favorite, but if he thinks to turn me into an unpaid spinster companion for mama's megrims, he may think again."

"No, of course he does *not*. Merely, you deal better with her at this moment than I could, and if it comes to that, he is using me as unpaid bailiff until we have come about a bit farther," Fanny cajoled. "Indeed, he is the best of kind brothers, Almy, but all is at a stand for a year in any case. Is it not better to see a new part of the country, make fresh acquaintance? I am sorry you cannot like it, but Harry is determined on it for the present."

"Well, I do *not* like it," Almina muttered, "and if Boltie is to be here, why should I not return when mama is settled? I'm sure I could learn something of management that would be helpful, or—or occupy myself with new songs and the mending."

"I expect so, but Harry does not wish it. You have ever come to cuffs with him, Almy, and he is overstrained as it is. Besides," Fanny said absently, "Robin is not like to be back any time soon. You would be moped to death to no purpose, and I'm sure Warwickshire will be more to the point."

"What d'you mean 'Robin is not like to be back'?" Almina pounced. "Not that it matters, but where had you such intelligence?"

"Oh, the devil!" Fanny sighed. "He might have come home with Harry, but Bordeaux was more amusing. That's all. Lord Ullastone said the same, Almy."

Almina narrowed her eyes. "That is *not* all. Tell me the truth!"

Fanny's temper slipped. "Well, if you *will* have it," she said evenly, "the reason Robin did not return with Harry was a rich widow. She wanted a ring for her fifty thousand pounds, but the money smelled too much of the shop. Robin bet Harry fifty guineas he'd bed her within the month and without the ring . . . and they both won: it took Robin more than a month, but he got *her* to give him the money to send Harry."

"How—vile!" Almina whispered, white-faced.

"I don't know that," Fanny observed. "I fancy all young blades are much the same in such matters, Almy. Harry should not have told me, it was a slip of the tongue, and he strictly forbade me to repeat it. Nor I would not have, but that I do not like you to be sitting on the doorstep, waiting for him when he *does* return."

Almina straightened her shoulders. "Never fear!"

Two days later, Mrs. Cherill and her Dark Incomparable bowled away for Warwickshire at an early

hour, escorted as far as the turn for London by Major
Cherill's curricle. At noon, a post chaise turned into
the Cherley drive and deposited a gray-haired little
woman with twinkling eyes and a merry smile. "Boltie!" Fanny shrieked, rushing to embrace her. "Oh, famous! I never expected you so soon."

"I never expected me so soon, either," Miss Bolting
remarked in an astonishingly deep voice for so small a
woman, "but to say truth: I was moped to death in
Cumberland with my sister. Such a *good* woman, so
sincerely happy to have me *forever*—for you must
know she and her husband are very well to pass, my
bit of money would not be needed, not the least suggestion of 'poor relation, let her do the housework for
her keep.' No, indeed! Sarah would scarce allow me to
peel a potato, if you please."

Fanny was bubbling with mirth, tugging the governess up the stairs. "Poor Boltie! She expected you to sit
in the parlor and sew a fine seam? How dismal!"

"Well, it was, for both Sarah and Thomas took it almost as a tragedy that I should be consulting the papers for a new situation. How had they failed, did I not
love my sister that I should wish to live among total
strangers when there was not the slightest financial
need . . . and so forth." Miss Bolting sighed. "Goodness can be very wearing, very wearing indeed! *Nothing* could have been more fortuitous than Major Cherill's letter, I assure you.

"An appeal for assistance in a time of mourning
from children I had instructed? A return to familiar
surroundings? Loyalty required instant acceptance,
Sarah and Thomas entirely understood, and though
desolated to part with me, would have been *shocked* at
anything less than immediate compliance," she finished
in a saintly tone, "and now I'm nicely away, demmed if
I'll ever go back!"

"Oh, Boltie, how good it is to have you," Fanny
hugged her heartily. "I've such masses to tell you, we
shall be talking for days!"

But the surface was barely scratched by four o'clock when Pitcock entered the salon to announce expressionlessly, "His Grace, the Duke of Wyvern, Miss Fanny. I have told him Mrs. Cherill and Miss Almina are from home, but he asks if you will receive him."

"Of course I will." Fanny jumped to her feet and ran to the door, "Pray, come in, Your Grace. How delightful it is to see you again. Pitcock, bring the tea tray and whatever wine His Grace would fancy. Let me make known to Your Grace my governess, Miss Bolting. Boltie, this is His Grace, the Duke of Wyvern, a most particular friend of Almina's."

Almost there was an expression on His Grace's stolid countenance as Fanny settled him in the most comfortable chair, then seated herself and beamed at him like a happy child. "If only this were yesterday, you might have seen Almina, but she has accompanied our mother to Warwick for a visit with mama's sister, Lady Kenelm. However, her loss is my good fortune."

"Why, I might say much the same, Miss Fanny," he said gravely. "I have some small property near Hythe that required my attention, and realizing how close was Cherley, I thought to wait upon Mrs. Cherill for my personal expression of sympathy."

"Indeed, they will be very sorry to have missed you."

"And do they make a long stay?"

"The length is not determined, but it is hoped that the change of scene and company will cheer mama from her megrims before she returns to us," Fanny said limpidly. "For you must know that her nerves have been much afflicted upon this unhappy occasion, Your Grace, to a point that my brother insisted upon her removing, fearing a complete decline."

This time there was a definite twitch to the Duke's lips. "I am sorry to hear it," he observed. "I trust the disorder does not extend to your sister?"

"Oh, not in the least," she assured him, "although between attendance on our mother and the necessary withdrawal from her accustomed society, I fear Almina is not in spirits. I suppose it is too much to hope that Your Grace also possesses some property in Warwickshire requiring supervision?"

Under her teasing twinkle, the twitch broadened to a sudden boyish grin. "As it happens, I do not—but I believe there are some cousins living in that county whom I have not seen in some years."

Fanny laughed outright. "It must surely be time to renew the acquaintance, Your Grace!"

While not fully in possession of the facts as yet, Miss Bolting felt Fanny was verging on impropriety. "Fanny!" she reproved. "Do not allow your tongue to run away. What must His Grace think of such audacity?"

"Why, that Miss Fanny's music entitles her to far more audacity than she has yet displayed, Miss Bolting. Is it too much to hope for one of your improvisations, Miss Fanny?"

"Of course not!"

Blithely she seated herself and let her fingers express her private elation: that the Duke of Wyvern should have called, should ask to be received when his real object was not present . . . it must mean his interest in Almina was serious.

At last the Duke took his leave with formal thanks for the hospitality, "It is most kind of you to receive me without prior notice, Miss Fanny."

"Indeed, my family would be distressed if Your Grace did *not* feel able to turn aside at any time for a space to rest the horses. Pray, let us see you again, should you be passing this way." As soon as the outer door closed, the coach was moving away, Fanny turned to the governess in high fettle. "Well?" she demanded. "What did you think of him, Boltie? For my part, I think he is shy, although Almina doesn't agree. She says, with so much money and consequence, what has he to be shy about?"

"His money and consequence," said Miss Bolting. "I

believe you are right: it weighs him down. At first glance he appears unduly reserved, self-important; when he is made to feel liked, and is comfortable in his surroundings, there is a very different side to him. I found him most conversable, when he was at ease during the music."

"Music is the passport," Fanny declared. "I wish Almy could have observed without being seen, for I believe he is a man she could truly respect, could she but see him when he unbends."

"Shall you write her of this visit?"

Fanny stared into space. "I think I shall not," she said slowly, "but you shall advise me, if you please. Let me tell you the whole." When she had finished: "I think it may be too soon, Boltie. Were mama to learn, she would instantly be *cap-à-pie*, pressing Almy to make every effort for such an eligible connection, and at this moment, when I have just jolted her with Robin's escapade, do you not think Almy would accept anyone at all, out of pique?"

"I fear so."

"Well, I think if she can be made to forget Robin, she can be made to see Wyvern as himself. I should like one of us to be happy," Fanny said wistfully, "so I think I shall say nothing, Boltie."

"Will there not be a scold for your secrecy when he visits in Warwickshire and reveals this call?"

"Oh, I shall think of some explanation, and by then it will not matter . . ."

However, in Almina's letters there was no mention of Wyvern. Conversely, it appeared His Grace's property at Hythe was in a bad way, requiring inspection once—sometimes twice—in a week. Upon each occasion he turned aside to rest his horses at Cherley en route to London. With each visit he was more at ease, more at home, better able to talk freely of his travels, even of his childhood, to which Fanny countered with tales of Almina's nursery naughtinesses. On the day His Grace literally roared with laughter, she gave herself the palm—because Harry entered unexpectedly and thus met the Duke at his most natural best.

Not possible for His Grace to poker-up under the relaxed friendliness of Major Cherill. "Your servant, Wyvern! I see Fanny's offered hospitality, including laughter."

"I was relating the time Almy spread glue on the Alsop's pew because Jane called her a nasty sneak—and by ill luck, *that* Sunday Mrs. Alsop entered first, so she got the glue."

Harry threw back his head, "Lud, if I hadn't forgot that, and the devil of a fuss it made, I can tell you, Wyvern!"

"Indeed it did," Miss Bolting inserted with a shudder, "for you must know that Mr. Alsop possesses the best stretch of trout water in the locality, Your Grace —and Mr. Cherill had no wish to be at odds with *him!*"

Wyvern laughed again. "Do not keep me in suspense, how was it settled?"

"Well, by the greatest good luck, Mrs. Robinson had still enough *mousseline de soie* to replace the back breadth of Mrs. Alsop's skirt," Fanny said demurely, "and although mama said Almy must stay in the nursery in disgrace for a month, when papa understood the whole—about Jane, I mean—he said she need *not,* for it was undue provocation, and if Almy would guarantee to get the glue on the correct section of the pew next time, he would buy another pot." She sighed faintly, "He was a great gun when we were young, wasn't he, Harry?"

"How fortunate you were to have him," Wyvern murmured. "My father died before I was seven." He got to his feet, "I must be off for London. Miss Bolting, your servant, ma'am—Miss Fanny, if I were to bring music paper, could we attempt to set down some of your improvisations? It seems a pity they cannot be heard by others." In a spate of graceful bows, handshakes, and smiles, the Duke took his departure, escorted to his carriage by Major Cherill, who returned to eye his sister inscrutably.

"I thought Wyvern was Almina's beau," he remarked. "According to Pitcock, that's twice this week he's called in at teatime. What are you about, kitten?"

"Impressing him with my suitability as sister-in-law. Did you like him, Harry?"

"Yes, on the whole," he decided. "A bit pompous, perhaps, but I fancy he's a man of good sense beneath it. You think he still wants Almy?"

"I am sure of it, and Boltie agrees. Given time, she will get over Robin—and I am sorry if you are not quite pleased with me, Harry, but I told her about the widow in Bordeaux," Fanny apologized, "for she did not at all wish to leave Cherley, you know."

"The devil you did," he frowned. "I told you *not!*"

"Well, I am sorry," she said again, "but I fancy it was best. I didn't want her to be standing at the door with her heart on her sleeve, waiting until he grew bored enough to come home. You know very well that if he had the least *tendresse* for Almy, he would have returned when he heard of papa's death. Even if he felt himself ineligible, he would not have failed to be at hand at this time, let alone remaining away for *such* a reason.

"And if you could not like an alliance in any case, I think it is better for her to be disillusioned at once," she finished. "Then, later she may come to view Wyvern differently. Indeed, I do myself, for you are entirely right that he is a man of sense, Harry, and a very pleasant amusing person when he is made to feel at ease."

"*Amusing?*"

She nodded firmly. "He does not often *say* anything humorous, but he is extremely quick to appreciate the wit of other people," she said earnestly. "I assure you, Harry, nothing escapes him, and he enjoys it the more from the inability to do it himself."

"Well, I will leave it in your hands, puss," Harry grinned, "although I shall not be surprised if it ends in his offering for *you!*"

CHAPTER X

No more than Major Cherill did Teake and Pitcock know what Miss Fanny would be about, and unlike their employer, they were unable to ask. It was the more disturbing in that the old days of conferring at the Spotted Dog were gone. Pitcock was now permanently at Cherley; Teake went back and forth with the Major, but on no fixed schedule. So, too, did Somers, accompanying Lord Waterbury between Basings and London. On rare occasions, Teake and Somers meshed for a report; more often they could only leave a message with Jem, the bartender.

It was all most unsatisfactory, no one of them was really abreast of events, and by the time Teake caught up with Somers or managed to relay his news to Pitcock, there was no knowing whether it represented the true position at any given moment.

Thus, while Teake was aware of an interview between His Lordship and the Major, it was more than a week before he was able to mention this to Somers—who instantly deduced the rejected offer. *"Very* nervy he was that morning, all of a twitch and spoiling three neckerchiefs, which is a thing His Lordship never does in the usual way, Mr. Teake. Naturally, I knew there was something of importance, and it hadn't gone to suit him," Somers shook his head. "An hour later he's home again, saying we'll return to Basings at once, where we've been ever since with His Lordship in the glooms such as I've never seen before. In general, his spirits can't be lowered for more than a day, not even when the Dowager rings a peal over him, but depend upon it, Mr. Teake: he offered, and was refused."

"In course he would be, right now," Teake frowned. "The Major wouldn't take it serious."

"His Lordship does," Somers said after a moment. "He told me in so many words, 'I mean to marry her—if not now, as soon as may be.' Nor he hasn't changed his mind, I'll be bound, Mr. Teake. What I wonder: has Miss Fanny?"

But Teake was unable to say, and neither could Pitcock, although highly titillated by their deductions. "She is not in her usual spirits, but nobody is, madam most of all," the butler said frankly. "The vapors and complaints you wouldn't believe, Mr. Teake! I will say Miss Almina's pulled around a treat—not the same girl as before London, nor it ain't to be expected. After two seasons, she's more mature-like, but no repining, no sharp words, patience itself with Mrs. Cherill and very sweet with Miss Fanny. Mrs. Hodge passed the comment only yesterday how it seems the master's death has drawn them together as sisters should be."

"What *I* wonder, Mr. Teake: would the Major object if His Lordship were to drive over for a condolence call?"

"Not him," the bâtman said positively. "He may have turned down the offer, but there weren't no unpleasantness. The Major even showed him out personal, laughing and clapping him on the shoulder, but wot about Miss Almina?"

"There's no knowing," Pitcock agreed. "Still, *if* His Lordship's still of a mind and Miss Fanny likewise, how's he ever to know if he don't make some sort of push?"

At Basings, this was exactly what Lord Waterbury was asking himself, but with no answer, nor anyone to consult. The Dowager Duchess had removed to Bath as usual, and Mr. Mattison was visiting relatives for a month, leaving his parish to a *locum tenens* of such surpassing dullness as to reinforce Charles' conclusion that Fanny had thought *anyone* preferable to the Cherley curate.

More and more he cursed himself for making a formal offer to her brother. "I should have waited until the air cleared, just explained how it all came about and left it for the moment, instead of trying to convince him I was serious," he thought gloomily. "Damme, what a clodpole! All I've done is close the door in my face. He says I've his permission to visit, but how can I? Ten to one he knows Fanny don't think of me, and meant to close the matter as easily as possible."

Conversely, Charles rarely forgot her. The memory of her lips, the feel of her in his arms, her pretty voice and gurgle of soft laughter—all were driving him to drink far more brandy than was good for him in the lonely evenings. While Somers was able to reassure him that Miss Fanny had received no word of reproach, Charles was discouraged to learn she was busily assisting the Major in estate management. Absorbed in Cherley and with an affectionate brother to protect her, what need had Fanny of himself?

At length he was impelled to get away from it all, and went up to London with a half idea of going on to Bath and his grandmother. Wandering into a club, he encountered Bertie Pakenham. "Hallo, Charlie, you *here?* Thought you was rusticating."

"I was, but I got bored with it," Charles said briefly. "What are you doing in town? Thought you'd be gone to Pakenham."

"Would have, but no point to it; only have to come back again," Bertie returned gloomily. "You ain't heard: my mother managed it. Griffies came up to scratch for Edie."

"Good God, did he?"

Mr. Pakenham nodded. "Thing is, the amount of complications that arise before we get 'em tied up, you wouldn't believe, Charlie! It's more than settlements, lawyers handle those. There's banns, and bride clothes, and betrothal dinners. *I* don't know where it'll end. M'mother *would* have me here to deputize. My fa's gone off to Ireland . . . well, *he* knew what he was about, he'd been through it before with my older sister," Bertie observed. "As soon as the papers was signed, he left. Got clean away."

"Lord, yes, only thing to do. My fa did the same when he settled Louisa. How long's it going on?"

"Finished tomorrow, with a whacking great dinner for all the connections on all sides. After that there's nothing until the wedding, but the summer's ruined: too late for trout, too early for grouse," Bertie said moodily. "*I* don't know—half-thought I'd drive out to you, but if you're here, I can't."

"I could go back, couldn't I? What about Tomaston and Spenning? There's no sport aside from rabbits and wood pigeons, but we can hack about," Charles urged. "Fill in the time before Scotland? To tell you the truth, Bertie, I'm blue-deviled at the moment. It'd be true friendship if you'd bear me company."

Mr. Pakenham looked at him fixedly. "Well, I don't mind if I do," he conceded. "Very pleasant little property, anxious to see how you've come on. Tomaston's in town, not sure about Spenning, but we'll find someone." Bertie cleared his throat and said, "No wish to pry, old boy, but confess I wondered how you brushed through that scrape?"

"Oh, tol-lol. You were right, m'grandmother brought me off. Turned out she was a friend of Fanny's grandmother, but all passed off easily enough in the confusion of Cherill's death."

"Yes, that was a bad thing, but maybe for the best: he hadn't had time to lose everything," Bertie said. "How's Miss Fanny?"

"At Cherley with the rest of 'em," Charles shrugged. "The Major gave me permission to call, but I don't know if it mightn't reopen the whole thing. Can't risk that—kindest thing is to hedge off, stay out of the way."

Mr. Pakenham was struggling with An Idea. "You *serious* about Miss Fanny?" he asked cautiously. "I mean—seeing Harry. What for?"

"Explain the circumstances, make my apologies," His Lordship colored slightly beneath Bertie's steady gaze. "Oh, devil take it. *Yes,* I'm serious," Charles admitted. "Made my offer, he was perfectly pleasant but wouldn't take it seriously, y'know. Said Fanny's only seventeen, no scandal developed, formal offer not required, it'd all blow over and so on." Charles sighed. "He's right, of course. No matter how well I come about, he can do better for her when the time comes."

"Shouldn't think that'd weigh with him," Bertie murmured. "Very straightforward chap, apt to let his sisters take what they fancy. You ain't that far off course, Charlie: got a decent holding, enough money to settle. If Fanny wants you, he'd probably agree."

"Yes, that's the heart of the matter, ain't it?" Charles said defenselessly. "I'm old enough to know my mind, Bertie. Fanny isn't. Thing is, I muffed it. Should have held it to getting permission to visit, waited to see how the land lay before asking to pay my addresses. Made a fool of myself, curse it."

Mr. Pakenham rubbed his nose thoughtfully. "I don't know that," he observed. "He's turned you off at present, but he ain't closed the door. I'd say you're in good shape: go visiting, carry on as before being friendly, driving around the countryside. How can she make up her mind if she don't see you?"

"That's true enough, but you don't know the whole."

"No need to tell me, old boy," Bertie said hastily. "In fact, rather not know. Just saying, if you want her, you'll have to go get her."

Fate continued to be capricious, however. By the time Teake managed to get word to Somers that Pitcock suggested a visit, His Lordship was entertaining a house party . . . and by the time it disbanded, the *Gazette* announced that the Honorable Mrs. Cherill had removed to her sister, Lady Kenelm, for an extended sojourn in Warwickshire.

"Oh, the devil!" said Charles. "I may as well come to Scotland with you, Bertie. She'll have taken the girls with her."

Accordingly, Teake's scrawled message that Miss Fanny remained at home lay unclaimed at the Spotted Dog for more than six weeks, and by the time Somers retrieved it, he learned simultaneously from the Duke of Wyvern's man that His Grace was now a regular visitor at Cherley.

This information was such a jolt to Somers that he dared not reveal it to Lord Waterbury. "Perhaps he'll get over her," Somers told himself hopefully. "He was in better spirits these last weeks. Best to say nothing, give him a chance to forget. He sounded serious at the time, but out of sight, out of mind. No point in bringing it up again."

Mr. Pakenham disagreed, although it took him a few days of cogitation. "If you're still of a mind to Fanny Cherill, you'd best make a push, Charlie."

"What d'you mean? I can't be driving up to Warwickshire and some old lady I never heard of."

"Thing is, Fanny ain't in Warwickshire."

"What?"

"She's been at Cherley all the while. Had it from my man, who got it from some curst tavern they all frequent . . ."

"The Spotted Dog."

"Well, you've got a rival, or so they say," Bertie said carefully. "The Duke of Wyvern's been calling several times a week."

"Good God!" Lord Waterbury went a bit white about the mouth, tossed off his brandy and refilled the glass, staring moodily into space.

"Thing is: she's at Cherley, got a female to chaperone, but no reason not to drive out to see her. Miss Cherill ain't there, she's with the mother. I'll come with you, if you like," Bertie offered handsomely.

"Say we're stopping in to see Harry; nothing wrong with that, known him for years. Besides, he said you could call; if I'm there, makes it look more casual."

Charles shook his head slowly. "No point in it, Bertie. It'd only embarrass her," he said simply. "I can see now, I was right she never thought of me. Her brother knew it, did his best to let me down gently. If she can attach Wyvern, how can I interfere—because she *liked* him. Told me so, when he came in unexpectedly one day. No, that's that. It's all up for me. I suppose I'll get over it, but damme, it's hard, Bertie."

"She was so perfect in every way: loved Basings, knew just how to go on, had the Skinners round her finger in a trice," Charles groaned. "The rector approved, covered the whole locally. Everything's in a way to be done, Fletcher's pulling me straight with my land; Rowbotham's cleared some of the encumbrances already. But if she can get Wyvern, where's the point?"

"Basings?" Bertie repeated bewilderedly.

"Oh, the devil! Don't know why I curse you for a loose tongue, Bertie; mine's even worse."

Mr. Pakenham frowned. "I can keep the bone-box shut when I'm *told*," he said with dignity. "Thing is: you *didn't* tell me before. Collect Basings is the rest of it, but no need to explain."

"Oh, you may as well know," Charles shrugged recklessly, but when he'd finished detailing the abortive elopement, Mr. Pakenham was more than astonished. In fact, his eyes bulged dangerously.

"No need to ask secrecy," he stuttered. "Good God, old boy, wouldn't breathe a word! Damme, what a story—but all the more reason to go over at once."

"How can I? I've nothing to offer compared to Wyvern."

"You ain't thinking," Bertie said severely. "If Fanny was willing to marry you—over the anvil, good God!—she won't have changed her mind. Ten to one, by now she thinks *you* wasn't serious. As for Wyvern, she can't refuse to receive him when her sister was moving heaven and earth to attach him."

"Maybe, but he'd be a fool to take Miss Cherill if he could get Fanny."

"*You* think so, but you're prejudiced," Bertie pointed out. "If you want to know what *I* think: Wyvern's still after the Dark Incomparable, putting his toe in the door to be a family friend until she gets back. In fact, think I'll put it in the book at White's. They scratched all the bets when Cherill died, but no reason not to make a new one."

"The devil with your wagers," Charles said impatiently. "D'you really think Fanny'd have me, Bertie? She's so young, have I a right to try to attach her before she's of an age to understand?"

"Flummery! She ain't a coquettish miss, liked you well enough to risk her reputation by meeting you on the sly," Bertie returned stubbornly. "As for her age, my fa always says 'Catch 'em young, before they've time to make comparisons.' "

"Well—well, maybe you're right. I hadn't thought of that: maybe Fanny thinks *I* didn't mean it. Damme, what would I do without you, Bertie!" Charles exclaimed admiringly. "Every time I come a cropper, you put me in the way of a recover. I'll drive out tomorrow, demmed if I won't!"

That Lord Waterbury went instead to Norfolk was due to an express informing him that his uncle was on his deathbed and expressed a wish to see his godson. Somers had just enough time to pen a note for Teake at the Spotted Dog. "Make sure Miss Fanny knows!"

It was still some days before that message went from Teake to Pitcock, and the butler found a suitable moment to say, "I was sorry to hear of the illness of Sir Charles Thwaite. You might not recall him, Miss Fanny, but he was often in company with your father. Lord Waterbury is his godson. I understand he's in attendance at the bedside in Norfolk."

"Oh?" said Fanny, suppressing a leap of the pulse. "I trust the gentleman will recover, and will you ask Mrs. Hodge to make the special cakes, please. I rather expect the Duke of Wyvern, if not today, then tomorrow."

October passed and November, while Lord Waterbury stayed in King's Lynn with his godfather. Sir Charles was quite certainly dying, although not in agonizing pain, and His Lordship could not bring himself to leave while he might cheer his uncle's last days. In fact, he was so occupied in contriving comfort and small diversions for the old man that he scarcely thought of Fanny. When she came to mind, he felt certain she would not have had him do otherwise than all his possible at such a moment.

Nor would she, although matters were becoming entangled at Cherley and required so much consideration as to leave little time for missing Lord Waterbury.

Under Miss Bolting's eye of propriety, the younger Miss Cherill and the Duke of Wyvern were become "Fanny and Edward." Mrs. Hodge automatically made crumpets and sent in the blackberry jam for tea; Mr. Pitcock automatically produced the Canary, which His Grace preferred to Madeira. The Duke brought his violin, the newest music from town, and was often heard to laugh. Occasionally Harry came in at teatime and added a baritone to the Duke's basso for a country song, with Fanny taking the soprano and Boltie contributing an uncertain alto. They were not very good, but they all sang out lustily and enjoyed themselves, while giggling over mistakes.

Fanny had never yet written Mrs. Cherill or Almina of the Duke's visits, and had seriously enjoined Harry from any mention. "I am more and more certain I am right. He talks constantly of Almy, looks forward to singing with her and playing accompaniments. If I can but contrive to let her see this side of him, I fancy she will be truly catched."

"Are you certain it is not *you* who is catched?" he asked keenly.

Fanny looked at the floor. "Quite certain," she said

in a low voice, and ran from the room with an unmistakable sob.

"God bless my soul," said Harry Cherill, astounded. "I believe the puss wants Waterbury!"

"Of course she does," said Miss Bolting when he put it to her. "The question is whether he wants her."

"Well, he *offered* for her, but would you take it as more than a conventional gesture, Boltie?" Harry looked dubious. "I gave him permission to call. If he were serious, would you not expect him to do so?"

"I can't say," the governess sighed. "He may have felt an awkwardness at encountering Almina, or your rejection may have seemed to represent Fanny's sentiments. He would suppose you to know her feelings, Harry, and as a gentleman he would not embarrass her by any further pursuit. I could wish you had not refused out of hand, but left some chance for the matter to develop. Fanny may be young, but she's ever known her own mind—and I may say, she's never yet failed to judge people correctly. If she thinks Waterbury will suit her, and if she thinks Wyvern and Almina can be brought to a love match, she is probably right.

"I will add," said Miss Bolting austerely, "that I have long known Almina's fancy for Robin Elvey and long wished he had not been made so at home here through your friendship for him. However, I suggest you leave the entire affair to Fanny. She has matured amazingly, Harry. Girls do, when they are in love."

"God bless my soul," Harry said again blankly. "Well, if you say so, Boltie . . . and I expect it will be fun to watch."

Thus, while Charles was doing his duty in Norfolk, Fanny was establishing a very particular friendship with the man she intended for her brother-in-law. She felt increasing confidence in the outcome. His Grace arrived and stode into the house with informality; he smiled, he was eager to show what he'd brought of new music. His mastery of the violin was excellent, forcing Fanny to practice faithfully for accompaniment. Most of all, he talked with growing fluency, slowly unloosening to reveal a wry sense of humor.

"I think he will do very well," said Fanny. "Almina has a sufficient quickness that will help him on but never outface him. If we could but contrive to get her home and leave mama at Kenelm . . ."

The Honorable Mrs. Cherill settled the question by deciding to remain for the present in Warwickshire. "Mama's found herself a small house," Harry reported, tossing a letter into Fanny's lap. "She's sending Almy home to pack up."

"She doesn't expect Almy to live with her, does she?"

"Probably, but Almina lives where her guardian decides," Harry said with a twinkle, "so where does Almy live, Fanny?"

"Here, of course! When does she arrive?"

"A week or so hence."

Sir Robin Elvey arrived the following day. With the freedom of old acquaintance he walked up from the stables and let himself in through the French doors of the salon, where he found Fanny and the Duke of Wyvern trying over a new piece by Herr Beethoven, while Miss Bolting knitted placidly behind the tea tray.

"Oh, the devil! At your curst caterwauling again?" said Sir Robin unceremoniously. "How are you, kitten? Hello, Boltie. I'm home."

Observing the Duke's instant curling-up withdrawal, Fanny was infuriated. "So I see," she returned sweetly. "What happened? Was the widow too close for comfort? Make you known to His Grace, the Duke of Wyvern—Sir Robin Elvey—and now you're here, you can go away again, Robin. We're busy."

"Oh, well, if you're busy," Robin said sulkily. "Your servant, Duke. I'll leave you to your music, go talk to Harry."

"By all means," said Fanny, "and close the door quietly behind you, Robin."

But the practice session was ruined. "Shall we take a

short turn about the garden before tea? Boltie, do you care to join us?"

With one piercing glance, Miss Bolting said she fancied the air was oversharp. "I will ring for tea. Do not wander too far, or you will be overchilled, Fanny."

Pacing beside Wyvern toward the barren rose garden, "My sister returns shortly," Fanny remarked. "Mama means to settle in Warwickshire for the moment, and Almy comes to supervise the packing."

"Ah?" the Duke's arm tensed slightly. "I shall hope to see Miss Cherill while she is here."

"Oh, no fear," Fanny said cheerfully. "Once she arrives, she will stay. Harry says she is not to be mewed up with elderly people, and since he is now her guardian, his decision is final. It will be good to have her at home. She will add so much to our music."

"Her mere presence adds more than music," the Duke muttered, and turned to her suddenly. "Fanny, we are friends, are we not? You will not take it amiss that I ask you . . . say to you what perhaps should only be said to your brother?"

"Of course we are friends, and you may say anything at all to me," she patted his arm encouragingly, but when he seemed unable to go further, "Is it Almina? You are not sure of your course?"

"Yes, that's it. I want her for my wife, Fanny. She is so very beautiful, there is a delicacy of touch," he yearned disjointedly, "but I'm such a dullard. It is only my rank and wealth that make me acceptable, I'm aware, and yet . . . That is, I do not hope for your sister's heart, but I should not like it given elsewhere. That were to make her truly unhappy, which I could not bear."

"Hmph, I told Harry you always saw more than anyone said," Fanny chuckled. "I wish you will not underrate yourself, Edward. You are not a dullard; you think more quickly than you are able to find words, that's all. I have never known you fail to get a point, no matter how subtle, and when you feel at ease, you are most conversable.

"As for Almina, you are right that she has had a partiality for Robin Elvey, who's run tame in our home since we were children," Fanny went on soberly, "but her heart is far from given. Disillusion has already begun; the contrast between you will complete the cure. My sister is not trivial; she will sincerely delight in your musical ability. I am convinced you will deal excessively well together. She has every social quality to grace your rank, her natural spirits will lighten your shyness in company, and I believe her capable of a lasting affection for you, Edward. We all grow up and change as we grow—except Robin, who hasn't changed a jot since college, but what was amusing at twenty ill-becomes a man of near thirty. Let Almina see that for herself first. Later she will be able truly to appreciate you."

However, what Almina saw first was her sister at the piano and the Duke of Wyvern suspending the bow over his violin to laugh full-throated. Wide-eyed, she stood unnoticed in the salon doorway observing a scene of the most perfect felicity, completely bewildered by this easy laughing man teasing Fanny and drawing chuckles from Miss Bolting.

Behind her, Pitcock cleared his throat genteelly. "We had not expected you so soon, Miss Almina, but your room will be readied at once. Will you wish to change your dress before joining the practice?"

"Practice?"

"His Grace comes frequently to play with Miss Fanny," Pitcock observed. "I believe he finds her an exceptionally good accompanist. When the Major is at home, he often joins them for quartet singing, but now you are come, the music will improve. I have several times overhead His Grace remark that your voice was badly needed. Shall I have hot water sent up?"

"No. No," Almina said, "I'll go in as I am." Pushing back the door she went forward, "Fanny, I'm home. Boltie, it is so good to see you . . . and Your Grace, what an unexpected pleasure. You'll pardon all my travel dirt?" She kissed Fanny lightly. "I could not wait to be tidied before making my entrance."

Caught off balance, His Grace was unable to stiffen. He beamed, he kissed her hand most elegantly, holding it long enough to leave no doubt of delight in seeing her. In a matter of minutes, Almina was divested of traveling cloak, examining some of the new songs and exclaiming at the Duke's violin, "for you never told me you played an instrument, Your Grace. I take it very unkind in you to conceal it."

"Oh, the veriest amateur, I assure you," he disclaimed, "but Fanny is so good as to bear with me."

"Nonsense!" said Fanny. "Do not believe him, Almina. Have a cup of tea to refresh yourself. Come along, Edward. Let us finish the sonata, and perhaps we can try the new madrigal afterwards."

Exactly as they finished, Harry strode in. "Hallo, Almy; they told me you was come home," he kissed her casually. "Your servant, Wyvern. Well, now we shall have some real singing, eh? Boltie, give me a cup of tea for once in a way. Devilish cold outside!"

When at last the Duke took his leave, with a definite engagement for Friday next, "because if you are to be dispatching boxes to Mrs. Cherill, I doubt you can spare time before then," Almina whirled on her sister the instant the door closed.

"What is this, Fanny? What does he here, on such familiar terms?" she demanded sharply. "Pitcock says he has been a frequent visitor."

"Yes! He arrived first not six hours after you left, Almy, on the thinnest excuse: some property at Hythe requiring attention, but in reality he wanted to see *you!*" Fanny crowed. "And Boltie was come, I made him welcome . . . now he feels completely at home with us, and do you not see that I was right, Almy? There is a very different man underneath the society façade!"

"I could scarce believe my eyes," Almina agreed. "To see him *laughing,* calling you by your first name, condescending to Boltie . . . such *familiarity*."

"He thinks me barely out of the nursery," Fanny said blithely, "and it is hard to be formal when one is playing wrong notes. Besides, he likes very well to be free of his consequence without in the least knowing how to achieve it himself."

Almina was still frowning suspiciously. "Why did you never mention this in your letters? I do not understand such slyness, Fanny."

"Mama," Fanny said tersely. "You know very well she'd have rushed back at once in the hope of securing him, Almy, and quite apart from Harry not wanting her here, it would ruin all. I think it is why he did not offer long since, she was too eager. Besides, you were having this foolish fancy for Robin, and Edward would not wish to go farther until you are over it. Indeed, you cannot expect him to want a wife who holds his bank account in more respect than his person, Almy.

"Robin is come home, by the way," Fanny added artlessly.

Almina stiffened. "Oh? How is he?"

"The same little boy as ever," Fanny shrugged. "Isn't it strange: Harry is a full year the younger, but he's a grown man taking charge of all of us, Almina, while Robin is still Boxing the Watch like a sprig fresh from Oxford."

In the next days, the girls packed Mrs. Cherill's possessions for dispatch by the carter. "You can send along the demmed épergne," said Harry. "*I* don't want it, nor those fancy plates she's so fond of. Of course she can have her dressing room furnishings. She'd better keep the carriage, too, although what will you use? I'd rather not set up another just yet."

"The gig or the pony cart will do, we shan't travel more than locally."

"Shall you tell mama about Wyvern?" Fanny asked privately.

"No. I think you are right she'd return, and—I *can't* go through it all again," Almina said in a low voice.

"She never stopped telling Aunt Kenelm every detail, and blaming papa for ending all my chances—if I ever had any. No, I shall say nothing. We have Boltie for propriety, after all."

Coincident with Miss Cherill's return to Cherley, His Grace's property at Hythe appeared to have taken a turn for the worse, requiring him to remove there from London. Since the distance from Hythe was far shorter than to town, they now saw rather more of him than before. Harry made amused eyebrows at Fanny, but welcomed him with hearty informality. "Why leave so early, Duke? Eat your mutton with us and we'll have a real musicale after. It's full moon, easy for night driving."

In all of this, Robin Elvey was necessarily an outsider. He played no instrument, could not carry a tune, and had no ear of appreciation. This exclusion made him first impatient, then mischievous. "I must say, her season's gone completely to Almy's head," he complained. "All these airs and graces, musical dukes, forever practicing some demmed song to impress him— not that it will answer. I heard the betting was all against her until they scratched when your father died, and if she couldn't get him in London, she'll not do it here."

"She's not trying, she merely enjoys the music. It's a pity you don't."

"I've a good mind to cut him out," Robin declared sulkily. "See if I don't!"

"It's a farthing to a guinea you can't do it this time," Fanny said promptly, drawing a coin from her reticule. "Let's see the color of your money. Boltie," as the governess came into the room, "you can hold the stakes. I'll give you a month, Robin, and you'll have a clear field for at least two weeks of it, because Edward must hold Christmas in Gloucestershire."

"Done!" Robin slapped a guinea in Miss Bolting's hand. "Don't spend 'em, Boltie. I'll get 'em back in a few weeks."

He might have accomplished it, but Fanny was in a

fighting mood. She did not fear any attempt at seduction, Robin was not an out-and-outer, but with no clue to Almina's present view of Wyvern, Fanny did fear it might not be sufficiently established to resist Robin's expert cajolery. Until His Grace departed for Wyvern Castle, Robin made small headway. Almina was too immersed in new songs. With the Duke no longer at hand, not to be expected before mid-January, she was vulnerable.

"Oh!" Fanny made a show of disappointment as her sister came downstairs in her driving coat. "Off again? I hoped you'd have time to work on the quartet."

Almina colored faintly. "Robin is driving me to pay calls on mama's friends, for Christmas, you know. I do not like to be backward in any attentions in the locality, Fanny," she murmured, "and after all, it is more comfortable to be driven in the phaeton than to use the pony cart. Besides, there will be plenty of time to practice before Wyvern returns."

Fanny chuckled. "Robin up to his tricks again! What a scamp!"

"What d'you mean?"

"Hah! I think I see Robin Elvey squiring you about from Mrs. Egerton to Mrs. Hastings to the *vicarage* in order to pay holiday calls!" Fanny laughed. "Make use of him, by all means, but never take him seriously."

Almina stared at her suspiciously. "Why should he not visit old acquaintances? I think it very pretty in him to suggest it."

"Did you ever know Robin waste a second on *boring* old acquaintances?" Fanny scoffed. "Ullastone drives out to pay his respects, but even when Robin was home on leave, he didn't go with his father."

"Perhaps Robin thinks me better company than Ullastone."

"What he thinks is that a farthing is better than nothing," Fanny said cryptically, "and at the rate he goes, it probably is."

"I wish you will stop talking in this nonsensical fashion," Almina complained. "What is this folderol of far-things, pray?"

"Never mind."

"I insist on explanation!" Almina drew herself up stormily. "Let me tell you, you are become altogether too pert, Fanny. I vow I'll tell Harry to send you to mama, you have been far too much indulged."

"Oh, fiddle! If you will have it, Robin bet me a guinea to a farthing, he'd cut out Wyvern while he's away for Christmas," Fanny said impatiently. When Almina recoiled with a gasp, "Well, at least it's not fifty guineas on the likelihood of seducing you—but how you can be such a green-goose as to be taken in by Robin! I'm sorry, Almy, but I hate him to think he's only to whistle and you'll dance to his piping."

"Never fear, I shan't," Almina said after a moment. "So I'm only worth a guinea?"

Very sweetly, Fanny added the *coup de grâce*. "Don't feel badly, darling," she urged. "Fifty is enough for a shopkeeper's widow, but he must know he couldn't possibly afford you."

CHAPTER XI

On the first of December, Lord Waterbury was awakened with the sad news of his uncle's death during the night. "Doctor says it was entirely peaceful, milord. Sir Charles just slept away."

His Lordship drew a long breath in and out. "Well, I'm glad of it," he said somberly, "not but what I feel I should have been with him."

"He'd not have known, milord," the butler shook his head, "nor he'd not have wanted you kept from your bed. He was contented enough to have you here these weeks; it was a comfort to all of us, I assure you."

"It was a comfort to me, too," Lord Waterbury murmured. "He was a grand old gentleman, he'll be sorely missed in the neighborhood. Well, I'd best be up and dressed for whatever I can do."

A death, he discovered, required innumerable expresses and intelligences to be sent far and wide, as well as receiving formal calls of condolence and giving orders for such things as opening unused bedrooms or provisioning for a funeral breakfast. "Good God, what do *I* know of such things?" he demanded, harassed.

"Nothing, milord," the butler agreed indulgently, "but the staff must have show of authority from a family member or we shall not know how to go on."

"I see. Then do as you think best, and let me know your arrangements, so *I* shall know how to go on next time," Charles remarked.

Four days later, following the interment of Sir Charles Thwaite, his will stated that aside from bequests to servants, his estate was left to Lord Charles Waterbury. It was not a magnificent inheritance. The house was not so large even as Basings, and the acreage was insignificant, but the Funds produced near seven thousand pounds a year.

"Lord, I'd no idea he was so well to pass!" said Charles.

The Duchess of Pevency looked at her son censoriously. "My brother was always one to hold household," she stated, "and I only trust you will do likewise, Charles."

"What will you do with the land?" the Duke inquired. "Pity it's so far separate from Basings. A hundred acres added to what you have would be helpful."

"I don't know what I'll do with any of it, but no need to decide overnight, after all." Charles pursed his lips thoughtfully. "With this small Golconda, I *may* get married."

"D'you suppose he was serious?" Her Grace asked as the coach rolled away from King's Lynn. "He's a dear boy, I must admit privately he's my favorite, Reggie—but who'd have such a rascal?"

"With seven thousand a year, I fancy he'll have no difficulty in finding a number of takers, m'dear!" the Duke of Pevency snorted. "Demmed if I ever expected your brother to cut up so handsome! Be interesting to see what the boy does with it. He's come on amazingly well. Don't scruple to tell you, Melsham's all my heir should be, but he's demmed *dull,* Lavinia!"

"Well, that's a charge no one will ever level at Charles," Her Grace remarked. "Hmmm, there's the Lovelace girl . . . or that older daughter of Lady Vesey . . ."

"Don't waste time on matchmaking," the Duke advised. "It's ten to one he's got the female in his eye already. I wonder who she is . . ."

Left behind at Thwaite House, Charles was both elated and overwhelmed by his good fortune. While

Basings was the bigger, and better placed for his taste, his uncle's home was a going concern: a gentleman's residence in every way, complete to a shade. At a glance, it could not be hastily disposed of; everything must be gone through, carefully examined for keep or discard. Charles blanched at the prospect, it'd take *weeks,* but it was the measure of his growing maturity that he did not dream of shirking.

If only Fanny were with him! At every turn, he longed for her more keenly. Every impulse urged him to go straight down to Kent and lay all his perplexities in her lap: Fanny would know exactly what to do. On the other hand, it was nearing Christmas; she'd be immersed in holiday plans, perhaps gone into Warwickshire. All over England families were coalescing for the yearly reunion, Charles himself was expected automatically at Pevency.

"Best take it slowly," he decided. "Go to London, consult Rowbotham, see how I'll stand. He'll know my position, what I could settle on Fanny. Leave Harry Cherill for after the holidays, when I'll have all in shape and he'll be of a mind to attend to me. Yes, that's the dandy: have to buy Christmas presents and get my formal clothes for Pevency, in any case. Can't go rushing out, saying 'I want Fanny, but have to leave for Leicestershire at once—sorry.' "

He left Thwaite House fully staffed for the moment. While not best placed for hunting, the terrain afforded some decent sport. "Make up a snug little party for the spring," Charles thought. "Bertie'll give me the office, very sound man about property. Demmed if I don't write him to join me here for a few days when I'm squared away. He'll tell me how to go on."

Arrived in London, he found it thin of company. More than half the knockers were off the doors. The clubs contained only a sprinkling of old gentlemen whose relatives found them too disagreeable for invitations. Such members of the *ton* who were in town were frantically getting the presents they had forgotten until now. Among them was Lord Waterbury. Armed with a succinct list prepared by Somers (6 aunts, 5 uncles, 5 sisters, 10 nieces, 14 nephews . . .), His Lordship dashed from Hatchards to Fanchette to the small shops along Bond Street, pointing at random. "I'll take that, and that, and this."

As he was passing Asprey's, a fan caught his eye in the display window. Delicately painted, it portrayed a balloon ascension. Compulsively, he went in and bought it for Fanny without even asking the cost. Thrusting the box into the pocket of his greatcoat, he left the shop and literally blundered into Tomaston. "Beg pardon," he lifted his hat automatically. "Oh, the devil! What are you doing in town, Tommy, not that I ain't demmed glad to see someone I know."

"Same as yourself: getting presents," Mr. Tomaston returned gloomily. "I'll tell you what it is, Charlie: it's getting so I hate Christmas. Buying a lot of things for people you don't give a curse for, and they do the same—ends in having to pretend you're enraptured by stuff you wouldn't give a crossing sweeper. Dashed good to see you, old boy! Join me for dinner?"

"Happy to accept," Charles said promptly. "Anyone else around? Been away so long I'm out of all touch."

"Heard your uncle died, offer my sympathy," Tomaston said mechanically. "Don't know who's available, but send my man out to see, and expect you later."

Much cheered by some company to anticipate, Lord Waterbury completed his shopping in one reckless sweep from Bond to Regent Streets, and sent everything to his lodgings by a chairman together with a message that he was dining out. Subsequently he filled time by a session at Jackson's, where the great boxer was permitting each of his favored patrons to get in one hit as a Christmas present. "Ah, yes, *vairy* pretty, milord," dancing lightly about while His Lordship lunged. "You want to keep that right hand *up*—ah, *there* you are!"

Later he stopped at White's, where the betting book revealed nothing of much interest aside from Bertie's wager on Miss Cherill's attaching the Duke of Wyvern within six months. It was so handsomely covered that the eventual settlement would be substantial, either way. Charles was tempted to add his bet to Bertie's, but had a superstitious sense it might be bad luck. Six months, after all—Bertie might have been right that Fanny was not one to change her mind, but six *months?* He was even more tempted to cancel everything, drive out to Cherley at once no matter what time he arrived, and settle the matter—but if Fanny were not there, he would only look a fool.

He spread the fan before his shaving mirror and studied it while he changed his clothes for dinner. Somehow the frivolous trifle was cheering to his spirits; he thought Fanny would surely like it. "Send it by express tomorrow, with a letter presenting compliments of the season," he decided hopefully. "Nothing wrong with that, sort of thing anyone could do . . . and I can explain casually that I've been out of town, unable to call."

The fan was still opened when Charles trotted downstairs to shrug into his coat, set his hat at the correct angle, and depart for Tomaston's lodgings. As Somers tidied the room, he eyed it speculatively: a fan for Miss Fanny, with a scene of reminiscence. "He *ain't* forgotten her, means to try for her again, I'll be bound!" Somers thought with satisfaction, setting out for the Spotted Dog. Tonight luck favored him, he was scarcely seated when Teake walked in.

"Well, thank goodness! I hadn't dared hope to see you, Mr. Teake," Somers exhaled with relief.

"Nor me, neither," said the bâtman, "not that I been here very often. The Major's been back and forth to our property in Suffolk, nor he don't go through London but crosses at Tilbury. We wasn't due to return before week's end, but he got an express that brought him down this morning. So he says we'll stay a few days, get some presents for the girls, and go along to Cherley for Christmas Eve."

"His Lordship's already bought a present for Miss Fanny," Somers remarked. "It's a fan with a balloon painted on it. You wouldn't know, Mr. Teake, but it was a balloon began the whole thing: he took her to witness an ascension. Well, it is good to see you. We was so many weeks in Norfolk before the old gentleman died, I feel quite out of touch, although between us, that death changes all. His Lordship's the heir. There's a very neat little house, a bit of land, *and* Funds in the region of seven thousand a year, I believe."

"Whoo! With wot he had, His Lordship should be well fixed."

Somers nodded complacently. "I fancy we're in good shape. All the same, he ain't happy, Mr. Teake, nor he hasn't got over Miss Fanny. How do things progress at Cherley?"

"I don't know about the last ten days, we been in Suffolk, but before that," Teake squinted in memory. "Well, we're rid of the old lady; she's moved her vapors and complaints to Warwickshire. Miss Almina come home to pack the boxes, and the Major wouldn't send her back."

"I did hear the Duke of Wyvern was a constant visitor?"

Teake nodded. "At first, me and Mr. Pitcock *wondered,* but it's all music. Miss Fanny's a beautiful pianist, Duke plays the violin and sings; the Major's got a good voice, too. Very friendly they were, with the Duke driving in once or twice a week for a musicale, using Christian names informal-like. Well, in course we wondered, but it ain't Miss Fanny. Soon's Miss Almina got home, His Grace moved out to his property in Hythe, wot's much closer than town, Mr. Somers, and he's driving over nearly every day! Gone off to his castle by now, I expect, but Mr. Pitcock is confident of the outcome. He says Miss Almina's looking very dreamy-eyed, and quite got over her fancy for Sir Robin Elvey, which is a great relief to us all."

"Hmmm," Somers murmured. "What about Miss Fanny?"

"Pitcock says she ain't happy. She don't *say* nothing," Teake reported, "goes about her business managing the house and playing her music, but Pitcock says they can tell she ain't *happy*. Now, if this here fan means what you think, I'd say it's time to step up and tell His Lordship to see the Major again."

While they considered this, a cheerful voice said, "How are you, Mr. Somers?"

"Very well, Mr. Higgins, and yourself? This here's Mr. Teake who is bâtman to Major Cherill—Mr. Higgins is the Duke of Wyvern's gentleman—and what brings you to town, Mr. Higgins?"

"An appointment with a certain Major Cherill," Higgins said slowly, and sat down without waiting for an invitation. "There was an express come night afore last from Kent," he looked from one to another of the men significantly. "That's not unusual, but yesterday morning His Grace says he's coming up to town and don't know when he'll return. I understand from the butler it caused considerable surprise, not to say *words* from the family, for him to leave his house party, but in course he gave no explanation. We stopped over at Oxford, reached Berkeley Square for tea today, when His Grace sent a footman straight off to Major Cherill, instructed to wait for a reply.

"He's dined at home, telling me to wake him at nine because he's got an important engagement in the morning," Higgins finished. "So, what d'you make of that, gentlemen?"

"I should say we're all going to be related, in a manner o' speaking," Teake said promptly, "and it calls for a proper drink. Jem, give us each a glass of the good brandy . . ."

By the time they parted, each man had his responsibility. "If we don't straighten 'em out, they'll never manage on their own," said Mr. Teake.

He had no difficulty; after fighting a war together, he stood on the easiest terms with his employer. "Me and Mr. Somers had a *chisme* tonight. Seems His Lordship's inherited a nice little property from that uncle in Norfolk, but he ain't happy. Pitcock says Miss Fanny ain't happy, neither. We been thinking: if His Lordship was to ask for her again, would you maybe take it more serious? Looks as if he's more the thing with this money; seven thousand a year was the figure Mr. Somers mentioned—might make a difference?"

"The deuce of a difference," Major Cherill agreed blankly. "If they really want each other, *I've* no objection."

"Right! I'll just step around and tell Mr. Somers to send His Lordship over tomorrow," Teake said briskly. "You'll have time when you've finished with the Duke. Makes a nice Christmas present for the girls: a couple of husbands."

"Very nice," Harry chuckled, "if a bit unusual."

Higgins' task was to apprise the Duke that Lord Waterbury might be his brother-in-law. While His Grace did not encourage backstairs gossip in general, he was in an approachable mood tonight. Higgins was able to inform him obliquely that, due to an inheritance, it was surmised Lord Waterbury might decide to settle.

"Ah? Not well acquainted, but always found him a very pleasant chap," the Duke observed. "Who is the fortunate young lady?"

"Miss Fanny Cherill was the name mentioned, Your Grace."

"Fanny?" The Duke stared thunderstruck for a moment, then slowly he smiled. "Well, that *is* good news! Thank you, Higgins, that will be all. Good night."

In Holton Square, Somers rehearsed his report carefully, much encouraged by Mr. Teake's information that the Major was receptive, but it was past midnight before Lord Waterbury returned. "Needn't have waited up for me, Somers. Go along to your bed, man; we're for Leicestershire tomorrow."

"Yes, milord, but as for tomorrow, it appears there is a development."

"Good God, never tell me m'grandmother's in town?" Charles asked in alarm. "Dashed if I'll escort her again! The last time it took three days at two miles an hour."

"No, it ain't the Dowager, milord—merely that I encountered Mr. Teake at the Spotted Dog, as well as Mr. Higgins, who is the Duke of Wyvern's man."

"All right, tell me the worst," Charles said harshly.

"It ain't worst, but best, milord. That is, you did once condescend to inform me you meant to marry Miss Fanny Cherill? Not wishing to intrude on personal matters, milord, but we think you should know the Duke has an appointment with Major Cherill in the morning, nor it ain't for Miss Fanny," Somers said earnestly. "It's *Miss* Cherill he wants, Mr. Higgins was very positive on that."

Charles sank limply into a chair. "What are you trying to tell me, Somers?"

"Present yourself to the Major at noon, and ask for Miss Fanny again, milord. You'll not be refused, nor it ain't your inheritance. The Major don't want his sister unhappy, which she is at the moment. Mr. Teake has it from Mr. Pitcock: there's no cross words between the sisters, the Major enjoys his home and the music. Mr. Pitcock says the house has never been so easy . . . but for all that, Miss Fanny ain't *happy*."

Lord Waterbury stared into space for so long that Somers shook inside. "If so be you're not of the same view as formerly, milord, you'll forgive the presumption?" he murmured anxiously.

"Oh, I still want her—more than ever," His Lordship smiled wryly. "It'd all be so much easier if I had her to talk to, Somers. If only I could be sure . . ."

"Me and Mr. Teake think you'd best find out, milord . . . although there ain't no reason Miss Fanny'd be unhappy aside from missing *you*. Now if you was to take the little fan around with you, and maybe a note for the Major to give her?"

His Lordship drew a long breath. "Very well, Somers. Wake me at ten, please."

All that sustained Lord Waterbury, ascending the steps of Major Cherill's lodgings with a firm tread, was the feel of the fan box in his greatcoat pocket. Exactly as he reached the top, the door swung back for the exit of the Duke of Wyvern, with Harry clapping his shoulder and laughing jovially.

"Oh, damme, here's another!" Harry exclaimed. "Come in, come in, Waterbury. Your servant, Wyvern. Bid you good day."

Bemused, Charles stood aside while Wyvern clapped on his high-crowned beaver with a shy smile for the new visitor. "Wish me happy, Waterbury," he said softly, "and I'll wish you the same."

"Uh, thank you kindly, Duke," Charles stuttered as His Grace walked down to the waiting carriage.

Dazedly, he went forward to take Harry's hand and leave his coat with Teake, who was smiling pontifically. "Arrr, that's the dandy, and I hope I see you well, milord?"

"And yourself, Teake," His Lordship returned mechanically. He had a sense this was all a dream from which he would presently wake to be handed his dressing gown and hot water, although a tentative finger to his chin assured him he was already shaved.

Major Cherill was courteously ushering him along the hall to the study, "Expect you've guessed Wyvern's business with me, Waterbury? He's offered for Almina! That'll put m'mother in prime twig, I can tell you."

"Bertie Pakenham'll be glad of it, too," Charles chuckled. "He was betting on your sister, got it handsomely covered at White's."

Harry laughed. "Ask you to say nothing until the formal announcement," he said. "Bertie can wait to collect—never knew such a chap for wagers! Well, that's one of 'em settled," he waved Charles to a chair with a grin, "and what can I do for *you*, milord?"

"I've come for the other one," Charles said helplessly. "That's if she'll have me, Cherill."

"Oh, she will," Harry nodded. "Afraid I wasn't too alive on that suit last time. Well, the circumstances, y'know: seemed you were only doing the pretty, and the puss was too young to be shackled, best let you both think it over—but I see I didn't read the situation correctly. Fanny's a very gallant spirit," he said soberly, "but she isn't happy, some of her sparkle is missing. Suggest you come out to Cherley and address her directly as soon as you have time."

"This afternoon?"

Harry looked startled. "Ain't you off to Pevency for Christmas?"

"Fanny," said Lord Waterbury firmly, "is more important than Christmas. If you've no objection, I'll get it settled today. The details can wait, I'm in better shape than I was; inherited a bit from my uncle, I'll have something to spare for a jointure."

"Her dowry was twenty thousand pounds originally, there's only five left," Harry grunted, "but I can probably raise another five."

"The devil with it," Charles shrugged impatiently. "One way or another, there'll be enough. We may be poor relations compared to Wyvern, but we won't need to be pensioners, Cherill." He stood up, "I'll be off, confess I can't wait to see Fanny—and *thanks*, Cherill!"

"Don't mention it," Harry said politely. "If anything, I should thank you. It's not every day a man gets rid of both his sisters at a single clip!"

At Cherley, Fanny was still masterminding her sister's future. The revelation of Robin's wager did the trick. Thereafter, Almina was thoroughly intransigent. She canceled appointments with no excuse, or kept Robin waiting to the limits of his patience. She made every use of the Ullastone carriage for her local errands, and dismissed Robin as soon as the parcels were carried into the house. When he sulked, she told him to go away until he could be better company; when he complained stormily, she smiled in sweet wonderment and said, "Surely, I needn't stand upon ceremony with you? I count you quite as a second brother, Robin."

"All the same," said Fanny to Miss Bolting, "I think it is time for Edward to speak to Harry. Have you any shillings for some expresses, Boltie? I'll give you them back out of Robin's guinea."

"Are you so sure?"

"Are not you? It is a nuisance everyone is away at this moment, but Edward will come back as soon as I tell him, and I shall write Harry that we need a vast long list of stores for Christmas, which will require him to pass through London."

"And when Almina is settled, what about yourself, my dear?"

"Well, the gypsy said I'd have a dark love, I'd never be rich but never be poor, and it would end the same way whatever I did, and now I see she was right," Fanny smiled and sighed faintly. "Either way, I should have ended at Cherley, and I *did* have a dark love, but she never said I should keep him, Boltie. Do you mind to ring the bell for Perkins to take my letters?"

In the ensuing days Almina was fretful. "I don't mind practicing, but it does not sound the same without the male voice," she complained. "I cannot tell how it will be, and here is Harry gone off to Suffolk *again*. What shall we do for Christmas gifts? I should have thought to ask him for some money, although what can be bought in a market town? I declare it will not seem at all like Christmas with no more than a tree."

"I fancy you might find some small trinkets in Biddeford. Fresh ribbons, or a length of muslin," Miss Bolting suggested, "and any of the tradesmen would give credit until Harry returns."

Almina brightened. "New dresses!" She was ruth-lessly hauling forth the London finery. "Let us alter some things for Fanny. It is stupid to pack them away, we should salvage all we can." She would brook no ob-jections, "I shall never wear them again, they are al-ready *demodé*. Never mind that Fanny is not Out, we can remove some of the trimmings for simplicity, and Harry will llke to see us prettily robed."

Refurbishing their wardrobes kept the sisters pleas-antly busied, but Fanny noticed Almina often spoke of Wyvern. "I think you were right that he is shy, though one could not believe it, but however, he is not at all *dull,* Fanny. He is not lively, he lacks the ability to command a frothy conversation, but when he talks, he is extremely well informed."

"He's a demmed sight more comfortable than Robin," Fanny said flatly. "Edward is *kindly,* Almina. He always spares a smile or thank-you for the servants, and look at the courtesy he gives to Boltie. He treats her quite like a family relative. Besides, Harry likes Edward, and I will tell you he declared firmly he wouldn't consent to Robin. He said a man might have intimates he wouldn't have in the family, and you know Harry's well able to judge. In plain English, Robin was the greatest fun when we were children, but he's grown into a dashed loose screw."

Almina bent over her sewing and said nothing for a few moments. "Has the tree been brought?" she asked. "When shall we trim it?"

"When Harry gets home," said Fanny. "He'll surely be here by Christmas Eve, Almy."

In fact, he was even then on his way—preceded some three hours ahead by the Duke of Wyvern, whose carriage was followed an hour later by ˉord Waterbury . . . all of which would vastly have amused the Major had he known it. Like Charles, he had gone hastily the length of Bond Street and pointed at random, while Teake procured the items on Fanny's list. The curricle was now bulging with boxes lashed behind and before, with Teake's massive boots perched high over the remainder.

When Wyvern's carriage rolled to a stop, the girls were immersed in fitting one of Almina's gowns to Fanny's diminutive figure. They had just got the hem pinned into place when Pitcock knocked at the sewing room door. "The Duke of Wyvern has called to see Miss Cherill."

"Wyvern? Merciful heavens, what does he here? I thought he was gone to Gloucestershire," Almina said, flustered.

"Probably some business with that property at Hythe," Fanny shrugged. "You're dressed, you go down to receive him, Almy. I'll come as soon as I'm ready."

"Well—all right," Almina said helplessly, "but do not be long, Fanny. Boltie, come with me?"

"In a few minutes. Let me get Fanny out of these pins, Almina."

The instant she had gone, Fanny hugged the governess rapturously. "He has offered! I knew how it would be," she chortled. "He's seen Harry in London and got permission to speak. Oh, Boltie, isn't it wonderful?"

"It would be more wonderful if you would release me, my love," Miss Bolting returned. "Those pins are stabbing me to death!"

Since Lord Waterbury was springing his team, his curricle reached Cherley a scant thirty minutes behind the Duke. He had never felt more nervous in his life as the front door opened to reveal Pitcock's astonished eyes, however quickly the butler controlled himself. "Afternoon, Pitcock. Is Miss Fanny at home?"

"She is, milord, and I venture to say will be happy to see you," Pitcock murmured, "as I am myself. If you will allow me . . . ." he divested Charles of coat and hat, "I will inform her of your arrival."

"Wait in here, shall I?" Charles plunged across to the slightly opened salon door before the butler could stop him . . . took one look at the Duke of Wyvern with Miss Cherill's head nestled comfortably on his shoulder, and said aghast, "Oh, the devil! Beg pardon, no wish to intrude . . . only called to bring a present for Fanny . . . Miss Cherill, y'r servant . . ."

"No, no, come in!" The Duke released Almina and stood up, beaming widely. "Wish me happy, milord: Miss Cherill's accepted me!"

"I wish you happy indeed, Wyvern—you'll never know *how* happy!" Charles grinned. "Miss Cherill," he bowed over her hand, "my felicitations."

"Thank you, milord," she said demurely, her glance sliding over his shoulder.

Fanny stood in the doorway. She still wore the pure white evening gown they had been altering abovestairs, with part of the hem trailing. "Charles!"

"I came to bring you this fan, your brother gave me permission," he began and stopped, holding out his arms wordlessly. He was aware of nothing but the sweet clean scent of her, the warmth of her lips, the feel of her arms about his neck. "My dear and only love," he muttered huskily, "your brother says yes; do you? Will you have me, Fanny darling?"

"You cannot suppose me in the habit of kissing gentlemen in this abandoned manner," she whispered. "Oh, Charles, it has been so long!"

"Well, we will have a lifetime in which to make it up," he said, "and what the *deuce* is sticking into my ankles?"

"Pins and a needle, for we had not quite finished," she apologized, "but when Pitcock said you were here, I could not wait. You recall my eagerness was always shocking?"

"One of your most endearing qualities," he murmured against her hair, "but could we remove the needle for the moment?"

"Well, if we sat down, I could finish the hem. It is

only the overdress, after all, although I don't know what difference it would make for you to view my ankle now, when presumably you will become well acquainted with it later."

"True enough," he agreed, "but I do not wish to share its shapeliness with Wyvern, even if he is my brother-in-law."

"Oh, lud," she whispered, stricken. "I'd forgot. Is *he* here? Oh, Charles!"

Lord Waterbury chuckled deeply, "He's here, so's your sister, as well as a female I suspect is Miss Bolting, and if I know Pitcock, he's listening in the hall. There never was such a public declaration, my love— but you said yes, and you'll not get out of it now. I've too many witnesses."

"Oh, heavens!" Fanny pulled away to peer about, blushing rosily. "Well—well, then I have as many witnesses for you. Almy—Edward—is it true? How happy I am! Boltie, this is Charles, and perhaps you should pull out that needle; we can finish later. Someone ring the bell for tea, please, although I expect Pitcock has already gone for it. *Almy,* I am so happy! Edward, welcome!"

Charles stood bemused, lapped in felicity, watching his intended moving lightly from person to person with soft hugs and kisses. How natural and graceful her movements, how beautiful she was!

"I trust you like music, milord?"

"Eh?" He turned to face the governess, "Oh, as for that, I can take it or leave it, ma'am."

"If you plan to marry Fanny, you'll take it," she remarked, "but unless you're a clodpole like Robin Elvey, you'll find it no hardship. Do you sing?"

"I can carry a tune," he admitted.

"Good!" she nodded briskly. "You'll soon get in the way of it, and I present my congratulations, milord."

"Uh, thank you," he murmured blankly, moving aside for the majestic entrance of Pitcock, carrying the tea service and followed by Perkins with decanters,

Edith and Janet with plates of sandwiches and cakes.

"How cozy this is," Fanny sighed. "I wish Harry were come. Then we might have in the tree and trim it together."

"By all means," said Major Cherill from the hall doorway. Setting his hands on his hips, he laughed heartily at the group about the tea table. "No need to tell me," he said. "I see my Christmas presents have arrived, and I hope you're pleased with 'em, girls, because they ain't like to get away soon. There's a swirling snow coming down from the north. You'll not make London today, gentlemen."

"Good God," said Charles blankly. "Ask nothing better than to be stormstaid with Fanny, but dash it, I've no clothes."

"Nor I," said Wyvern, rising to peer from the salon window, "but I've a house near Hythe. I fancy my coachman can make it and return before we're closed in." He turned to smile gently, "You ain't my size, Waterbury, but a shirt is a shirt, after all—and we'll all keep our first Christmas together, eh?"

At Pevency, when the first mail coach got through from London, His Grace received a letter.

"Dear fa—Have the honor to inform you I am betrothed to Miss Fanny Cherill, daughter of the late Hon. Edgar, and am keeping Christmas at Cherley, near Biddeford in Kent. Accept my apologies for failing to attend you and my mother at this moment. Yrs, etc. Charles."

The Duke of Pevency stalked unceremoniously into his wife's bedchamber and tossed the paper on her chocolate tray. "There you are," he said with a wicked grin. "I *told* you not to invite Lady Vesey and her daughter. Of all dismal females! *Now* what'll we do with the girl?"

"Bless my soul!" said Her Grace, perusing her son's intelligence. "Well—well, there's always Bertie Pakenham . . ."

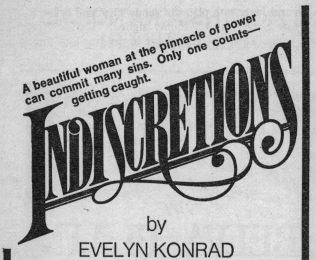

8 MONTHS A NATIONAL BESTSELLER!

EVERGREEN

by

BELVA PLAIN

From shtetl to mansion—Evergreen is the wonderfully rich epic of Anna Friedman, who emigrates from Poland to New York, in search of a better life. Swirling from New York sweatshops to Viennese ballrooms, from suburban mansions to Nazi death camps, from riot-torn campuses to Israeli Kibbutzim, Evergreen evokes the dramatic life of one woman, a family's fortune and a century's hopes and tragedies.

A Dell Book $2.75   (13294-0)

Bestsellers